7-24-15

OF MICE & MECHANICALS

A STEAMPUNK NOVEL OF SUSPENSE

BY KIRSTEN WEISS

Thank you!

The publisher does not have any control over and does not assume any responsibility for author or third-party websites and their content.

Cover Art: The Book Cover Machine

Visit the author website: http://kirstenweiss.com

The publisher does not have any control over and does not assume any responsibility for author or third-party websites and their content.

Misterio Press / paperback edition April, 2015

ISBN-13: 978-0-9908864-3-3

ISBN-10: 0990886433

CONTENTS

CHAPTER 1

San Francisco, California Territory. March, 1849

The drum beat folded into the clatter of construction, a counterpoint to the scrape of saws, the pounding of nails. Inside her workshop, Sensibility Grey's grip tightened on the screwdriver. She preferred the rumble of construction to the damnable parade outside, but neither were conducive to her work.

But she would not fall behind schedule. She glanced at her friend, Jane Algrave, frowning at a damaged mechanical pinioned to the wall. Sensibility bent her head to the array of gears fitted together on the table.

A shot rang out, and her shoulders twitched, her gaze flicking to the paned windows. They had cost her a small fortune, but she loved the natural light they provided.

The tops of flags and banners bobbed past the glass. Her spine stiffened, better conforming to the lines of her stays.

Inhaling the scent of freshly cut wood, her grip on the tool relaxed. She was in her own workshop – hers! – and all would be well. Flasks and glass condensers and retorts lined the shelves. Metal tubes, gears and coils of wire lay stacked in wooden boxes. Partially assembled mechanicals hung, gleaming, from the walls.

She touched the copper pocket watch dangling from her waistcoat. This was where she belonged. As long as she could work, it did not matter what went on outside in boomtown San Francisco. And if the skin beneath her eyes was the color of a bruise, and her gowns fit a trifle loosely, what of it? She was young and would recover from the long hours caused by this excess of employment. Never again would her stomach pinch with hunger. Never again would she depend on the charity of others. Never again would fear of the future be her constant companion.

Never.

Her friend raised her voice above the din. "It's been nearly a year, and all we've got are a few prototypes that don't work for more than a minute or two." Jane paced the length of the workshop, her blue-satin skirts swirling in a froth of crinolines at each turn. Her chestnut curls bounced beneath her delicately cocked hat. "My superiors are beginning to think you'd be more productive back in the States."

"But not nearly as prosperous." Frowning, Sensibility shoved the gears aside. She bent over her latest plans for a mining mechanical, laying the screwdriver on one edge of the wide paper to prevent it from curling. The violet-colored apron skirt that she wore over her leather trousers slipped lower on her hips.

She'd once seen aether technology used to control a mechanical remotely. But thus far, she'd been unable to replicate it, and the problem was driving her mad. Without remote control, her new design would require a man inside to manage the excavator's angle of descent. Not only would that expose the operator to hazardous conditions, but space for him was a problem. A tremendous steam engine would be required to power the device and as it stood, the mechanical was simply too unwieldy. Without the remote control, she'd need to develop a more efficient compression device—

"Are you even listening to me?" Jane asked.

"Yes, yes." Sensibility waved her hand, dismissive, and noticed a new chemical stain on the hem of her white sleeve. She rolled it up, hiding the umber blotch. "Your superiors in

Washington are disappointed that I haven't progressed on my late father's aether research. Though I might point out that I've gone further than any of their scientists in the States. And you want me to give my complete attention to government work, rather than continuing with my own private endeavors. Your government may consider itself fortunate that I devote any time to their little problems."

"*Their* problems? First off, you're living in an American territory. It's your government too."

She snorted. "In the California Territory, we barely have any government at all."

"And it's not as if you're really English. You might as well be an American," Jane said.

"I was born in England and raised by an Englishman, even if I did come by way of Peru." A miniature mechanical with a broom for a skirt bumped into Sensibility's booted foot. Brass gears whirring, it chirped and swiveled to sweep in the other direction.

"And your father made a problem for everyone when he discovered aether could be used as an energy source. Our enemies have already developed aether as a method to control mechanicals remotely. There are others working on the same questions. When they get the answers, they'll use aether first for weapons and next to overturn the world's governments. They've come close once already. The revolutions last year in Europe—"

"I am aware!" A headache bloomed behind her eyes. Sensibility straightened, one hand sliding off the drawing. It curled up with a snap. Pressing her lips together, she spread it flat, weighting its other end with a heavy wrench.

She did know, and that was the real problem. She knew better than Jane, better than the American government, the implications of her father's discoveries. That was why she toiled late into the night, chipping at the solution in secret. Not even Jane could know how much she cared about finding the answers.

"You *know*," Jane said, "but—"

"And you know the costs of daily life in San Francisco. Yesterday, I spent two dollars for an egg. A single egg! Have you any idea how much the ores and metals I require cost? Why do you think I've been leaving my mechanicals naked, with their gears exposed for all the world to see?"

"I thought that was your trademark style."

"Style! It's a scandal! I can't afford metal plating to cover them, and neither can my clients afford the additional cost. And you wonder why I take commissions from the miners."

"I told you, the government will fund your research. They would have paid for this whole lab."

"And made me indebted to them? No, thank you. I find I'd like to keep my independence now that I have it."

Across from her, Jane braced her hands on the table, her fingertips brushing a red globe of putty. "Independent like me, you mean?"

"Indeed, you are an admirable example."

"And I work for the government."

There was a soft knock at the wooden door.

"Yes?" Sensibility called.

The door swung inward, and a middle-aged man stepped inside, his black cloak flowing about his ankles. White brows hooded his dark eyes. Sweeping his top hat from his head, he exposed a shock of platinum hair and bowed low. "Good day, ladies. I am searching for the inventor, Miss Sensibility Grey."

Sensibility moved around the table. "That is I. How can I help you?"

"Who are you?" Jane's blue eyes narrowed.

"Apologies, dear lady. My name is Nicholas Hermeticus. I am in need of an unusual device, and everyone I inquired of gave me Miss Grey's name."

"Sorry," Jane said. "Miss Grey is too busy right now to take on new clients."

Sensibility canted her head. "But I'm intrigued by—"

He took another step within, drawing back his cloak.

Jane's hand moved in a blur. She aimed a revolver at the man. "Far too busy."

He bowed, backing out the door. "My apologies for the intrusion." The door closed softly behind him.

Sensibility's face heated. "You had no right—"

"I had every right! You can't be distracted by every Tom, Dick and Nicholas who stops by with a demand for your time."

"The only person *demanding* my time is you. What is wrong with you?"

Jane picked up the putty, squeezed it. "What is wrong with *you*? After the—" She lowered her voice. "—troubles with the Mark last year, you were committed to unlocking the secrets of aether technology. It was all you could think about. Aether as an energy source. Aether as a method for controlling devices from afar – which so far you haven't been able to replicate, in spite of the models and plans we discovered last year at that rancho."

"Several of which you sent to Washington. The scientists there have had no better luck than I at solving that riddle."

"Maybe if you spent less time building things for the miners, you'd already have figured out aether control. Now it's all miners and money."

"Our troubles with that organization were, as you said, a year ago, and there have been no problems of that sort since. And you know why I prefer taking commissions from miners rather than committing all my resources to your government. Diversification is only prudent."

Jane frowned at the putty in her hands. "You've been keeping things from me."

As this was true, Sensibility said nothing,

"Something's been bothering you," Jane said. "Is it Mr. Night?"

Sensibility's cheeks flamed anew, and she turned away, examining an empty vial. Dried chemicals crusted its lip, and she picked at them with her fingernail. "Mr. Night is in

Monterey with the other politicians and lawyers. I haven't seen him in months."

"Throwing yourself into work so you don't have to think of him, eh?"

Sensibility placed the vial in a metal bucket, to be washed later. If she thought much about it (and she did, late at night), her work and his were the cause of their separation, not the balm. But what of it? Her lungs constricted. They had no formal understanding...

"Look," Jane said, "I'm sorry. It's none of my business."

"No, it is not."

"What is this?" Jane lifted the ball of putty to the light. Dust motes floated around it. "It feels like rubber."

"Just a toy I've been working on."

"Oh? Does it bounce?" Jane pitched it to the floor at her feet.

"No!"

There was a muffled explosion, and clouds of pink smoke engulfed Jane.

Sensibility pressed her face to the crook of her elbow, and her friend collapsed in a graceful, rose-tinged heap.

"Dash it!" Handkerchief to her nose, Sensibility ran to the windows. Her booted feet tangling in her apron skirt, she shoved one open, then another. The skirt slipped to the floor, unnoticed.

She regarded Jane, snoring on the floor. The corners of Sensibility's mouth curved, trembled. No, this was by no means amusing, and under no circumstances would she laugh. She pressed the handkerchief to her mouth more firmly, stifling a cough. As a spy, Jane should appreciate this invention, with its defensive capabilities. Or at least, she would when she awakened.

If she didn't kill Sensibility first.

Striding past a wall lined with tools, she opened a closet and stepped inside. She lit the wall sconce, illuminating a narrow cot and short bedside table.

Her hand drifted across a knothole. It hid a switch that would open another, secret room behind her makeshift bed. Crawling over the cot to get to the hidden door was inconvenient, but getting locked in a madhouse would be even less convenient. And if others knew the secrets behind that wall, they *would* think her mad. Because her father had believed that the key to aether was magic. Of course, magic was just another word for a scientific principle which had not yet been understood. But not even Sensibility could call the incantations and formulas locked on the other side of that door science.

She grabbed a pillow from the cot. Jane would be furious when she awoke, but at least the agent could sleep comfortably. Dangling the pillow from one hand, she gave a last, longing look at the wall and backed from the tiny room.

"So where is it?" A rough voice asked.

She yelped and whirled, heart in her throat. "What?"

Two men stood before her, their faces darkened by the sun, hands broad and roughened by work. One was tall and lanky, the other squat and muscular. Both wore miner's clothes – stained trousers and patched shirts and battered hats.

She reached down to smooth her apron skirt, discovered its absence, and curled her hands around her middle. The odor of unwashed bodies stung Sensibility's nostrils. Eyes watering, she resisted the urge to bury her nose in the pillow clutched to her chest.

"Pardon me, sirs." She smoothed back the lock of mahogany-colored hair that had worked its way free from her chignon. "I did not know you were there. How may I help you?"

"You can give us the mechanical you promised," the short one said.

"I?" She bit her lip, certain she'd never laid eyes upon the two men in her life. While she frequently forgot names and faces, she never forgot a client. "Are you certain you are in the correct workshop?"

"You Sensibility Grey?"

"I am Miss Grey. I'm afraid you have the advantage of me, however, Mr...?"

"Pacalioglu," the short one said.

The tall one stood silent, impassive.

"Er, quite right," she said. "And you say you placed an order for a mechanical with me?"

Pacalioglu snorted. "With your agent. Now don't you try to put one over on us. We paid good money, and we expect satisfaction."

"I'm sorry, sir, but I have no agent." She raked her hands through her hair, freeing more locks. "There must have been some mistake."

Nostrils flaring, he planted his legs wide. "We paid for it, and you owe it to us."

A delicate snore rose from behind the tables.

"What was that?" he asked.

Her stomach churned. Why had Jane picked now of all times to lose consciousness? And what would these men do if they found her friend, helpless? "My... pet pug. It's terribly noisy. But that is neither here nor there. I have no agent, I have no order from you, I've never heard of you before, and I have no idea what type of mechanical you claim to have purchased."

His face reddened, and he stepped closer.

Sensibility turned her head from the invisible cloud of garlic and tobacco and stale beer.

"Claim?" He roared. "There's no claim about it. Now if you don't give us what we want, we'll take it."

Sensibility's hand fumbled on the closet latch behind her. It snicked open. "Perhaps if you return later and give me some time to better understand exactly what has happened?" She turned.

Something struck her in the head. A crack of red, blazing pain. A sense of movement, and then all went black.

CHAPTER 2

Flora stood in the shadow of a warehouse, her mourning gown fading into the dark gray of the wood-plank building. Gulls cawed, wheeling in the fog above her like carrion crows, and her flesh crept.

Miss Grey stumbled out the door opposite, propped between two miners. Another man approached from the opposite direction. The newcomer nodded to the trio, and the men laughed. The third man walked on.

Her eyes narrowed. She'd watched Miss Grey long enough to know she was neither a drinker nor a lady of loose character. Were it not for the girl's interest in mechanicals, she'd be decidedly dull. Could it be an abduction?

The girl's head lolled back, mouth hanging open.

Flora's brows rose. Definitely, an abduction. She scrutinized the men, certain she'd never seen them before. And she would know if she had. She was condemned to remember.

Her father had called it a gift. Every page she read, every diagram she examined, engraved in her memory as if chiseled in a stone tablet. She closed her eyes, and her father's laboratory was there, and her father...

Shuddering, she turned away from the street, her face to the wall. She trailed her chemical-stained fingers over the wood. It was uneven, soft, as if corroded by the salt air. Picking at a sliver of wood, she inhaled deeply, scenting rot, forcing herself to think about anything other than the unchangeable, unforgiving past.

She could not afford to lose herself. Miss Grey was being abducted. Now, what was she going to do about it? She hadn't come all this way to watch her quarry be killed.

She trailed after the trio. Killing Miss Grey was Flora's job.

CHAPTER 3

Spinning. Her head whirled, her stomach roiled... Sensibility groaned, tasting something sour in her mouth. She tried to bring her hands to clutch her aching skull, but they wouldn't move. She couldn't move.

Sensibility's eyelids fluttered open.

Light seeped beneath a closed door to her right, the room's only illumination. The place smelled of damp and brine. Somewhere near the docks? She shook her head to clear it, setting off rockets of pain, but she couldn't shake that sensation of movement, of swaying. Her stomach heaved, and she clenched her mouth and throat shut, willing herself not to vomit.

She was on a ship. Good gad, where were they taking her?

She slowed her ragged breath. Calm, she must remain calm. Stilling her trembling limbs, she closed her eyes and drew in a slow, deep breath. The thundering beneath her ribs diminished. *Assess the situation.*

It was the rare ship that departed San Francisco these days, and this ship was stationary. She was alone – which meant Jane was... Sensibility swallowed, head swimming. Likely, it meant the men who'd taken her hadn't noticed Jane. And even if they had, unconscious, the federal agent was no threat. Surely they wouldn't have harmed her. Sweat beaded her lip, and she licked it, tasting salt. Surely.

The back of her head throbbed.

Assess the situation. Don't think about what might be. Understand what is.

Her hands were bound. Experimentally, she wiggled her wrists and winced. Tightly bound. Low, masculine voices drifted to her from behind the door.

So. She'd been abducted and likely taken to one of the abandoned ships in the harbor. Well, she had not spent the last months evading drunken miners on San Francisco's streets without learning a few things.

She wriggled her arms. There was a snick, and the spring-loaded knife beneath her sleeve snapped forward.

Sensibility glanced at the door, but the men's voices continued. Could they be part of the Mark, a criminal society she and Jane had encountered nearly a year ago? She dismissed the notion. The Mark was sophisticated. These gentlemen were not.

She sawed at the ropes. Hot pain sliced her wrists. It was the first time she'd used her invention for anything other than cutting string. Slicing the ropes that bound her was considerably more difficult. The knife scraped along her opposite arm. Biting back a cry, she moved more slowly.

Too slowly.

Another trail of fire pricked her thumb, followed by a trickle of warmth. Another cut. Why hadn't she practiced for this? She banged the back of her head on the wall, setting off a fresh cascade of pain.

The ropes loosened. Sighing, she wrenched off the ropes. Returning the knife to its sheath on her forearm, she rubbed her bloodied wrists. In the dim light, welts gleamed red, wet, angry.

She lurched to her feet, planting one hand on the wall to steady herself.

The voices continued.

Creeping to the door, she bent her head to it.

"If we kill her, we'll never get it," an unfamiliar voice said. The tall, silent man from her workshop?

"Well, we can't take her with us," Pacalioglu said. "And I don't reckon those mechanicals can be built overnight. If we kept her in the workshop, someone would notice. The girl's got to have friends."

"I don't like the idea of them getting away with stealing our gold. I worked too hard for it."

"*We* worked too hard for it."

Sensibility extracted the copper pocket watch from her waistcoat. Angling it toward the light, she checked the time. Colorful planets circled its face, marking the planetary hours. An hour and minute hand ticked away. Just over one hour had passed. Jane should have reawakened by now. If she could. If the men hadn't harmed her.

No, she mustn't think of that. Sensibility pushed up her sleeves. They had no reason to injure her. Jane was well. But the agent would have no idea what had happened to Sensibility. She could not count on rescue from that quarter.

Neither did Sensibility like her odds of getting past the two men on her own. Aside from her little knife, she was unarmed. Her gas "toy" would have come in useful now. She patted her trouser pockets, hoping to discover something she could use and found only some matches wrapped in a bit of sandpaper. The men must have removed all her useful tools.

Sensibility returned her attention to her prison, her eyes adjusting to the gloom. Four, shadowy walls, a ceiling with a swinging lantern… A lantern! She tiptoed to it, stretching upward, and lifted it off its hook. A bit of candle remained within its four glass walls.

Jane is well.

She edged back. Her heel caught on something, and there was a clank of metal. She stumbled, froze, the unlit lantern clutched to her breast.

The murmur of voices continued. Her muscles relaxed, shoulders caving inward. They hadn't heard.

Kneeling, she lowered the square lantern to the floor. She ran her hands over the floorboards, and her fingertips touched cool metal, a thick ring. Her heart leapt. Surely her captors hadn't been foolish enough to put her in a room with an escape route? She felt about the wooden floor until she found a thin crack, running perpendicular to the wood planks. Edging off the trapdoor, she grasped the handle, pulled.

It creaked opened, revealing a square of blackness.

One corner of her mouth slipped upward. She'd found a use for the lamp at last, but did she dare light it? If she could see the men's light seeping beneath the door, they might notice hers.

She considered the hole yawning before her. If the room below was deep, there should be a stair leading down to it. But if it was shallow – perhaps a cargo hold – she could jump. In either case, the lantern would not be needed.

She dangled her limbs over the edge, stretching, feeling for a floor, a step. Nothing. Beneath her was a void. Her confidence evaporated, sweat breaking out on her brow. What if she was wrong? She would have to risk the lamp. If she jumped and injured herself, or if there was no escape, she'd only worsen her predicament.

Rolling onto her stomach, she unlatched the lantern. She dangled it beneath the edge of the trapdoor with one hand, struck a match with the other. It flared, smelling of phosphorous, and she lit the candlewick.

The light revealed a low cargo hold beneath her. Its floor had been just beyond her toes. She leaned further inside. *Yes!* The hold stretched beyond the small room she was trapped in. Smiling grimly, she closed the lantern's glass door and dropped into the hold.

Her feet thunked on the floor. She paused, not daring to breathe. The ship creaked around her, a plaintive groan.

Stooping, she scuttled forward, lantern grasped tight, head craning upward. The lamp swayed, making grotesque shadows of her form. Footsteps thudded above her in the room where her captors argued.

There had to be another exit from the hold. If it led to where her captors' waited, she was ruined. But the hold was long, surely it extended beyond those two rooms?

She paced, trailing one hand on the ceiling, feeling for what her eyes might miss. A splinter dug beneath her fingernail, and she smothered a curse. She wrenched it out, and a drop of blood oozed from beneath her nail.

Swearing, she looked up, stilled. Above her was a square cut in the ceiling, a trapdoor. Pain forgotten, she edged forward, head cocked, listening.

Silence.

Putting her shoulders to the door, she heaved. Light flooded down.

Two masculine hands grasped her arms, hauling her upward.

Kicking, her feet found solid ground, and she staggered backwards. The hands released her, and she rubbed her arms.

A strange man grinned at her, his blue eyes bright against skin bronzed by sun and wind. He tipped back his black hat. "Sorry if I was a bit rough," he said in a low voice, not sounding at all sorry. "Miss Grey, I presume?" He stood six inches taller than Sensibility and was likely a decade older, in his late twenties or early thirties. The man was absent any sort of overcoat on this brisk March day. He wore a gray tweed waistcoat over a blindingly white shirt with a silken cravat the color of a sunset. His trousers were an elegant gray. He made an odd sort of dandy, with his roughened skin and fine garments.

"Yes," she whispered. "Who are you?"

"A friend of Miss Algrave's. You can call me Mr. Sterling."

She pointed to the stairs. "Well, Mr. Sterling, I suggest we leave before—"

The door behind him burst open. Mr. Sterling shoved her back and turned.

Paclioglu glowered on the threshold. "Where do you think you're going?"

"Out," Sterling said and punched him in the jaw.

The stocky man stumbled backwards. His tall companion pushed him aside, throwing himself at Sterling.

Sterling slipped sideways, and the force of the tall man's rush carried him past. Turning, Sterling kicked him in the rear. Her abductor crashed headfirst into the wall.

Sensibility covered her mouth with her hands. "Oh, dear."

Paclioglu surged through the door.

She backed against the wall. "Behind—"

Paclioglu grabbed Mr. Sterling, wrapping his arms around him in a bear hug and lifting him off the floor.

Sterling grimaced, bracing his hands on his attacker's and arching backward. But Paclioglu's grip held. Sterling paled.

The room was empty – there was no bottle she could break over Paclioglu's head, no chair she could throw. So she did the only thing sensible.

She screamed.

Jane and a second man, tall and ungainly, rushed down the stairs. His face was cheerfully ugly, lantern-jawed and raw-boned. He flashed past her and kicked the back of Paclioglu's knee.

The villain collapsed, Sterling on top of him. They rolled, fists flying.

Jane grasped Sensibility's arm, dragged her up the stairs. They emerged on the ship's deck.

Sensibility took a gulp of fresh sea air. A narrow strip of low, gray clouds obscured the sun. Two seagulls dove at each other, screaming, tangling mid-air. They broke apart and flapped away, disappearing behind the masts of ships.

"They'll take care of things from here," Jane said.

"They? Who are they?"

Jane's eyes flashed. "A better question is, who are those two who brought you here? What the devil have you gotten yourself into?"

"I don't—"

"And what do you mean testing that stunning gas on me?" A vein pulsed in Jane's forehead.

"I didn't—"

"I'm supposed to be protecting you. And I can't very well do that if I'm asleep on the floor! What if that gas had been dangerous? I could have been killed!"

Thumps and shouts echoed from below.

"I'll have you know that gas was thoroughly tested. It has no long-term effects."

"How did you test it?" Jane's voice lowered dangerously.

"On myself, of course. Mrs. Watson thought I should pay volunteers, but that didn't seem quite right."

"I want to strangle you."

Sensibility gestured toward the stairwell door. "I can hardly be blamed for the abduction. And I did try to stop you from activating the gas. I'm sure it must have been disorienting waking up on the floor with me gone—"

"You don't know beans."

"I do not understand that expression."

From below, a grunt, two thumps, and the sound of the trapdoor slamming shut.

"I hope your friends are the victors," Sensibility said, "or we'll be right back in the stew. Er, you do have your revolver?"

Jane sighed, shoulders slumping. "Of course I do. But I won't need it. They always win."

Sterling emerged on the deck and brushed dust from his jacket sleeve. His companion followed, straightening his narrow tie.

Sterling bowed and clapped his hat on his head. "Ladies, perhaps one of you should tell us what that was all about."

"A misunderstanding," Sensibility said. "They insisted I had sold them a mechanical, but I've never seen them before in my life. When I tried to explain there had been some mistake…" She rubbed the back of her head. "They must have knocked me unconscious and brought me here."

"And as charming as here is," the second man said, his voice a pleasing baritone, "I suggest we continue this conversation elsewhere."

"This is Mr. Crane," Jane said to Sensibility. "And I believe you've already met Mr. Sterling. They're federal agents, like me, from Washington."

"You've come a long way," Sensibility said.

Mr. Crane frowned. "Let's hope it's worth it."

"I'm sure it will be." Mr. Sterling motioned them forward. "Shall we?"

They exited the ship to a rickety dock floating on the water. Its narrow planks zig-zagged between a clutter of abandoned ships, pinning them in a swaying maze.

Feeling small and fragile sandwiched between the high-masted ships, Sensibility quickened her pace. A stiff breeze whistled through the ghost fleet, and she shivered.

Jane prodded her in the back, nudging her forward.

"Where are we going?" Sensibility asked, the makeshift pier swaying and bouncing beneath her feet.

"My office," Jane said.

"Oh." Sensibility's heart sank. She had come to love San Francisco, with its eerie fogs and steep hills and sparkling waters. But she was not enamored of its burgeoning crowds of gold seekers, and Jane's "office" sat above a gambling hell, a favorite destination for the Argonaut hoards.

She stepped off the pier, and her boots sank ankle-deep in mud. Tucking her arm inside Jane's for balance, she wrenched free.

They sloshed forward, slipping and sliding, through crowds of shouting miners. A cluster of sailors stopped to gawk at the women. Clad in leather work trousers, feminine bodice and man's waistcoat, Sensibility looked as disreputable as the ladies who worked in the gambling hells. She sagged. No, in truth she looked worse.

A miner pushed forward, hand pressed to his chest. "Marry me!"

"Take a bath," Jane snarled.

Men nearby hooted with laughter, and the miner joined in.

Mr. Sterling stepped forward, offering Sensibility his arm. "I imagine you receive a good bit of attention in San Francisco. I've seen few ladies since I've arrived."

"It is rather tiresome." Sensibility released Jane and took his arm. As much as she disliked requiring male protection, it was dashed useful.

With a flourish, Mr. Crane bowed and held out his arm to Jane. She glared, lifted her nose, and strode off. The rest hurried to follow.

Against the door to a ramshackle saloon leaned a United States flag. A raucous drumbeat pounded from within, and the shouts of drunken men rose to a roar.

Sensibility wrinkled her nose. "The Hounds at play."

"The what?" Sterling asked.

"They came together calling themselves a safety committee," Jane said over her shoulder. "But they're brainless thugs who use their committee as a cloak to harass foreigners, mainly Chilenos. You might have seen their parade this morning."

"Little surprise the march ended in a saloon," Sensibility said.

Mr. Crane glanced at his partner, and a silent communication seemed to pass between the two.

They sloshed onward. Reaching a wood plank walk, she scraped the mud from her boots on its edge and stepped upon it.

A donkey hee-hawed, its cart tipped down for loading. The creature hung in the air, feet dangling, helpless, indignant. Sensibility shook her head with sympathy at the beast.

They passed more saloons, gambling hells, and mercantile shops displaying gold mining equipment.

"Here." Jane turned the corner at a freshly-painted saloon. She led them up a flight of exterior stairs to a solid wood door. Drawing a key from her bodice, she unlocked it, swung it open. "My office."

Music from an out-of-tune piano drifted up through the floorboards. A heavy mahogany desk anchored a thick, oriental carpet in place. Beside it stood an ornate, rosewood gun cabinet. Lighting a lamp, Jane drew the blue-velvet curtains.

"We can speak privately here," she said to Mr. Sterling. "And you can tell us why you've come all the way from Washington to meet Miss Grey."

"Not all the way from Washington," Mr. Sterling said. "From Monterey. Do you know it, Miss Grey?"

"Of course," she said. "The village is not far. Why do you ask?"

"Your uncle was there." Mr. Sterling crossed his arms over his broad chest.

"Really? I'd heard he'd gone to the gold fields. Monterey is in the opposite direction. Are you saying you saw him there?"

Mr. Crane grimaced, the planes of his crooked face shifting. "In a manner of speaking."

"What manner?" Sensibility asked.

"I'm afraid your uncle is dead."

"Dead!" Sensibility's mouth slackened, ice spreading through her core. She didn't know her uncle well, and had several excellent reasons to dislike him. But he was her only living relative. And he could not possibly be dead. "I don't believe it."

"Sensibility—" Jane began.

"This is just like him." Sensibility braced her hands on her hips. "We both know he's done this sort of thing before."

Jane lowered her chin, her eyes dark with pity. "Mr. Sterling and Mr. Crane are well-respected agents. If they say he's dead... I'm sorry."

"There's no need to be sorry." She turned to the agents. "No. No! You are mistaken, sirs. My uncle is not dead."

"We saw the body," Mr. Crane said, his voice gentle.

"You may have seen *a* body, but I doubt you saw his. My uncle has an uncanny ability to worm his way out of difficult situations."

"She's right about that," Jane said. "Are you quite sure it was Mr. Grey?"

"The identification was positive." Mr. Crane gestured helplessly.

Scowling, Sensibility went to the window and stared at the brick wall of the building next door. "I see little point in arguing. He'll no doubt turn up, alive and well, and then you shall believe me. Now tell me, what happened to lead to his so-called death?"

"It seems he was selling your mechanicals to the miners." Mr. Crane perched on the edge of Jane's desk and stuck his bony fingers in the pockets of his waistcoat. "Some very special mechanicals."

"But... I don't understand." Sensibility grasped the back of one of the chairs. "My mechanicals? I had no such arrangement with him."

"As we suspected." Mr. Sterling removed his hat. "He swindled the miner's out of their gold on the promise that you would deliver the merchandise."

Sensibility's mouth opened. Closed. That explained the strange demands of her abductors. "But what you are saying makes no sense. Why sell my mechanicals in Monterey? The gold fields are far to the east of there. Surely Sacramento or San Francisco or even Virginia City would make a better base to sell equipment."

"He could hardly sell them here with you so close," Jane said.

Sensibility's face heated. Of course.

"Like you said," Jane continued, "you never had any such arrangement."

The men shared another look.

Mr. Sterling slouched against the gun cabinet, arms crossed over his broad chest. "If it makes you feel any better, the miners should have known it was bunkum. Your uncle promised a massive drilling device capable of burrowing through solid rock. As he described it, it's big as a wagon, shaped something like a great animal, and could be operated from afar."

"What?! But…" Sensibility sank into the chair. "That's impossible."

"Of course it's impossible," Mr. Sterling said. "But the miners wanted to believe it."

"You misunderstand me," Sensibility said. "I am working on such a device – without the distance control, of course. I have not yet mastered that branch of aether technology."

Mr. Sterling started forward. "What?"

"I sent reports on her work to Washington, along with a pack of mechanicals we confiscated from the Mark's rancho last year." Jane's brow furrowed. "Didn't you read my reports?"

"I did," Mr. Crane said, "and I don't remember seeing a mechanical that could mine for gold."

"But you should know it's within Miss Grey's capabilities to build such a device," Jane said tartly, "even if this is the first I've heard of this digging machine too." She scowled at Sensibility. "Why didn't you tell me?"

"It's for a private client, and he is concerned someone may steal the concept. And as it is an excavating mechanical and not a weapon, I didn't think you'd be interested. If you want to see them, I'm happy to share the schematics. But my uncle could not have known of the excavator. I haven't shown the plans to anyone but the buyer, and the plans are kept locked in my warehouse. If you're suggesting that my uncle was committing some sort of fraud, it…" She wanted to say it was impossible, but knowing her uncle, it was all too possible. "It explains quite a bit, including his supposed death. He must have annoyed a so-called client and had to pretend his own death to escape."

"I'm sorry we're the ones to break the news," Mr. Sterling said, "but his death was no fake."

She shook her head. "As I said, my uncle is quite good at what he does."

Shifting his weight, Mr. Sterling rested his hand on the gun holstered at his hip. It was a curiously relaxed gesture. "Miss Grey—"

She rose. "That my uncle is a scoundrel and a rogue is unquestionable. But he is not dead. Who identified the body?"

Mr. Sterling hesitated. "A lady."

"Ah, there, you see? A confederate of his, no doubt. He's simply pulled the wool over everyone's eyes – again – in order to make good his escape. Make no mistake, he'll turn up elsewhere, no doubt selling more of my purloined inventions. The question is, how did he learn about my plans for the excavator? They're less than two months old, and I haven't seen my uncle since last October."

Jane grinned. "That was a near thing. I was sure they'd tar and feather him when he won that card game."

"He cheats at cards too?" Mr. Crane quirked a brow.

"Certainly not," Sensibility snapped. "He hasn't fallen that low. He is simply deucedly clever when it comes to card games."

"Miss Grey." Mr. Crane ran a hand through his curly hair. "I know it's hard for you to accept, but the Sheriff was quite adamant that your uncle is, well, dead."

"Of course, he would think that," Sensibility said. "He's the sheriff, the most important person for my uncle to fool. Thank you for letting me know and for aiding my escape from that ship. I suppose there will be other angry customers afoot." She'd toyed with the idea of installing some sort of alarums in her shop, but had been too busy with new clients to find the time. She should delay no longer. "How did you find me, by the way?"

"It wasn't hard." Mr. Sterling's eyes crinkled, blazing blue in his tanned skin. "None of your neighbors really believed you were drunk."

"Drunk?!"

"That's what your abductors told the men they passed," Jane said, "as they dragged you between them."

"Oh, good gad. I see I shall have to do some work repairing my reputation."

"Don't bother," Mr. Sterling said. "We're here to take you back with us to Washington."

"Washington?" Sensibility stared, incredulous. Her heart flipped. "But that's in the United States!"

"Why?" Jane strolled behind her desk and sat, her eyes narrowing.

"I'd think today's events should be reason enough," Mr. Crane said.

Jane tugged at her frothy, lace cuff. "A couple of miners get carried away, and you want to cart her off to Washington?"

"Her uncle has brought unwanted attention to Miss Grey and her devices," Mr. Sterling said. "Here in the California Territory, it would be easy for something to happen to her."

"Which is why I'm still here in San Francisco," Jane said.

Mr. Sterling reached inside his coat, withdrew an envelope, and handed it to her.

Swiveling her chair away from him, she whipped out a knife sheathed in her boot and slit open the envelope. She read the letter, her brow furrowing. Her lips pressed into a white slash. "I see."

"We should leave as soon as possible." Mr. Sterling revolved his hat in his hand.

"Yes," Sensibility said, "you should, for you have wasted a trip. I'm not leaving San Francisco."

Mr. Crane opened his long arms, pacifying. "But, Miss Grey—"

"What nonsense!" Sensibility's nostrils flared. "In the first place, I am not an employee of your government to be commanded. And in the second place, even if I were, this is but a Territory and your authority here is loose at best. Miss Algrave and I have functioned quite well for the past year and shall go on doing so. I thank you for your warning of my uncle's activities. We shall carry on from here."

"Your uncle isn't the problem," Mr. Sterling said, an edge creeping into his voice. "Your secrets are."

"I have no secrets. All of my research associated with aether technology has been recorded and sent on to your government's scientists, along with samples of the devices. They can—"

"They're dead," Mr. Sterling said.

She paled. "Dead? What, all of them?"

"In fairness, there were only six. All murdered."

"Dead." Sensibility blinked. "But I just received a correspondence from Dr. Mathers. He was having some difficulty replicating the aether power source."

"He wasn't the only one," Mr Crane said. "When was the letter dated?"

"Months ago. It arrived remarkably quickly."

"It must have been sent just before he died," Mr. Sterling said. "I'd like to see that letter."

"Of course," Sensibility said, numb. Dr. Mathers, dead?

"We believe the Mark is behind the killings," Sterling continued. "They may be trying to rebuild their operations here on the California Territory."

A lead weight settled beneath Sensibility's stays. She clutched the arms of her chair. "The Mark?"

"A secret society that's been exerting influence on various foreign governments," Mr. Crane said. "We believe they were behind the revolutions in Europe last year—"

"I know what it is," Sensibility said, her voice faint. She'd hoped she was done with them, yet she had known that the hope was irrational. Last year the criminal society had followed her from Lima to San Francisco in search of her late father's secrets.

Jane quirked a brow. "You really don't read my reports, do you? Miss Grey was instrumental in dismantling the Mark's base in the California territory."

"Miss Grey." Mr. Crane knelt beside her chair, the stark planes of his face softening. "You, more than anyone, know how dangerous these people are. Last year you were clever and brave, but you were also fortunate. You must see the wisdom of removing yourself and your work to a safer location."

"You say your scientists in the United States were murdered," Sensibility said. "Your answer is to move me to the same place where they were killed. I fail to see the wisdom."

"The last scientist was murdered in Kansas City," Mr. Sterling said. "The killer is making his way west. He may know of your existence, particularly given your uncle's recent activities. We can provide better protection for you in the United States."

"It is out of the question," Sensibility said.

"Why?" Mr. Crane asked.

A lump formed in her throat, and she looked away. How to explain?

When she'd first arrived in San Francisco, it had seemed an ugly backwater. And while at times she preferred her memories of the simple village it once had been to the boomtown it had become, San Francisco was home. She would not leave it or Mr. Night. "My reasons are immaterial. I thank you for your concern, but I will not go. Your fears are overblown. As you said, the men who abducted me had nothing to do with the Mark. There is no reason to believe the Mark has any interest in me."

Jane's gaze skidded sideways.

"That's not entirely true," Mr. Sterling said.

"Then stop dribbling bits of information to me as if I were a slow-witted child and tell me what you are withholding," Sensibility said.

"Miss Algrave can explain better than I," Mr. Sterling said.

Jane examined her fingernails. "The Mark sent an assassin here last month." She locked gazes with Sensibility. "You were the target."

"An assassin? But—"

"I caught him before he could do any damage." Jane rubbed her shoulder.

Sensibility crossed her arms over her bodice. "And you were too busy to tell me?"

"The military swore me to secrecy."

"And when has that stopped you?"

"I'm still a U.S. agent, Miss Grey."

"And your government wanted me to keep on with their projects like an obedient child, is that it?"

Mr. Sterling cleared his throat. "Ladies, there's another option, instead of moving to the East."

Mr. Crane rose. "You can't."

"I don't see what choice we have," he said. "The Mark's back, and it's a good bet they'll be looking for Miss Grey." He shook his head at Sensibility. "The only way you'll ever be safe is when their organization is destroyed. We suspect they'll try to recruit you."

"Why?" Jane asked. "It's a big jump from killing scientists to rebuilding their western operations. What aren't you telling us?"

"There's a lot we're not telling you," Mr. Sterling said. "You know how this business works."

"Trust us," Mr. Crane soothed. "We have our reasons."

"I, however, am not a part of your business," Sensibility said. "And if you want my cooperation, I will require more information."

"Things are happening in Monterey," Mr. Sterling said. "California statehood will have big implications for the United States."

"The slavery question, you mean," Sensibility said. If California entered the union as a free state, it would upset the balance. And oh, how she hoped it would.

"That, and other things. This is a rich territory. The men who control it will wield power. This is an ideal place for the Mark."

"Speculation," Jane said.

"More than speculation, but for the moment that's all we can share," Mr. Sterling said.

"If, by some chance," Sensibility said, "the Mark does approach me, what do you want me to do?"

Sterling smiled. "We want you to say, 'yes.'"

CHAPTER 4

The agent leaned against the hitching post, watching the hell without appearing to do so. A miner trudged past leading a limping horse, its head lowered.

The abduction had been an opportunity missed, and he couldn't afford to miss anything. Grimacing, the agent swatted at a fly. It buzzed away, unscathed.

He shifted against the post. Things hadn't been going right since he'd arrived in the territory. His contact had vanished. Hell, the whole damn operation had vanished. Still, he had his orders, and the Mark didn't tolerate excuses. He'd get it done or… He wouldn't think about the alternative.

Getting it done meant building resources, hiring men, using deceit to co-opt the unwary. And still, it was only luck that his two best men had found the Grey girl's uncle before he could do too much damage. His gut twisted. He couldn't afford to rely on luck.

When those two buffoons had dragged the girl out of her laboratory, he'd been first startled, later intrigued. It was the perfect opportunity for him to gain her trust, to affect a rescue. It would have brought her close to him, made him her protector.

But something had held him back. Had that sixth sense that had kept him from past disasters rung its warning bell? Or was it a distaste for the whole business? Whatever the cause, he'd listened.

And when the whore had arrived with the two federal agents in tow, he had understood the source of his unease.

He'd crossed swords with those two gentlemen before. He'd looked quite different then, and they'd likely not have recognized him.

But.

He would have to step from the shadows in his new identity soon, deal with the agents. And when he did confront them, it would be on his own terms.

Removing his broad-brimmed hat, he ruffled his hair, inhaling the scent of fresh sawdust. In an instant, he was a child back in his father's carpentry shop, the sun making magic of the wood shavings. The pleasurable memory was quickly followed by one of pain.

He closed his eyes for a moment. The dark days had ended when he'd joined the Mark. Now the organization was calling in its debt. There could be no more mistakes. He couldn't lose what he'd gained – his family, wealth, security.

A man on horseback trotted past, spattering mud. The agent took a step backwards and checked the hems of his trousers. Clean. And now he needed to figure out a way to clean up this mess of an operation.

The Algrave woman had surprised him. For weeks he'd thought she was just what she appeared – the owner of a gaming hell, selling her charms to those who caught her fancy or could pay her price. Under the circumstances, her friendship with the proper Miss Grey wasn't wholly unlikely. The chaos of the gold rush had led to many strange companions. That odd friendship was surely more believable than Algrave being a female agent. But incredible as it seemed, she was the girl's minder.

And now two more government agents from Washington had arrived. Something had roused their suspicions. Their interest in Miss Grey meant his instincts had been right – the girl was valuable.

He strolled inside the mercantile shop, crowded with shouting, swearing gold seekers. Ignoring them, he went to the window and gazed through it, past the display of gold pans and pick axes – poor man's equipment, fool's gold. Not like the girl's creations.

Outside, a group of men passed, ruffians, thugs, his Hounds. They weren't the caliber of his usual associates, but they were quick to violence and easily manipulated. And with his contacts here vanished, he needed to build his own network.

Clapping each other on the back, the Hounds swaggered into the gaming hell.

His eyes narrowed. Was now the time to set them in motion?

The bare outlines of a plan formed in his head. He would set one of his Hounds to watch the lady inventor for now. And later…

He didn't like the idea of killing a woman. But this was a fight for survival. If it was between his life and hers, that was no choice at all.

CHAPTER 5

"So you're not concerned Miss Grey will be spirited away by the Mark." Jane ran her fingers along the blade in her hand. "You're afraid she'll turn traitor."

Sensibility glared at her. If Jane thought she could wheedle her way back into her good graces after her betrayal—

"I hope she will." Mr. Sterling dropped his hat on Jane's desk blotter. "We've been trying to get someone inside their organization for years."

"And why haven't you?" Jane flicked his hat aside with the tip of her knife. "Because everyone who's gone in has come out in a pine box. And now you're asking an untrained civilian to try? Don't do it, Miss Grey."

Mr. Crane sat in the chair across from Sensibility and leaned toward her, his brown eyes wide and serious. "It would be dangerous, but we'd be with you every step of the way."

"I have a better idea." Sensibility stood. "When and if someone from the Mark approaches me, I'll tell you, and you can apprehend them. I have neither the talent nor the inclination toward dissembling. I'm a tinkerer, not a spy. And now if you will excuse me, I need to get back to my workshop."

Sensibility strode out the office door. Drawing deep, furious breaths, she paused on the landing. Mist from the lowering clouds dampened her skin.

She closed her eyes. They were all treating her like a child. Worse – like a puppet. Even Jane. It was infuriating.

An assassin had come for her, and Jane had hidden that fact? How *could* she?

She hugged herself to contain her fury.

No, not fury.

Fear.

She walked disjointedly down the wooden steps, her knees stiff. Forcing herself not to break into a run, she stepped into the street.

A horse thundered past, its rider whooping.

She staggered back, steadying herself on the porch railing. Her knuckles whitened on the painted wood. She could have been trampled, killed, done an assassin's work for him.

An assassin had been here, in San Francisco! She could barely credit it. But she needed to cool her emotions and think. If one killer had come for her and failed, would another follow? *If* an assassin actually had come for her, *if* Jane was telling the truth.

She strode along the edge of the road, blinking rapidly. If? And now she doubted her best friend? But Jane had lied by a rather deadly omission. Who could Sensibility really trust? What could she do?

She could run. Or she could do what the agents had demanded, return with them to Washington, to safety. But the Mark would be there, too, wouldn't they? The organization had infiltrated governments around the world. Who was to say that the two agents hadn't been sent at the Mark's behest?

Biting her lip, she stepped onto a set of wood planks laid across narrow logs, a crude walkway. Now she was being fanciful, letting her fears run away with her. San Francisco was her home, and she would not be driven away. Not like she'd been driven from Lima. Her booted feet stomped hollowly on the wood planks.

A barking terrier raced past, tin cans tied to its tail. Down the street, a group of miners slapped their filthy trousers, stooping, roaring with laughter.

"Oh, for goodness… Hooligans!" Shaking her fist at them, she hopped from the walkway and ran after the dog, glad for the diversion from her dark thoughts. The terrier dodged beneath a wagon and darted across the mud. She slid, nearly falling, pursued by the coarse laughter of men.

The dog slipped beneath a wooden walk, and she stopped, panting, and braced one hand on a hitching post. It was just a poor beast, afraid, and did not know any better. But she did wish it would allow her to remove the cans from its tail.

The back of her scalp prickled. Casually, she looked behind her. The street was a bustle of activity, men shouting, hurrying with packs on their backs, regarding her with considering looks. While she attempted to observe the street without appearing to, everyone seemed to unabashedly watch her. As a woman in San Francisco, and particularly one wearing men's trousers, she stood out as well as a giraffe.

A wagon stuck in the mud, its driver tugging on his mule's reins. He caught Sensibility's eye and tipped his hat, grinning.

A shout, a crash, a burst of laughter. A man staggered from a tent with a sign proclaiming pans for sale. Its aproned proprietor ran after him, cursing. Sighting Sensibility, he waved.

There was a rattle of cans and a howl, and the dog streaked from beneath the walk and into the street.

"Dash it!" She ran after the animal.

It rounded a house of ill-repute and raced into a blind alley.

"Ha! Now, I've got you." She trotted around the corner, slowing. The dog huddled beside a rain barrel, its legs trembling, tail low.

Squatting, she held out her hand to the dog. "Come now. I am here to help, and I cannot do that if you insist on fleeing." She leaned closer, her hand extended.

The dog leaped past her.

She lunged, missed, one foot skidding from beneath her. Struggling for purchase, her hand plunged into the mud. "Blast!" She levered herself to her feet, and shook the mud from her hand. Would nothing go right today?

A man coughed. "Your dog?"

Startled, she looked up. The man Jane had driven from her workshop walked toward her. His black cloak swirled, seeming to fill the narrow alley with his mass. The terrier twisted in his arms, depositing muddy paw prints across his ebony, satin vest. He smiled, teeth gleaming, and removed his hat with one hand, loosing a shock of platinum-colored hair.

The dog writhed, and he whisked his hat onto his head, clasping the dog more securely.

She wiped her hand on the wooden wall of the hell, leaving a five-fingered stain. "No. The dog is a stray or someone else's pet, and it is determined not to let me rescue him."

"Him?" His brown eyes were deep set, hooded, twinkling. "I'm fairly certain he is a she. Perhaps that is the problem. Ladies can be remarkably stubborn."

"It is, I've found, often the best way to win a point." She lifted the string of cans tied to the animal's tail. They were hopelessly knotted. "Have you a knife?"

"Naturally." With one broad hand, he reached for the knife sheathed at his belt, and the dog thrashed. "Ah. I seem to be having some trouble reaching it. Perhaps if you…?"

"Never mind." She twisted her wrist, wincing, and the knife beneath her sleeve shot forward.

The man raised his brows. She sliced through the string, and the tin cans plopped to the mud.

The man set the dog on the ground.

It barked at the cans and raced from the alley.

"Not particularly grateful," he said.

"No, but I am." She clicked the knife back into place. A gob of drying blood crusted one of her wrists, lined with red marks. She tugged down her sleeve, hiding the damage from the morning's abduction. "And I must apologize for your ejection from my workshop earlier today. I hope you will forgive my friend."

Removing his top hat, he bowed. "Think nothing of it, for I have quite forgotten the incident, Miss Grey."

"Thank you, Mr... Hermeticus, was it?"

"Yes. And now I fear I have detained you long enough. Good day, Miss Grey."

He turned to leave.

"Mr. Hermeticus."

He swiveled back to her, his hooded eyes probing.

"You didn't get a chance earlier to tell me about the device you required," she said. "If you have not yet obtained one, I'd be interested in learning more. Perhaps I can assist you."

"Well, then. May I escort you to your workshop and tell you along the way?" He offered his arm.

"Thank you, but perhaps not." She held up her mud-stained hands. "While I appreciate the offer—"

He roared with laughter. "Do you think me afraid of a little dirt?" He tucked her arm in his. Stepping carefully, they made their way down the muddy streets.

"I am looking for someone to build a device that senses the presence of spirits," he said.

Sensibility blinked. "Of... what?"

"Spirits. I am a channel. The spirits speak through me."

She smoothed her expression. "I see." On its face, it sounded ridiculous. But on its face, so were her experiments with her father's incantations. And she had seen strange things in her short life.

"Have you, perhaps, heard of the Fox sisters?" he asked.

"No."

"I am not surprised. The news is but a year old, and communications between the States and this territory are abysmal. Last spring, the Fox sisters set New York on its heels when they communicated with a spirit haunting their home." His brow creased. "It claimed to be the restless soul of a murdered tinker, buried in their basement."

"That, at least, should be simple enough to prove. Did they dig up the basement?"

He nodded. "They found human bones."

"And they are quite certain the bones are human?"

He grinned. "Your doubt is palpable, my dear lady, and quite understandable. I take it you do not believe in the existence of spirits?"

"Belief is not my purview. As a scientist, lacking evidence I must remain open-minded. I cannot deny the possibility spirits may exist, but I also require proof."

"Precisely. This is why I have come to you. I experience the spirits. But my experience is impossible for others to observe, and observation is the crux of the scientific method, is it not?"

Sensibility nodded. "And you believe the existence of spirits can be proven scientifically?"

"It must be so, for they do exist." A cart lumbered past, its driver cursing his mules as the cart bounced from one muddy rut to the next. "I know it."

"And how can one prove it?" she asked.

"There are two methods. The first is to create a device the ghost can use to communicate directly with the living, without the aid of a human channel such as myself."

"And the second?"

"In my experience, the presence of spirits tends to make the room colder. It is as if there is a shift, or a drawing of energy."

Sensibility's grip on his woolen sleeve tightened. Energy in the atmosphere, the occult — what he described veered dangerously close to her father's — and now her own — research. "I'm afraid you overestimate my abilities. I work with clockwork and steam, not the supernatural."

"But that is ideal for what I have in mind. A highly sensitive clockwork device that would require the barest effort to control. I have drawings." He rummaged in the interior pocket of his cloak and looked up with a pained expression. "I am afraid I've left them in my hotel room." He glanced down the fog-shrouded street.

"Ah." Sensibility released his arm and stepped back. Sadly, she had encountered the my-plans-are-in-my-hotel-room ploy before. "Perhaps if you would be so good as to bring them by my workshop, we can review them together."

Two vaqueros walked past speaking in rapid Spanish, vivid blankets draped over their shoulders. Silver flashed on their boots and hips.

"I shall, but…" He canted his head. "What are my ideas after all? I am neither inventor nor scientist. Perhaps you should see the problem – so to speak – first hand. I am holding a séance tonight. Several of the first ladies of San Francisco will be in attendance. Would you come as my guest?"

"Tonight!" Sensibility recoiled. The contretemps with the kidnappers and the federal agents had set behind her work schedule. And what if Mr. Hermeticus, with his interest in magic and unseen energies, was a part of the Mark? His thick, mercury moustache could be a disguise. But if he were a member, and she said "no" to his invitation, would that force his hand? Perhaps she should play along and drop this problem in the laps of the irritating agents.

"I realize this is short notice," he said, "but it will be at least a week before my next performance. And oh yes, it is a performance, but a genuine one."

"Of course I will come. I simply do not move in high society. I do not know what I shall wear."

He threw back his head and laughed. "I use that term generously. Society in San Francisco is a far cry from that in the east, and far more entertaining. Come as you are. You are *the* inventor, the shaman of technology. All of San Francisco knows you or wishes to know you for the sake of your creations. There may be an even greater interest in you than in my spirits."

That was what she feared.

CHAPTER 6

The door to her workshop stood ajar.

Sensibility froze, heart thumping, then shook herself. Of course it was open. She'd been dragged from it, unconscious, by two ruffians who hadn't bothered to lock up and neither had Jane.

She strode inside, and a woeful noise escaped her throat. Tables lay overturned, gears and coils of wire scattered on the wood plank floor. Her sweepers zipped about the room, too small to dispose of the major detritus, bumping into a mechanical arm here, a cracked alembic there.

Sighing, Sensibility knelt, righting a barrel of gunpowder. A sweeper mechanical caromed into her side, wobbled to a halt, and attacked the gray powder on the floor.

"At last," Sensibility said, "a task you can manage. What I need are bigger automatons." Finding her lilac-colored apron skirt upon the floor, she wrestled the knot loose and wrapped the skirt about her waist. She smoothed it about her hips. There, she was at last presentable.

Sensibility walked to a window facing the bay and slid it up. A breeze flowed through, teasing the loose strands of her hair. Leaning out, she admired the slate-gray view, the leaden clouds brushing the masts of abandoned ships. To the north, great white sand dunes rolled like waves into the lowering fog.

Her workshop was perfect, aside from the recent destruction. Close to the harbor, so she could be one of the first at hand when a new ship came in. Above a warehouse, where she could store her materials. And it was next to an open yard, where she could use her forge without fear of burning the place down. Not even her father could have dreamed of a working space so delightfully situated, if poorly stocked.

All she needed was another abandoned steamship to scavenge. However, the last dozen ships to float into port had sails. The sailing ships occasionally held interesting things in their cargo holds. But she wanted a big, fat steam engine, with all its tubing and metal, levers and gears.

There was a knock on the door. "Miss Grey?" a masculine voice boomed.

Recognizing the voice, she smiled warmly. "Mr. Durand. I wasn't expecting you today." With his twinkly blue eyes, her client reminded her a bit of Father Christmas, his simple butternut waistcoat straining against his well-padded stomach.

"No, it's a surprise for me as well." Graying head twisting this way and that, he stepped over a copper distiller, catching the hem of his great coat. He twitched it free. "What's happened here?"

"It is nothing. A confidence man has been selling my work to miners without informing me of the fact – or paying me for them. I only learned of it today, when two irate clients appeared at my door, determined to take possession of the goods they'd been promised."

His eyes widened "Good heavens. Were you hurt?"

"No, I am quite well." Her reputation, however, may have suffered a black eye. She shuddered. Perhaps mingling with the first ladies of San Francisco tonight was not such a terrible idea. "But what has brought you to my workshop today?"

"Need I an excuse?" One corner of his mouth edged upward. "Very well, I shall give it to you. I was at the docks and thought to see how our plans are coming."

"Quite well. As you know, the challenge lies in the size of our power source. But I have an idea for a new compression device that is smaller but provides increased output. I will need to build a prototype, of course, but the problem is, as always, materials." Gloomy, she glanced out the window. Was one big, fat steamship too much to ask for?

"That is excellent news." But he frowned.

"What is wrong?"

"We had another cave-in last week."

She pressed a hand to her chest. "Oh, no! How bad?"

"Only minor injuries, fortunately. But your device cannot be completed too soon." He came to stand beside her at the window.

"You take every safety precaution. I know you care for the safety of the men who work for you."

"If you are delicately edging around my guilt in this disaster, you need not. The recent collapse only convinces me that this machine is essential. Your invention could revolutionize mining – not only increasing the ease with which ore is extracted, but saving lives. I am proud of what we are doing here. But these are your mechanicals, your inventions, so I'm afraid my pride is entirely misplaced."

"As you are funding the venture, you have every right to take credit."

"And you are too modest. It is not good for profits, young lady." A sweeper automaton bumped against his boot. Chuckling, he picked it up. "Remarkable. Remarkable. I shipped the one you built for me to the States, to my wife. I wonder when she will receive it, or if she will be able to understand my instructions on its use?"

"I hope she enjoys it."

"Oh, she'll enjoy showing it off to her high-society friends. The maids will enjoy not having to work quite so hard." His expression grew serious. "Now, how long will it take for you to develop this new compressor?"

"I should have it finished by next week," she lied. It would be finished in days, but she did not like to promise things ahead of schedule. "If it performs as I expect, we will be able to complete your device. But as you know, this work is a matter of trial and error, leading to more ideas and different solutions. A prototype of your mechanical is only the beginning."

"I understand. I ask much of you." He bowed. "I am a patient man, and in the meantime, the mining continues."

Sensibility nodded. The mining would continue, and men would continue to be injured and die in collapses. His message was clear. And she could not be annoyed at him for applying this sort of pressure, because he was correct. The device was crucial.

There was a soft knock on her open door.

Mr. Sterling leaned against the doorframe, his black hat in hand. He wore a coal-colored frockcoat now, and Sensibility wondered where he'd gotten it. "Miss Grey." Smiling, he nodded and straightened off the frame, walking to them. "And I don't believe we've been introduced," he said to Mr. Durand.

Something passed over Durand's face. But her client stuck his hand out, and the two men shook. "Durand."

"Sterling."

"What brings you to the territory?" Mr. Durand asked.

"Gold. And other things."

Mr. Durand ran his gaze over Mr. Sterling's wardrobe. "Take care about those other things. It's a remarkable territory, but sometimes a man gets more than he bargained for. I know I did." He tipped his hat to Sensibility and strode out.

"Were you following me?" Sensibility asked.

"Of course. Though even if I hadn't been, it wouldn't be hard to guess where you'd go. I enjoyed watching you chase that dog."

"A gentleman would have come to my aid." She jerked down the hem of her waistcoat.

"Another gentleman got there first. Who was he?"

Stooping, she retrieved a brass gear by her foot. "Mr. Hermeticus. A new client."

"And Durand?"

"It was his plans for an excavator which my uncle purloined." She found another gear beneath a workbench and added it to the growing collection in her palm. "I still cannot understand how my uncle got hold of them. Had he come to San Francisco, surely I would have known." Which meant he must have a confederate. Small objects *had* been going missing lately – gears and scraps of metal. She thought she'd just misplaced the things, and had not fretted much, assuming they would turn up in good time. Had someone taken them?

But how could a thief have gotten inside? True, she could be rather haphazard about locking up her workshop when she went out during the day. But anyone coming upstairs would have to go through the warehouse below. Usually there were men there, delivering or receiving goods and acting as a sort of guard. But "usually" was not "always." And those "guards" had let her two abductors slip past with her draped drunkenly between them. She had been shamefully careless.

"I saw those plans your uncle was flashing about. Heavy equipment for a simple miner. And expensive."

"Mr. Durand is no simple miner. He has a company and employs others to mine the gold. It is unusual in the territory, I know, but he is a man of means from the East with mining experience." Righting a glass jug filled with a green chemical, she thanked the heavens its cork had remained in place, and hefted it into her arms.

"Allow me." Mr. Sterling took the jug from her, his fingers brushing her bodice. "Er, where does this go?"

"There." Sensibility pointed, her cheeks warming. "Beneath that table beside the others." She focused on sweeping up the remains of a mechanical limb.

"What's that?"

"An arm for an automaton."

"It doesn't look like an arm."

"That's because it's broken, and lately I've been modeling my automatons after animals. Insects, I've found, are particularly efficient. Their appearance can, however, be rather startling."

"Speaking of startling, tell me more about that ghoul who approached you on the street. A new client, you said?"

"Ghoul? Mr. Hermeticus, you mean? He's quite likely a Mark agent. You should do better following him than me."

"Oh?" Crossing his arms over his broad chest, he sat against a table, one muscular leg braced on the floor, the other dangling.

"Mr. Hermeticus said he is a traveling showman of sorts. His last name is likely a pseudonym. He calls himself a channel for spirits and has invited me to a séance tonight at his hotel."

"And are you planning to attend?"

"Since there is a slim possibility the man is innocent, and he may prove to be an intriguing client, yes. If I uncover anything suspicious, I shall inform you, and you can do whatever it is you need to do in such circumstances."

Booted feet pounded up the steps, and Mr. Crane bounded into the room. "There you are."

"Miss Grey was just filling me in on the cast of suspects."

"We have an entire cast?" Mr. Crane rubbed his bony hands together.

"Miss Grey's been invited to a séance."

"I am not the only one," she said. "The first ladies of San Francisco – whoever they are – shall be in attendance." Another uncomfortable flush of heat rolled through her. It was quite ridiculous. California was but a territory, and there was no high society to speak of. She knew all these women.

So why did the thought of hobnobbing with them set her nerves on edge?

"Are they indeed?" Mr. Crane rubbed his chin, his expression speculative. "A town this size, I suppose everyone who's anyone knows everyone else."

The words echoed her own thoughts and startled, she regarded him.

"Miss Grey, do you have a list of your clients?" Mr. Sterling asked.

"Of course."

"I'd like to look through it, if you have no objection."

Mr. Crane picked a mechanical limb off the floor, tracing one long finger along its pulley system.

"I suppose you must," she said. It was an invasion of her clients' privacy – and her own – but the sooner this was over with the sooner she could get on with her work.

Pressing her lips together, she marched to a wooden filing cabinet and opened a drawer, withdrawing a book of accounts. "I suppose Miss Algrave will wish to review this as well."

"She won't be working with us," Mr. Sterling said.

Sensibility clasped the book to her chest. "What? Why not?"

Mr. Crane flexed the mechanical limb. "This is incredible."

"Orders from Washington," Mr. Sterling said.

Her fury at Jane's betrayal evaporated. "Orders from Washington? Then Washington is an ass. Miss Algrave is the premier expert on the Mark's operations in the territory." Sensibility was unsure if this was true, but Jane had dealt with the Mark in the California Territory before. "And she knows San Francisco better than anyone. Besides, as a lady she is best positioned to protect me. She can go anywhere I do without fear of impropriety."

"She didn't do a very good job protecting you this morning," Mr. Sterling said.

"That wasn't entirely her fault." Sensibility pressed her chin against the edge of the account book. "In point of fact, it was largely my own."

Mr. Crane picked up a sketch for an automaton and studied it, frowning. "Don't tease her, Sterling. That order from Washington is three months old. It's got nothing to do with the morning's events."

"But what is her order?" Sensibility asked.

"I can't say." Mr. Crane held the sketch away from him and tilted his head, his angular face contorting with thought.

Sensibility's mouth tightened.

"We don't know her orders," Mr. Sterling said. "It was a private communication. May I?" He grasped the account book in Sensibility's hands.

Reluctantly, she released it.

"You know," Mr. Crane pointed at the sketch. "If you use a smaller gear here and a larger one there, you'll get more force."

"And snap the pulley." Sensibility's gaze flicked upward. "I know."

"Just use a larger gauge wire."

She drummed her fingers on the top of the filing cabinet. "If I had a stronger wire, I would use it. But as you can see, I am forced to use whatever I can scavenge."

"But surely you can make wire."

She strode to him, her apron skirt tangling in her ankles. "I have no doubt that future generations of tinkerers and scientists will improve upon my devices. In fact, you yourself may feel at liberty to do so."

Sensibility whisked the sketch from his fingers. Yes, yes, she could make better wire. But it took time, and she was impatient and so were her clients. And what were Jane's orders? Why wasn't she here? "And now I need to put my workshop to rights. If you will excuse me?"

"Actually," Mr. Sterling said, "I'll need your help reviewing your client book. Mr. Crane can put your lab back together."

"What?" Mr. Crane shouted.

"After all, you've got a lab of your own," Mr. Sterling said. "You should know where everything goes."

Mr. Crane jammed his fists on his hips, his long arms akimbo. "Well, that's a fine thing."

"And you can kill two birds with one stone," he said.

"Oh." Mr. Crane dropped his hands to his sides. "Right. Fine."

"Rummaging through my workshop while I'm not looking you mean?" Sensibility asked. "What do you expect to find?"

"Merely curious, my good lady," Mr. Crane said. "I've seen the work you've done for our government, and it's quite remarkable."

"Your government, not mine."

Whoops and gunshots pierced the air. She glanced toward the windows, her neck stiffening.

"Who knows?" Mr. Crane said. "Someday, the territory may become a state, and then it will be your government as well."

She turned to Mr. Sterling. "Let us get on with this."

One corner of his mouth quirked upward. Leading her to an empty table in the center of the room, he spread the book open and drew her a chair. "Miss Grey?"

"Thank you." She sat, adjusting her apron skirt. They couldn't possibly be sending Jane away. Surely, this was a temporary situation. If Mr. Sterling and Mr. Crane were her new minders… But no, their plan had been to remove her to the States, not act as guard dogs. Once she discovered who the Mark agent was, she could hand the problem over to them, and life would return to normal.

More gunshots rang out, and there was a splintering of glass.

Sensibility leapt to her feet. A bullet hole cracked her window. As she watched, a fissure lengthened, made lace of the glass. Her new window! "No!"

"Get down, Miss Grey." Mr. Sterling shoved her beneath the table.

The men drew the revolvers from their belts. Mr. Sterling bolted from the room.

She wedged herself beneath a table, and stared vacantly at a gear wedged between the floorboards. Back to normal? She no longer knew what normal looked like.

CHAPTER 7

Pocketing her revolver, Flora watched from the shadows of a warehouse. A muscular young man bounded from Miss Grey's building and stormed toward the nearest Hound.

Smothering a laugh, she watched as they argued, the young man's teeth flashing. She could only hear bits of the argument, of the Hound's brayed denials. But of course he *had* been shooting moments earlier, and there *was* a revolver in his hand.

More men gathered, crowding the street, and for a moment it appeared the nice-looking young man would lose control of the situation. But he straightened his hat and stalked into the warehouse.

Interesting.

She'd almost like to put another bullet through the window to see what the handsome young man would do. But there was something about him, something that made her shiver. No. Another bullet would be reckless. And bullets cost silver.

Her supply of both bullets and silver was dwindling. It would continue to shrink until the day she would be forced to become the fallen woman she pretended at. She closed her eyes, the blood pounding in her ears. Good God, what had she come to?

One day she would fall. It was as certain as the sunset. But she would not go down before Miss Grey paid for her crimes. And that would happen when the time was right, when Miss Grey was unguarded, and Flora could escape to continue her work.

Miss Grey was the final piece of her puzzle, her mission.

Miss Grey would die. Flora would live on.

CHAPTER 8

Warm, golden light cascaded from the windows of the boarding house, making rectangles on the porch, stretching onto the street. Sensibility's heart lifted. Home.

She trudged up the steps to the front door and went inside. Shutting the door behind her, she paused on the doormat and lifted her hems for the boot scraper to do its job. The tiny mechanical's stiff brush whirred over her boots, polishing them to onyx. She dragged her feet over the tattered canvas mat, removing the bottom muck.

Mrs. Watson bustled out of the dining area, brandishing a large wooden spoon. A dwarf, she stood no higher than Sensibility's waist. She raked a flour-stained hand through her hair, turning the gray at her temples white. Her brow wrinkled. "Tiring day, dear?"

"You could say that." Sensibility fumbled with the ties of her brown cottage cloak and hung it on the coat stand by the door.

"Well, I've got something to cheer you right up. You've got a visitor in the parlor."

"Jane?" Sensibility hurried into the cheerful parlor and stopped short, drawing a quick breath.

A man rose from the Hitchcock chair, its tiny ball feet scraping against the wood floor as he pushed it back. He smiled broadly, his coppery eyes crinkling. "Sensibility. It's good to see you again." His hawk nose twitched. "No chemicals today? How have you been keeping yourself?"

"Krieg." She swayed, emotions bubbling, a chemical reaction. Disappointment at Jane's absence tamped the flames. Happy surprise at the sight of Mr. Krieg Night kindled them. And a strange tinge of guilt prickled at the edges of her awareness. "I didn't know you'd returned from Monterey."

"Three days ago."

Her eyes widened, her throat constricting. "Three days?!"

"I had to deliver a message from the governor to the Presidio, and then I got caught up with the Alcade—"

"I am surprised the military governor does not have troops to deliver his message to his own Army." She was being waspish. But three days! He had been in San Francisco for three entire days without sending her word, or coming to see her? She lifted her chin. Ah, well. No promises had been made, and she knew how passionately he felt about bringing statehood and rule of law to the territory. But an ache swelled in her chest. She pulled off her gloves and stared at her work-scarred hands.

"This was a different sort of message." He stepped closer, stumbling over a blue rag rug. Straightening, his cheeks darkened. He examined her, his expression intent. "Is anything wrong?"

He smelled of wood smoke, and musk, and soil dampened after a rain, his nearness soothing and unsettling her at the same time. Her heart shifted off balance, out of kilter. "No," she said. "A window was broken at my workshop. That is all." She wanted to tell him everything, but something – pride? – stopped her lips.

"Broken how?"

"A bullet. It was just those blasted Hounds."

A vein pulsed in Krieg's jaw. "You could have been killed."

"Hardly. You know how narrow that street is. The bullet went nearly straight into my ceiling. Another two inches to the west, and it would have missed the window entirely."

Krieg laughed. "I do believe you're more distressed by the loss of your window than by your brush with mortality."

"Have you any idea how much windows cost? Something must be done about the Hounds. They claim to protect us, but they're the real criminals."

He sobered. "I am afraid there is little we can do about the Hounds for now. The governance of California was thrust on the military, and it is ill-prepared for the task. They are a fighting force, not a governing body."

"You sound as if you are the governor's spokesman."

His smile was quick. "Do I? I was parroting the Colonel at the Presidio. The Alcade has been begging him for help bringing order to the town."

The position of alcade was a holdover from Spanish rule, and the hapless mayor had been utterly ineffectual in his post. "Is this why you were at the Presidio?"

"That, and some other business." His mouth turned down. "On my ride back from Monterey, I detoured to the rancho." He did not have to say which rancho. For them both, there was only one. The one they had nearly perished on last year.

"Why?"

"I don't know. Have you ever had a sense that you should do something, even though you had no good reason why?"

She sat upon the settee. "Yes, I have." And she rarely regretted following that instinct. It had been sharpened to a razor's edge over the past year.

"The place is still abandoned." He lowered himself beside her. "Cleaned out. It has a strange air." He shook himself. "I am being fanciful, though the place does have a damned odd feel."

"It is to be expected."

"What is?"

"All of it. The rancho has a tragic history, and our memory of it taints our perception of the place. Add to that it has been abandoned. Little wonder if its atmosphere is uncanny."

"It was more than that. I had the sense I was being watched."

She leaned closer to him. "And were you?"

"I did not catch the person, but yes, I am certain of it. It could have been an Indian, out looking for things to scavenge from the site."

"You do not believe that, or you would not be telling me about it."

"No." He laid a hand over hers, and her heart leapt. "Sensibility—"

Someone coughed from the doorway. "Am I interrupting something?" Mr. Sterling stepped into the parlor, his hat held loose in one hand. He nodded to them. "Good evening, Miss Grey."

Krieg rose. "I don't believe we've met."

"I'm Sterling." He extended his hand, and Krieg took it. "Night."

"And you're a boarder here too?"

"No."

"The rooms aren't bad."

"How would you know what the rooms are like?" Sensibility stood. She did not want these two men discussing her. And she wanted to be the one to tell Krieg about recent events.

"Because I've rented a room," Mr. Sterling said.

"You know this man?" Krieg asked her.

"A business associate," Mr. Sterling said. "We were just going to go over some plans."

"Oh, good gad." Sensibility pulled the copper pocket watch from her waistcoat. It had taken her longer than she'd expected to complete her business in town and return home. The scents from the kitchen tugged at her, and her stomach rumbled in protest. "I'm afraid I lost track of the time."

"I won't keep you." Krieg touched her elbow. "I'll see you tomorrow. We have much to speak about." Nodding to Mr. Sterling, he left the room. The front door closed quietly.

"Your fiancée?"

"No. Are you really staying at Mrs. Watson's?"

"Mr. Crane is too. Do you object?"

"Would you change your situation if I did?"

"No."

"Then why pose the question? I have not yet eaten. Would you mind if we continued this discussion elsewhere?" She canted her head toward the door and the kitchen beyond.

"Not at all." He bowed, waving her out the door.

Mr. Sterling at her heels, she breezed through the windowless dining area, where half a dozen men sat shoveling food into their mouths. Striding into the kitchen, she whipped a dish cloth from the oven door and removed a lidded pan from the stovetop.

"Mr. Sterling!" Mrs. Watson stood in the open door to the back yard, her mouth agape. "I do not allow guests into my kitchen."

"But, Miss Grey—"

"Miss Grey is not a guest. She lives here and may go where she pleases. You, however, must wait inside the dining area." She glared at Sensibility. "And you know better than to let him in."

She ducked her head, hiding a smile. "I apologize, Mrs. Watson."

"Now git!" She picked up a broom, cut in half to fit her size, and waved it, threatening.

Shooting Sensibility a look, he hunched his shoulders and backed from the kitchen. "I'm getting."

Mrs. Watson laid the broom in the corner. "Thanks to your mechanicals, that's the first time I've used that in months." She bent, hands on her knees, and peered beneath the table. Rows of steaming pies stretched out upon the crossbeam.

Sensibility sniffed, her mouth watering. After a year, she still was unused to seeing quite so much food in one place.

"There you are, you little imp," Mrs. Watson said. "Come to mama." A mechanical with a broom for a skirt and fashioned like a tiny woman rolled from beneath the table.

"Er, you know my automatons cannot understand commands," Sensibility said.

"She understands me just fine, doesn't she?"

"Well. I'm glad you like her." Sensibility put a pot on to boil.

"Like her? Between the sweepers and that steampowered washing contraption, I've got all the time in the world to bake my pies. It's a pity you don't have any mechanicals that can dust."

"Well, I do have a duster, after a fashion. When I lived in Lima I designed a mechanical with an exceedingly light touch. It used an over-large feather duster, which flowed over and around objects rather than knocking them over. It's not as effective as lifting each object and dusting beneath it, but my father was careless about housekeeping."

"Around is good enough for me. I'll take one. Figure out how many month's rent that will cost me and let me know. Is your young man staying for dinner?"

"If you are referring to Mr. Night, no." Her chest hitched. "And he isn't my young man."

"Oh, isn't he? Does he know that?"

"Considering how little time we've spent together lately, he ought to know."

"Well, you know how men are. Mr. Night's got strong feelings about statehood. I just hope he's not going to be disappointed."

Was Mrs. Watson referring to disappointment in her or in the territory achieving statehood? "I had better speak with my new client," she said stiffly.

"I'll bring your tea and dinner when it's hot."

"Thank you." Sensibility returned to the dining room.

Plates with half-eaten food lay abandoned on the blue and white, checkered table cloth. Alone at the table, Mr. Sterling slathered butter on a steaming biscuit. Lanterns cast pools of light on the table and sideboard.

Her brows rose. "Where is everybody?"

"They graciously agreed to give us some privacy."

"Graciously? I doubt that." The man had somehow frightened the other boarders off. He didn't appear fearsome, with his boyish grin and twinkling eyes. But he had demonstrated his capability with his fists in the abandoned ship. "Those men who abducted me, what have you done with them?"

He shrugged. "They're at the Presidio, waiting to be questioned. If they're part of the Mark, we'll find out."

"And if they're not?"

"Kidnapping's a crime. Are you still planning on attending the séance tonight?"

"Of course I am."

"I'm just asking, because earlier you didn't seem interested in helping us out."

"Mr. Hermeticus is a potential client, unless he is a part of the Mark. And if he is a Mark agent, it is to my benefit to learn the truth so you can take care of the matter."

He laid down his knife. "And how do you imagine I'll take care of it?" He asked, his voice a low rumble.

"By arresting him. Why? Did you have something else in mind?"

"No. I just know that in the past, Miss Algrave has had to take things into her own hands. My partner and I work a little differently."

Annoyed, she raised her brows. "I don't know what you've heard about Miss Algrave, but I assure you, her behavior has been perfectly proper. Today you have the benefit of the Army and the Presidio near at hand to act as your gaoler. But help was much farther away last year. And in no case did Miss Algrave forget that she was first an officer of the law. Such as it was."

"No case that you know of."

"Just what are you implying, sir?"

He grimaced. "Nothing. But you won't be alone at tonight's séance."

"I suppose you're coming with me."

"Nope, not I." He shoved back from the table and stretched. "I have to interrogate our prisoners from the ship. Don't worry, even though the séance will be at a public hotel, I'll make sure someone's watching."

"I take it someone shall be watching me until this is all over. I look forward to that day."

"Miss Grey, it will never be over. The secrets in your head must never fall into the wrong hands. You know too much."

"But… That's absurd." Wasn't it? She bit the inside of her cheek.

"Is it?" His blue eyes darkened. "Maybe Miss Algrave did what she needed to do. As long as the California Territory wasn't under the control of the United States, her authority here was weak. But that will change. The gold discovery has made sure of it. This territory will become a state. And then you'll have to decide what you'll do."

"Because then your government will be able to apply greater pressure on me to toe the line," she said bitterly. "For a government founded on the liberty of the individual, I find that ironic."

"So do I. But it's for your own protection. And that of others."

And there was the crux of the matter. For in her heart, she knew the man was at least partly right. Sensibility stared at the vase of poppies centered on the blue-checked tablecloth. "I must get ready for tonight."

He clapped his hat on his head and winked. "An evening with the first ladies of San Francisco? That will take some preparing for. Good luck." He strode to the door, hesitated, turned. "And I'm sorry about your uncle, whatever has happened to him."

"Thank you." Her voice cracked at the end.

He left her alone.

Fumbling her way to a chair, she sat at the table and shoved a dirty plate aside. How could this be happening? She had awoken this morning a moderately wealthy lady of business. With independence and friends. Family. And now her independence was threatened. Her best friend had been removed from the chess board, shunted aside, a fallen pawn.

And her uncle… She swallowed, tears pricking at the back of her eyes. Her uncle was alive. He would turn up when the time suited him.

The kitchen door swung open, and Mrs. Watson bustled in, the top of her head barely clearing the tabletop. "Dinner's ready." She laid the tray on the table before her. "You should eat up. A girl your age shouldn't be so thin." She nodded at the mug of brown liquid. "And your tea."

Sensibility stared at the chipped cup. Not even tea would solve this problem.

CHAPTER 9

Wrists aching, Sensibility buttoned the top of her winter pelisse. Like most items in her wardrobe, it was a deep, chocolate brown, a color that camouflaged stains from the lab and from the town's muddy streets. The pelisse gaped stylishly at the bottom, revealing her best violet gown – two years old and already one year out of season when she'd made it.

She glanced at herself in the wardrobe mirror and turned, frowning. And that, she thought, was the problem with having a fashionable friend. She hadn't concerned herself with such things before she'd met Jane. But Jane's finery had made her forcibly aware of her own lack.

Smoothing the front of her pelisse, she glanced down at the knife strap on the dresser. It had felt too good removing it from her cut and swollen wrist. She would not wear it tonight.

A sweeper automaton bumped into her skirts, chirped, and veered off.

"Ah, well. It is the best I can do, and that is all I can do." If she looked shabby beside the other ladies, so be it. Sensibility fluffed the short cape about her neck and plucked her reticule from off the bed. Dimming the lantern on her dresser, she walked downstairs, nearly treading upon her landlady in the entryway.

"Mrs. Watson! I'm terribly sorry. Are you all right? Are you going out?"

Beneath a hooded, black cottage cloak, the lady wore a deep-blue silk gown, its skirts puffed with crinolines and trimmed with Belgium lace. Spectacles dangled from a silver chain around her neck. She raised them to her eyes. "I'm fit as a fiddle, and don't you look a picture."

"I didn't know you wore spectacles," Sensibility said.

"Not usually, but if I'm going to a séance, I'm not going to miss the show because I'm too proud to wear my spectacles."

"You're going!" Sensibility smiled, relieved. "I thought I'd be alone."

Mrs. Watson pressed one finger to the side of her nose and winked. "We wouldn't let you go alone. But you're not afraid of spooks and spirits, are you?"

Sensibility blinked. Mr. Sterling had recruited Mrs. Watson to be her watchdog? Perhaps Jane had told him how handy her diminutive landlady was with her little shotgun. And beneath her cloak, Mrs. Watson could be hiding all sorts of weaponry. "Of course not." Sensibility opened the door, holding it for the lady, then stepped onto the porch behind her.

Scalp prickling, Sensibility stopped, scanned the foggy street. It was empty. Faint laughter and music wafted on the sea air, as if from another world. Light gleamed from the windows along the road, turning the mist golden. She felt for her watch, tucked into the pocket of her waistcoat, and ran her gloved fingers along its copper chain. Above, a seagull screeched, and she started.

"You forget something?" Mrs. Watson asked.

"No." Eyes straining, she peered into the fog. "My nerves are a bit frayed."

"You do look peaky. More red meat, that's what you need. Come on then, or we'll be late."

They sloshed down the street, struggling through the mud.

Prospectors in stained trousers and baggy shirts slouched past. The volume of music, laughter and shouting rose.

Gasping with exertion, they stumbled onto a wooden walkway. A man in a long black doctor's coat stepped off the platform, tipping his top hat as they passed.

"Thank you, sir," Mrs. Watson said. She plucked Sensibility's gown. "What time is it? Are we late?"

Sensibility checked her pocket watch. "It's nearly eight o'clock."

"Blast it! Well, we should make good time now that we're out of that mud. So what are you going to build for the magician?"

"I don't think he's a magician. But he requires a device that will prove he is not a fraud, and that may be difficult as he no doubt is a fraud."

"Well, either way, I expect a grand show tonight for my money."

"You paid?"

They pressed against the edge of the walkway. Two soldiers in blue walked by, tipping their hats.

"Course I did," Mrs. Watson said. "Man's got to make a living, hasn't he? Wasn't cheap, either." Huffing, she clambered up the steps to the hotel, her gait rolling like a sailor's.

A man in patched trousers and a worn, plaid shirt raced across the porch and held the door for them, bowing. "Madam. Miss? It is Miss, ain't it?" he asked, his expression hopeful.

"Not to you, she ain't." Mrs. Watson growled, shoving Sensibility inside. She slammed the door on him. "How you manage to stay unhitched, Sensibility, is a mystery."

"One simply says 'no,'" she murmured.

The hotel entry was homey, with a rag rug on the wood plank floor and overstuffed chairs around a low, polished table.

A clerk behind the high front desk looked up and yawned, scratching his mutton chop whiskers. "You here for the table rapping?"

"No. We're here to see spirits," Mrs. Watson said.

He frowned, stood, leaned over the desk. "Ah, Mrs. Watson. I didn't see you there."

Her lips curled. "It drives him mad that folks prefer my boarding house to his fancy hotel."

"Do they?" He raised a brow. "As my hotel is full, as usual, I couldn't rightly say."

Mrs. Watson pinked.

"Where is the table rapping?" Sensibility asked quickly. "We do not wish to be late."

Settling against the desk, he pointed toward an open double door. "Through there."

"Thank you," Sensibility said.

"Don't know what you're thanking him for." Raising her chin, Mrs. Watson sailed through the open doors. "No service at all," she called over her shoulder.

Shaking her head, Sensibility followed her landlady into a dimly lit room. Oil lamps in brass brackets flickered on the walls. Men in frock coats and women in shimmering gowns sat around a round table in the center of the room. Atop the table lay a violin, a drum, and a tambourine. A woodstove smoked in one corner, its door improperly fitted, and she itched to repair it.

The men rose, and introductions were made.

Sweat trickled down Sensibility's back. She unbuttoned her heavy pelisse, fanning herself with her hand.

"And where is our host," Sensibility said, "Mr. Hermeticus?"

"Here, my dear lady," a voice purred behind her.

She turned, and he was close, too close. She stepped back, bumping against the table. He took her hand and pressed his lips to it, his gaze capturing hers. "May I help you with your overcoat?"

He helped her remove her pelisse, his cool hands brushing the nape of her neck. "Thank you for accepting my invitation," he said. "I hope the séance will prove… inspiring."

"Sensibility," Mrs. Watson hissed, nudging her booted foot. "Your goggles."

"What?"

Sensibility reached for her belt and touched metal. Tingling swept up the back of her neck and across her cheeks. Good gad. She must have strapped them on without even knowing it, as she did every day when she set off for her workshop.

An old woman jabbed her in the side with a cane, and Sensibility jolted away. The lady peered at her through thick spectacles. "What are those contraptions? Some new fashion?"

Now everyone stared at her.

Sensibility laughed weakly. "How silly of me. I am so used to attaching them to my belt, I must have done it this evening without thinking."

"Oh, don't look so shocked." Mrs. Watson hopped onto one of the chairs around the table. "You've all heard Miss Grey's an inventor." She folded her hands in front of her. "Now, where are the ghosts?"

CHAPTER 10

Flora whisked into the shadow of the hotel. Miss Grey was a fool, striding down the streets as if she owned them. A fool to get involved with *him*. A fool to think her guard could keep her safe. A fool to think her sins would not find their way home.

The guard, disguised as a miner, lingered at the end of the alley, well-hidden. But she could hear his shifting feet, smell his bay rum scent. She'd imprinted the latter on her mind as soon as she'd seen the strange man trailing behind Miss Grey and the dwarf.

Reaching for the knife sheathed at her waist, she ran her fingers along its leather bindings. Against the soft pad of her thumb, its rough leather was a caress. She shivered. Soon the knife would slide across Miss Grey's neck, and then her little friends would go to work.

Her head came up, and she sniffed. A strong, fishy scent. A splashing sound. Her eyes narrowed. Whale oil?

Drawing the knife, she slunk forward.

Her chest tightened. *Little Mouse*, her father had called her when she'd crept up on him. Memories of her father broke on her like a Sierra storm, unexpected and treacherous. She forced them down, away.

The splashing and foul odor grew stronger. Miss Grey's guard emptied a canteen over a pile of refuse sloped against the side of the hotel. What was he playing at? Starting a fire... for what purpose? To smoke everyone out of the hotel? If that was her plan, Miss Grey was a bigger fool than Flora had thought. The buildings were close and made of wood. The entire block could catch fire, and that did not suit Flora's plans at all.

She slipped up behind him.

He was big, muscular – too big for her to disable. And with so many people about, her revolver would be too loud. Besides, she'd never cared much for using the gun.

She drew the knife. It would be like killing one of the swine in her father's yard. The memory pleased her.

Flora smiled, sliding the blade across his neck.

Burbling, he clutched himself, fell to the ground.

She wiped her blade on his filthy trousers and sheathed it. Reaching into the pocket of her skirt, she drew out a small, copper carrying case.

Her little friends would take care of the body.

CHAPTER 11

Dimming the final oil lamp, Mr. Hermeticus motioned Sensibility to a vacant chair near the woodstove. He took his place beside her, flipping his coattails free of the chair.

"I don't see why you've got to make it so dark," the old woman said. Her chin trembled with indignation, the dark hairs sprouting from a mole on her cheek quivering. "I won't be able to see a thing."

Sensibility studied the woman. She'd thought she knew all the ladies of San Francisco. There weren't many, and they came to her often enough for her labor saving devices. But the old woman was a stranger. Perhaps she was uninterested in Sensibility's inventions. Sensibility had noticed that the younger the person, the more interested they were in her mechanicals. And there was another stranger, a widow in black. Her ebony, bombazine gown bristled with ruffles along the sleeves and bodice.

"That's not a bad point," an elderly gentleman said. "It will make it harder for us to see if you're pulling any tricks, too."

Mr. Hermeticus sighed, lowering his head. "You see the doubt I must contend with?" he asked Sensibility in a low voice.

"The spirits require darkness and silence." The widow's voice boomed from beneath the heavy, black veil cascading past her shoulders. She laid her black-gloved hands on the table.

Sensibility canted her head, trying to place the accent. The American south? The widow's weeds provided a convenient disguise – and an excuse to attend the séance. Was she the showman's confederate? Or perhaps that was the old woman's role?

"Indeed they do," Mr. Hermeticus said. "Though I confess I do not know why. Perhaps they simply need calm to manifest, and the dark helps us to open our minds and look inward. Or perhaps I, myself am the problem. I must reach a deeply meditative state for the spirits to speak through me. But as to any tricks, I suggest we all grasp each other's hands. It is a simple thing, but I can think of no other way to assure you of my honesty."

He held out his hand to Sensibility, and she took it. It was cool and dry. Lightly, he squeezed her hand.

"And make sure it's a real hand." The old woman grabbed the widow, yanking her arm sideways.

The widow gasped.

"Give it a good hard tug," the old woman said. "Here, you can tug mine."

The widow's head turned, her veil floating in and out with each breath. "I will not tug your hand."

"Suit yourself." The old woman shrugged, her lips working as if chewing something.

The widow shuddered.

Mrs. Watson jammed her spectacles upon her nose and grasped Sensibility's hand. "I'm ready when you are."

"I am ready," Mr. Hermeticus said, his voice low and smooth. "Close your eyes, and relax."

"I won't see anything with my eyes closed," the old woman complained.

"We shall all open our eyes when we have reached the proper meditative state," Mr. Hermeticus said.

"Trying to mesmerize us all, he is," the old woman hissed.

The showman's grip tightened on Sensibility's hand. "Close your eyes and relax. Relax your muscles. Take slow, deep breaths."

His voice soothed her, and Sensibility's mind wandered. The séance now seemed ridiculous, and she hoped Mrs. Watson had not paid too much money to attend. She would offer to recompense the lady but knew Mrs. Watson would refuse.

Smoke from the leaky woodstove burned her eyes, and she squeezed them shut. No wonder her chair had been left vacant. Near the stove, the heat was suffocating. Was that part of the trick? To daze her into believing a mock vision?

As much as she hoped Mr. Hermeticus was indeed a member of the Mark, her doubts grew. His demonstration so far seemed like harmless fakery. True, the Mark had used occult societies to lure its aristocratic victims before. And it had a real interest in the supernatural. But so did Sensibility. Aether, which she'd once believed was a myth, was in fact a powerful energy source when properly harnessed. And the notes in her father's journal suggested magic and incantations could aid in tapping into that power. These were notes she had not shared with Jane's employer. They would not believe it anyway, and if they learned that she dabbled in magic, she was uncertain how they would react.

The occultist's grip on her hand relaxed. She opened her eyes, tightening her fingers around his before his hand slipped loose. Hellish orange light from the stove flickered weirdly on the carpet.

Mr. Hermeticus slumped in his chair, chin falling to his chest. He drew a deep, shuddering breath.

Around the table, the silhouettes of the guests leaned toward him.

"Mother?" The showman's voice was high-pitched, feminine.

Sensibility started.

The middle-aged lady on Sensibility's right, Mrs. Potter, craned forward. "Sarah? Is that you?"

"Why don't you come to see me, Mother?"

Mrs. Potter sobbed, a quick, choking sound. "See you? I don't..." Her eyes sought her husband's, and Sensibility imagined she could feel the tension vibrating from his still figure. "Your father and I visit your grave every Sunday."

"At home," the showman said in that eerie, feminine voice. "You're not at home anymore."

"At... home?" Mrs. Potter's voice grew anguished, taut. "But we're at home every day!"

Horror uncoiled beneath Sensibility's ribs, and anger.

"Our home. There are strangers there. Who are they, mother?"

The woman gasped.

"Stop this," Sensibility said to Hermeticus, her voice low. She had to put a stop to this fiendish trick.

"She's still at our old house?" the woman asked.

"It's nothing," the man beside her whispered. "Just a show."

"But how would he know we moved?" Mrs. Potter asked. "How would he know about Sarah?"

Her husband jerked to his feet. "Enough!" He cleared his throat and sat. "Enough."

Twitching, Hermeticus sank lower in his chair.

The tambourine rattled on the table. A violin string twanged.

The smoke, the heat, the flickering darkness, it was high time to expose this charlatan. Sensibility released Mrs. Watson's hand and pulled the goggles free from her belt.

The drum rattled, and hair lifted on the nape of Sensibility's neck.

How ridiculous.

Flipping a dark-seeing lens into place, she pressed one of the goggle lenses to her eyes with her free hand. The room glowed green. She could see Mrs. Potter's expression now, eyes wide and staring, lips parted. Scanning the table, Sensibility looked for the occultist's confederate, for the trick, the wires, the hidden hands.

The tambourine leapt off the table and rattled of its own accord.

Sensibility jolted forward, fumbled the goggles. She must have been looking in the wrong place. Tightening her grip on the goggles, she pressed them tighter against her skin.

A drum stick lifted into the air and thwacked the drum. The drum stick dropped to the table and rolled off, into the widow's lap.

"What was that?" the widow cried through her veil.

Heart pounding, Sensibility rubbed the lens on her bodice to clean it. She'd swear no one had lifted that stick. Sensibility ran her fingers along the edge of the other lens attachments, feeling the single pink and gold lens, and snapped it into place. With this lens, she could detect aether, the in-between energy, and if Hermeticus was no fraud... She lifted it to her eye.

A thick cloud of pink and gold sparks obscured the room. She blinked, focusing on the table, and shapes resolved themselves. The drum. The tambourine. The violin. The figures of Hermeticus's guests, shimmering with life.

Something sprang onto the table with a crash. She flinched and released a quick breath, relaxing. A cat with large, pointed ears prowled the tabletop. Just a...

It turned its face to her.

Sucking in her breath, her heart stilled. The creature's face was smooth, its nose narrow as a nutcracker's. A monocle widened one of its slanted eyes, unnaturally large, glowing topaz. Its ears were pointed, protruding from the top of its head like a cat's. It was dressed as if it had raced through a line of children's laundry and grabbed a random assortment of clothing – a cream-colored linen vest, a pair of blue trousers, a girl's yellow blouse.

The creature ran a claw across the violin strings. They thrummed, discordant.

Its gaze met hers, and the vibration of the strings cut, silenced.

The people in the room fell away, the stillness stretching taut. Sensibility was emptying out, and for a wild moment she wondered if she existed at all. Then all of nature poured inside of her. With each breath more of that clear, golden, life flowed in like a tide, and she knew all she needed do was breathe.

The creature tugged the brim of its top hat and vanished.

The tide ebbed.

Hands shaking, Sensibility hooked the goggles to her belt. What had happened? She drew a deep breath, half afraid, half desiring that tide to return.

She coughed, breaking the silence, smoke from the woodstove searing her lungs.

She must record what she'd seen. A creature the size of a monkey – could it have been a monkey? No. No monkey she knew of had such a pointed nose, such catlike ears. And there had been a strange intelligence in its gaze.

The aether – it had been thick, heavy. And that was not normal unless you were in one of those liminal spots where the veil between this world and the next was thin. The hotel parlor did not strike her as one of those mystical places. But perhaps there was more to this hotel than she'd thought.

Aether was a powerful energy source. In diffuse concentrations, it was everywhere, and one could harvest enough to power small mechanicals. But in liminal areas, such as sacred sites or places of death, aether ran stronger, denser. Since harvesting energy from death and sacred sites raised a host of ethical problems, Sensibility had buried that part of her father's research. There had to be another way to harvest aether more efficiently. If there was, she would find it.

Breathless, she grasped Mrs. Watson's hand.

She had to learn more about this hotel parlor. Either it was somehow connected to death or the sacred, or her understanding of aether concentrations was wrong.

She hoped very badly that she was wrong.

With a snort, Mr. Hermeticus released her hand. "What happened?"

Mr. Potter leapt to his feet and raised the light in the oil lamps. "I have had quite enough of this."

The room flared to life.

His wife shook her head, her face drawn. "But Sarah said—"

"She didn't say anything!" He pointed at Hermeticus. "It was all a trick. He learned about us before we arrived, that's all. We are leaving. Now."

"What did I say?" Face creased with concern, Mr. Hermeticus looked to Sensibility. Beads of sweat dotted his pale brow.

Mr. Potter bundled his wife out of the room.

"You spoke in the voice of a young girl and asked for her mother." What was real and what was a fraud? She had seen *something* move the instruments. It had not looked like a ghost, but neither had it been human. With such high concentrations of aether about, something appearing to be supernatural could have landed on that table, something which science had yet to explain. But if that creature had been real, what did that make Hermeticus?

"Is that it?" The old woman thumped her cane on the floor. "What about my ghost?"

Hermeticus drew a handkerchief from the pocket of his waistcoat. Something gold and circular fell from it, dangled from a chain against his round stomach. Pocketing the object, he blotted his forehead. "I do not control the spirits. They come as they will. We were fortunate tonight that any chose to visit, though I am sorry if they caused pain. I shall attempt to make amends to the Potters later. Perhaps I can bring them – and their daughter – a measure of peace."

"Hmph." The old woman pursed her lips. "Doesn't seem fair."

The widow pressed her palms flat upon the tabletop. "I had hoped… May we try again?"

Hermeticus nodded. "Very well. We shall try, but I make no promises." He dimmed the lamps. "Not so dark this time, I think."

Stretching their arms to make up for the missing Potters, they clasped hands around the table.

"Relax," Hermeticus commanded. "Breathe deeply, in and out. Feel each breath fill your lungs." He continued on, and Sensibility found her mind drifting on acrid clouds of wood smoke. Would the creature return? She sensed it would not, but could think of no rational reason why.

Hermeticus shuddered, his head lolling forward.

"It is happening?" the old woman whispered.

The widow gave a shake of her veiled head. "Shh!"

"Danger." The showman's voice pitched low.

A cold blow struck her core. She tightened her grip on Mrs. Watson's hand.

"Danger surrounds you," he said. "And lies, and betrayal. You cannot trust…"

"Trust who?" the old lady asked. "Danger for who? Who are you?"

He did not reply, and after a moment he raised his head, blinking. "Did I say something? Did something happened?"

"You warned of danger." The widow released the hands of those beside her.

The old lady sniffed. "Not very helpful, since you didn't say who the warning was for."

"If I spoke it, then it was likely for someone in this room. Miss Grey, have you any insights?"

Mouth dry, she swallowed. "None at all."

The voice had been her father's.

CHAPTER 12

"May we speak tomorrow of the device?" Hermeticus's eyes gleamed, feverish. His white hair lay limp on his brow, his too-tight grip dampening her gloves. He pressed a roll of papers into her hands. "Here are my ideas, but I am certain you can improve upon them."

"You wouldn't find a leaky stove like that in my parlor," Mrs. Watson muttered loudly.

The clerk at the reception desk glared at them. "Table turners!" He stomped into the back room.

Sensibility clutched the pages to her chest, her cheeks flushing with warmth. "Speak tomorrow? Yes, yes. Come to my workshop." Through the open doors to the hotel parlor, the brass fittings glittered. If only she could spend time alone there to investigate the unusual concentration of aether. But a hotel employee had already bustled inside. He whipped off the white table cloth and turned the table on its side.

Hermeticus's hooded eyes glittered. "Then you believe?"

"We experienced unusual phenomena, and I would like to explore them further," she said carefully. Was the creature that had plucked those instruments angel or demon, fae or spectre? And how was it connected to the aether? She clipped her goggles to her belt, and her breath caught. Her copper chain hung limp from the buttonhole of her waistcoat. "My pocket watch! It's gone."

"What? Are you certain you brought it here?"

She ran the chain through her fingers. "It is always attached to the chain."

"Perhaps it fell loose inside the séance room," Hermeticus said.

"Or someone pinched it." Mrs. Watson's eyes narrowed. "It was awful dark in there."

He shook his head. "But our hands were linked. And I cannot believe any of my guests would have done such a thing. Come, we will search the room."

They crawled about on the floor, searching beneath chairs, turning back carpets. But Sensibility's watch was gone.

She sat back on her heels, sickened.

He patted her hand. "There, there. The watch will turn up. Was it special to you?"

"A birthday gift from my father. The last…" She looked away, blinking rapidly. She must master her emotions. The last gift her father had given her, the watch held more than sentimental value. It ran on aether and was important. And if she had dropped it in the streets, she would never see it again.

"Someone took it," Mrs. Watson said. "They had to, because it's not in this room, and I remember it flashing on your waistcoat when you took your pelisse off in the parlor."

"Did you?" Sensibility sagged, relieved.

Hermeticus shook his head. "My dear lady—"

"Dear lady my Aunt Fanny! I should have known better than to come to one of these here shows," Mrs. Watson said. "I knew there was something wrong with it and with this hotel! Need the lights off indeed. It's a perfect opportunity for a sneak thief!" Mrs. Watson rummaged through her reticule and released a gusty sigh. "At least no one took nothing from me."

Sensibility swallowed the lump in her throat. "I'm sure the watch will turn up. Perhaps one of the housekeepers will find it."

"To be sure, to be sure!" The occultist wrung his hands. "Come, we will leave word with the desk clerk." He escorted the ladies to the front desk, rang the bell.

A few moments later, the clerk slouched from the back room. "Yeah?"

"This lady has lost her pocket watch," Mr. Hermeticus said.

The clerk squinted. "What's that to do with me?"

Mrs. Watson kicked the side of the counter. "It was lost in your hotel, you blamed fool. Now you tell your cleaning folks to keep a lookout for it if you don't want word to get out this hotel is full of thieves."

He leaned over the desk and bared his teeth. "Thieves? This girl loses a watch, and it's thieves now, is it? Don't think I don't know who's been blackening this hotel's good name all around San Francisco. It's libel."

"I've never spoken a word against your hotel, because it ain't worth talking about. Now you keep your eyes peeled for that watch."

He shrugged.

"It's rather unusual," Sensibility said, "made of copper with planets rotating about its face."

Something crashed behind the desk, and the clerk jumped. Swearing, he stamped his foot, as if trying to crush something beneath his heel. "A mouse! Dang it!" He stomped wildly, an angry dance. "Vermin!"

Mrs. Watson's lips curled upward. "No surprise there," she said beneath her breath. "Let's go, Miss Grey. We'll find your watch."

"I am sorry your evening was marred by the loss." The occultist hesitated. "I should confess that at times other objects have gone missing from séances – the spirits, you understand – but the items always return."

"This has happened before?" Mrs. Watson's nostrils flared. "Well, I never!"

"But they always return." He bowed to Sensibility. "Tomorrow then, dear lady."

Mrs. Watson snorted, her crinolines rustling.

Smile tight, Sensibility followed her landlady outside into the damp night air. The lanterns beside the hotel door barely penetrated the swirling fog. For a moment, the ladies stood, indecisive, on the porch.

"Well?" Mrs. Watson asked. "What do you think?"

A moth struck one of the lanterns with a thunk.

Sensibility drew her pelisse more closely around her. "I think there is something very odd going on in that hotel."

"They'll let just anybody in. Not like my boarding house. I'm more particular. I want a pleasant atmosphere for my guests."

"Mmm." She walked down the stairs, turning on the last step. Gazing at the hotel's porch, she unstrapped the goggles from her belt.

Mrs. Watson grasped her wrist. "Wait. Do you hear something?"

She tilted her head, listening. A piano played down the street. Men's laughter. The creak of a harness, the whicker of a horse. "Just the usual sounds."

"I don't like it."

Sensibility levered the aether lens into place and pressed the goggles to one eye. A handful of pink and gold sparks floated lazily in front of the hotel door. So the aether concentration was limited to the hotel parlor. Interesting.

"See anything?" Mrs. Watson asked.

Sensibility looked into the street, lips parting to reply in the negative. A stream of aether flowed along the ground, around one side of the hotel like a glittering ant trail. She frowned. "Possibly." Stepping down, her boots squished in the road, and she strapped the goggles to her head to keep her hands free.

"What is it?"

"There's something back here." Treading carefully so as not to slip, she walked around the corner of the hotel and into a narrow alleyway. It smelled of garbage and something foul, fishy.

Sensibility wrinkled her nose. The aether trail was denser now, seething. Senses straining, she walked past a squat pyramid of wooden barrels. A shape huddled on the ground, swarming with rose and gold-colored sparks.

She flipped the dark-seeing lenses into place, and the image resolved. A human skeleton lay in a pool of dark liquid, scraps of cloth and leather scattered about it. The scent of copper rose from the carcass, mingling with the odors of fish and waste. Bits of flesh clung to the bones, and Sensibility's stomach twisted.

"What is it?" Mrs. Watson huffed behind her.

Sensibility shoved the goggles up on her head, taking an involuntary step back, and bumping into her landlady. Her breath came in quick, shallow gasps. "A man. Dead." Swallowing, she knelt, hitching up her skirts. Blood. The liquid was blood. Her gorge rose.

"Oh, my." Mrs. Watson pressed a gloved hand to her heart. She gulped, wobbled. "Oh."

Sensibility clutched her landlady's shoulder, unsure who steadied whom. "One of us should… should go for help."

Hems held high, Mrs. Watson shook her head. "No helping him now." Her voice cracked.

"The blood is still fresh. What on earth could clean a man's bones like this?" More urgently, was it still nearby? Sensibility's gaze darted around the alley.

"It must have been animals." It was a question, threaded with hope. "You saw a coyote in San Francisco last month, didn't you?"

"Yes, but…" A part of her wanted to comfort Mrs. Watson, to comfort herself. But something dreadful had occurred, and animals had not been the cause. "The blood! Certainly no animal could pick the bones so clean while the blood was still fresh?"

Mrs. Watson studied the wall opposite. "Rats, maybe?"

Sensibility shuddered. "Rats did not kill this man." She must think, ignore the fear chilling her bones, shaking her heart. She pointed to a discarded knife beside the neck, its blade sharp, dripping.

"That's a good knife." Mrs. Watson nudged the handle with the toe of her boot. Blood trailed down the blade, sticking it with dirt. "What kind of fool would have left it there?"

"A fool who was interrupted. We should leave that knife where it lays for the authorities to view."

"Authorities! You know good and well there aren't any authorities. Besides, that knife might have been just lying there and the bones thrown on top of it."

"Nevertheless, we do have an alcade." But Mrs. Watson was correct. There were no functional authorities in San Francisco and wishing would not make it so. "Someone must be told. Perhaps you could speak with the hotel manager. I'll wait here and ensure the body is not disturbed."

"Not robbed you mean? If someone cut his throat, they likely already took care of that. You go. I'll stay with the bones. That hotel manager doesn't set much store by my opinions. I reckon it would be better if the news came from you."

"I don't like the idea of leaving you here alone."

"No one bothers with me." She drew back her cottage cloak, revealing a holstered revolver at her belt.

Sensibility forced a smile. "I wondered why you kept your cloak on during the séance."

"And it was blasted hot. But after I saw the way everyone reacted to your harmless goggles, I figured I'd better not draw more attention."

The revolver would have drawn less attention than her goggles, but Sensibility nodded and picked her way down the alley. A ripple of unease feathered her awareness. Something rustled behind her, and a knife, hard and sharp, pressed against the hollow of her neck. She froze, heart thumping, limbs rooted to the spot.

"Quickly, quietly," a woman's voice hissed behind her.

A hand gripped Sensibility's shoulder, edging her sideways. Was this how the man in the alley had perished?

Something whispered nearby, the rush of tiny feet, metallic clicking.

The threads of Sensibility's reason unraveled. She breathed deeply, knit them back together. "If this is a robbery—"

The knife dug into the flesh beneath her chin, and Sensibility gasped.

"Hallooo!" A woman called. "You there! What are you up to?"

The pressure released, and her attacker shoved Sensibility forward.

She banged her head against the wall of the hotel, the goggles digging into her scalp, her boots slipping, scrabbling. Sensibility wrenched the goggles off and rubbed her head.

Through the fog, the old woman from the séance marched toward her, cane thumping in the mire. "You there! What's going on?"

A dark apparition rose behind the old woman.

Sensibility levered herself off the wall, pointed. "Behind you!"

"What?" The old woman nimbly spun about, cane raised.

"Dang it!" The widow whipped off her long veil, revealing Jane's shock of chestnut-colored hair. "Club me with that, and I'll..."

"You'll what?" Quivering, the old woman drew herself up.

Jane cursed and stalked toward Sensibility. "What's happened?"

"We found a man, dead, just down the alley." Sensibility rubbed her neck, relief flooding her senses. "And then someone with a knife grabbed me from behind."

The old woman shouted a most unladylike remark and darted down the alley.

Jane put her hands on her hips. "I figured as much. There's nohow that could be an old lady."

"Then who is it?" Sensibility's anxiety gave way to irritation. "Why were you at the séance? Why didn't you tell me you'd be here?"

"I didn't tell you because those blasted agents from Washington are flitting around you like bees at a flower. Now where's the body?"

"Over here, with Mrs. Watson." Sensibility trudged through the alley, Jane at her heels. "He's right... Oh, no."

The bones lay coiled on the ground.

Mrs. Watson was gone.

Sensibility stared, unable to speak.

"Where is she?" Jane asked. "And where's the body?"

Sensibility pointed. "Right there, and I don't know where she is! Mrs. Watson?" she shouted. Chest tightening, she returned the goggles to her head and paced up the alley, peering into every dark corner.

"What, those old bones?" Jane laughed. "Someone's playing a trick on you."

Sensibility strode to the end of the alley, impatient, and tossed Jane her dark-seeing goggles. "Look at the blood. The bones are fresh." The alley opened onto a street lit with gambling hells and saloons. Women in colorful gowns leaned from a balcony above them.

"Hello, there!" Sensibility craned her neck. "Have you seen Mrs. Watson?"

"Who?" one of the ladies above shouted.

"Mrs. Watson. She's quite, er, petite, about this high?" Sensibility put her hand to her waist. "She would have come from this alley, perhaps in the company of another." Mrs. Watson would not have abandoned her post. Someone had drawn her away.

"The dwarf?" The women laughed, shook their heads.

Jane, black gown billowing, tugged on Sensibility's arm. "Stop running around like a chicken with its head cut off, and tell me what happened."

"After Mrs. Watson and I left the hotel, we decided to take a short-cut through the alley," Sensibility lied. She wanted to trust Jane, but she did not want Jane's government to know she had a device capable of tracking concentrations of aether. "We found the body. Mrs. Watson agreed to stay with it to ensure it would not be disturbed. I was to return to the hotel for help. But before I could leave the alley, someone – a woman – accosted me with a knife. Then the old lady from the séance arrived and frightened her off. It could not have been more than a minute between the time my attacker was driven off, and we returned to the body."

Jane handed her the goggles, and Sensibility returned them to her head.

"All right," Jane said, "so whoever attacked you probably had help."

"But if my attacker had confederates, then why would they allow an old woman to scare them off?"

"Maybe because they knew she wasn't an old woman."

"Who is she?"

"One of your new keepers is my guess."

Fear knotted beneath Sensibility's stays. "Whatever has happened, Mrs. Watson cannot have gotten far, and we know she did not come past us at the other end of the alley. She went this way."

"Come." Jane bundled her veil beneath her arm, and they questioned men on the street. No one had seen Mrs. Watson. All were keenly interested in Jane and Sensibility.

"It is impossible!" Sensibility stomped her foot, heedless of the mud spattering her hems. A cart rumbled past. "Mrs. Watson is quite distinctive-looking. How could no one have noticed her?"

"It is strange," Jane agreed.

Sensibility paled. "Oh, good gad." She ran to the alley and slipped inside. The old woman squatted over the bones and blood, her hair dangling from one hand, a lantern from the other. She looked up, and Sensibility started.

"Mr. Crane."

He grinned. "So you've seen through my disguise."

"It is not much of a disguise without the wig." She knelt beside him. "Where were you? You ran down the alley before Jane and I. Did you see Mrs. Watson?"

"Mrs. Watson? No."

"Where did you go?" Sensibility asked.

"I followed the lady who accosted you with a knife." He picked up the bloodied knife by the corpse, studying it. "She must have quite a collection. Or else someone else killed this man."

"Or the knife belonged to the victim," Sensibility said. "Perhaps whatever stripped his flesh was unable to, er, digest the blade. I assumed it was the murder weapon because of the blood on it, but there is so much blood about, and the woman who accosted me had a knife—"

"I can determine whether it was used to kill him or not," he said.

Jane arched a brow. "I take it you lost Miss Grey's attacker."

"Well, you don't have to sound so smug about it." He pointed at the corpse with the knife. "If I'd caught her, we might have some answers now about what happened to him. And what the devil are those things on your head, Miss Grey?"

"My goggles. To see in the dark." She cast about, and her heart leapt. One of the barrels was gone, leaving only a round imprint in the mud. Beside it, something glinted in the lantern light. She pounced on it: a three-inch piece of straight, copper wire, as thin as a strand of hair. Sensibility pressed her finger to one end, bending it slightly.

"What's that?" Mr. Crane asked.

"Only a twig." Pretending to toss it aside, she pocketed it. "I thought it might be a bit of wire I could use."

"You're quite the scavenger," he said.

"Never mind that," Sensibility said. "We must search for Mrs. Watson. Someone has clearly taken her."

"What have you found?" Jane asked.

"The man was attacked from behind," Mr. Crane said. "You can see from the blood splatter on the wall here." He pointed with a long finger.

"At least you agree he was killed with a knife and not eaten," Sensibility said. And Mrs. Watson had been abducted, not left for dead. There was hope.

"Yes, but what I can't figure out is what removed the flesh from his bones." He raised the lantern. "The mud and blood around the skeleton is a mess, and the tracks are incomprehensible. They barely made an imprint in the mud."

"No." Sensibility shifted her weight. The top of the earth around the corpse was scarred, as if tiny wheels and claws had churned it. A chill rippled her limbs.

"We can do nothing for what's left of this poor soul," Sensibility said. "But we may be able to help Mrs. Watson. She was taken from here in a barrel."

"Are you sure?" Jane asked.

"There were six barrels here when we found the body," Sensibility said. "Now there are but five. See how this puddle of... of blood is only beginning to seep into the indentation left by the missing barrel?"

"That would explain why nobody saw her," Jane said. "Stay here with Mr. Crane. I'll ask around."

Sensibility stepped toward her. "But—"

"No, Miss Grey," Jane said. "A man is dead, and Mrs. Watson has vanished. It would not do for you to disappear too. See what you can learn here." Jane whisked down the alley, disappearing around the corner.

"Are those really dark-seeing goggles?" Mr. Crane asked.

She pinched the bridge of her nose, shutting her eyes. If she was to be forced to remain here, then she must gather as much evidence as possible. "Yes." Drawing a breath, she opened her eyes and knelt, surveying the scene. Judging from the scraps of fabric – coarse wool and flannel – the man might have been a miner.

"Then perhaps you can read this." He handed her a folded sheet of paper. "I found it in the mud near the body.

There's no guarantee it belonged to the victim, and his clothing was too shredded for any other identification."

She adjusted the goggles and unfolded the paper. "It appears to be a bill for the Alhambra Hotel."

"Do you know it?"

She nodded. "It is not far from here."

"Ely!" Mr. Sterling shouted.

Sensibility turned toward the alley mouth and flinched away, blinded by a blaze of light. She tore the goggles from her head.

Holding a lantern high, Mr. Sterling strode toward them.

Spots floated before Sensibility's eyes, making him look like an elegant, otherwordly phantom in his black frockcoat and trousers.

"I got your message," Sterling said in a low voice. "What happened?"

"Murder." Mr. Crane straightened, his skirts rustling. "Just like the others. I don't suppose you recognize what's left of this fellow?"

"Others?" Sensibility rubbed her eyes.

Mr. Sterling raised the lantern above the bones. "Not likely. What of you? Any ideas?"

Mr. Crane shook his head.

Sterling grinned. "Nice disguise, by the way."

"Thanks." He whipped his gown over his head and plucked the mole from his chin. "Someone needs to inform the Alcade about the murder. And someone needs to get inside this man's hotel room before anyone else does."

"Murdered like the others?" Sensibility gritted her teeth. "What others?"

"You know the hotel?" Mr. Sterling asked.

He handed Mr. Sterling the receipt. "The Alhambra. Miss Grey knows where it is."

Mr. Sterling's jaw tightened. "I'm afraid there's no time for me to escort you to Mrs. Watson's."

She clenched her fists, her nails biting into her palms. These men had no authority over her, and Mrs. Watson needed her. But if the Mark was responsible for this man's death, and that cabal had taken her landlady… "I'll come with you."

"You'll be safe enough," Mr. Sterling said.

"You mistake my hesitation. Mrs. Watson, who escorted me here, appears to have been abducted."

Mr. Sterling glanced at his partner.

"Looks that way," Mr. Crane said.

"Miss Algrave is searching for her now," Sensibility said.

One corner of Mr. Sterling's mouth slanted upward. "If you're worried about Miss Algrave, I think she can take care of herself."

"I fear for Mrs. Watson."

Mr. Sterling nodded. "Then let's not waste any more time. We need to find out what this man has to do with her kidnapping."

CHAPTER 13

The agent rubbed his brow, head throbbing, fear coiling in his gut. Damp air flowed through the cracks in the plank walls, taking with it any heat emerging from the woodstove.

He stuffed his freezing hands in the pockets of his great coat and edged closer to the woodstove. His plans were unraveling. All he needed to do was pull one thread. One thread would put him into the Mark's good graces, stop California statehood, and position himself as the territory's puppet master. One thread that these idiots now threatened to snip.

He glared at the crude walls of the shack. And were the Hounds too stupid or too lazy to do something about the blasted draft?

A Hound flung open the door and stomped inside, leaving the door swinging in the wind.

"Shut the damn door," the agent growled, his question answered.

"Sorry, boss." The newcomer tugged on his battered hat brim and looked around the cramped room for a place to sit. As the only three chairs were taken, he leaned against the wall, slouching his hat forward, shielding his eyes.

The agent ground his teeth. "Why did you take the dwarf?"

One shrugged, crossing one booted foot over his knee. "She was standing over Pete's body." He laughed hollowly.

"Or what was left of it. Looked like she had something to do with it."

"A dwarf killed a man nearly six feet tall? And then what? Ate him?" He rapped his broad fingers on the crude table. Beneath the light pressure of his arm, it wobbled. "Do tell how she accomplished that."

A flush crept across the man's cheeks, light with stubble. "Well, she's involved somehow. She's a friend of that Grey girl. And she ain't right, with her peculiar little hands and feet. Like an elf or fairy or something."

"A well-respected elf," the agent said. "Did you stop to consider how the citizens of San Francisco might react to learn we'd taken her?"

"The dwarf ain't right," the man muttered. He raised his chin. "So what do you want us to do? Get rid of her, quiet like?"

"No." He thought of his wife, his sons, and had no illusions about what would happen to them if he failed. He had to fix this. There was too much at stake. His voice pitched low. "I've got a better idea. Does Mrs. Watson know who grabbed her off the street?"

"Doubt it. I tipped her into that barrel right quick, and there she's stayed."

"All right then." Rising, the agent clapped his hat on his head. "I'll fix this and keep the Hounds reputation clean. You boys clear out."

"What are you going to do?"

He blew out his breath. "I guess I'm going to become a hero."

CHAPTER 14

Sensibility led Mr. Sterling down streets sodden with fog to the hotel. One of the chains holding the Alhambra Hotel sign had snapped, and its name now hung, lopsided, above the door. The scent of brine hung thick in the fog, and she imagined she could hear waves from the bay. Jagged cracks streaked a window on the top floor. The hotel's wood plank walls seemed to bend, as if sagging from the weight of moisture in the air.

"You said others were killed using this method," she said. "Who?"

"The other scientists."

"They were also reduced to bone? Why didn't you mention that before?"

"Does it really matter?" Mr. Sterling asked.

"It's a rather pertinent detail! And their throats were also cut first?"

"Yes. Whoever our killer is, he isn't cruel. The death is quick."

"And the flesh was removed – why? To delay or obscure identification of the remains?"

"Oh, we identified them. They were killed in their homes and laboratories, and there was no question of who the victims were." Mr. Sterling consulted the receipt. "Room eight." Bowing to her, he swept open the door, and a bell tinkled.

She stepped inside the carpeted entryway. A tarnished brass lamp hung from the ceiling. On the right was an empty dining room, smelling of mold. *Why reduce the scientists to bone?*

A balding clerk emerged from a back room. He pressed his round stomach against the dusty counter. "We're full."

Removing his black hat, Mr. Sterling smiled and braced one elbow on the counter. "We're not interested in a room. My wife here would like to speak with your chef."

Sensibility's stomach rolled at the thought of food. And wife? Sterling was taking an awful chance that she and the clerk were unacquainted.

"Chef? You mean Cookie?"

"Exactly," Mr. Sterling said. "Cookie."

"What d'you want with him?"

"A recipe," Sterling said. "We ate lunch here on… What was it, darling? Tuesday?"

Sensibility's lips pinched. "Wednesday." Clearly, she was to be the diversion while Mr. Sterling searched the murder victim's room. It was quite annoying. There might be items inside that room which she would recognize as important. But she supposed she should be grateful Sterling had allowed her to come at all.

"Of course," Mr. Sterling said, "Wednesday."

"May I speak with your Mr. Cookie?" Sensibility asked.

The clerk's brows creased. "Well. I reckon it won't harm anything. Just a minute." He lumbered through the lobby and into an empty dining area.

"Keep him busy," Mr. Sterling muttered. Lightly he ran up the stairs, taking them two at a time, the tails of his dark frockcoat flapping behind him.

The clerk returned with a sleepy-eyed man in worn trousers and a stained plaid shirt, stretched taut across his muscles. He scratched his bald head. "You wanted to see me?"

"Yes," Sensibility said. "Last Wednesday, you made the most marvelous, er…"

"Stew?"

"Yes. Your stew. I was wondering if I could impose on you for the recipe?"

He squinted at her. "Don't rightly have a recipe."

"Well, that's quite all right." Rummaging in her reticule, she drew out a notepad and pencil. "Simply tell me what was in it, and I shall write it down for you."

"For critter stew?"

She grimaced. "That sounds right. Critter stew. What exactly is in it?"

"Whatever critters I can catch."

She pressed a hand to her stomach. Thank the heavens she did not dine here. "But surely I detected some additional flavoring? Perhaps a hint of spice or herbs or… vegetables?"

"Well, sure there are vegetables. Whatever scraps I've got left. Think I had potato peelings on Wednesday. Course, I've always got potato peelings."

"Where's your husband?" the clerk asked.

"He went outside to smoke a cigar."

"Awfully precious of him." The clerk sneered. "Nothing stopping him from smoking it in here."

"Nothing but me," Sensibility said.

"Probably just didn't want to have to offer you one, Fred." Cookie backhanded the clerk on the stomach, snickering.

"Well, maybe I'll just go outside and join him," the clerk said. "To be polite."

"He might have taken a walk," Sensibility said. "He likes to do that when he's smoking. But by all means, go ahead." She turned to the cook. "I'm simply fascinated by your culinary techniques. You made something positively delightful with such limited resources." Blathering about cigars and stews and walking, Sensibility resolutely did not look at the stairs or think about dead scientists. How long could it take the man to search a room? "Er, do you remember which particular critters were in Wednesday's stew?"

Cookie scratched his chin. "Well, I reckon there was a squirrel—"

Upstairs, something crashed. A man tumbled down the steps, smashing through the banister.

Mr. Sterling leapt after him. His hat flew from his head, drifting to the floor by her feet.

Sensibility gasped and skipped backwards.

Shoving Sensibility aside, the clerk threw himself at Mr. Sterling with a roar. "Cookie!"

The cook waded into the fray, fists swinging.

A chair flew past her, and she ducked beside the front desk. Good gad. She knew she should have gone with Miss Algrave. Crouching, she felt for her pocket watch, remembered it was gone and cursed beneath her breath. By her estimate, at least an hour had passed since Mrs. Watson's disappearance. She had taken the wrong path by following Mr. Sterling here. And she could only hope that meant Jane was on the right track, the one leading to Mrs. Watson. An image of the pooled blood rose in her mind, and her insides roiled.

Two strangers in rough mining clothes raced downstairs. One punched Mr. Sterling in the jaw.

Sensibility cried out, clapping a hand over her mouth.

The agent rolled backwards and to his feet, then plowed into the man's midsection. Five on one was decidedly unfair, though Mr. Sterling did appear to be holding his own. But they could dally here no longer. Mrs. Watson and Jane needed her help.

"Mr. Sterling?" She rummaged in her reticule. "Did Miss Algrave tell you what brought about her faint this morning?"

"Ooof!" He stumbled backwards onto a chair, and it fell over. "Yes. Could we discuss this later?" He kicked one of the men in the gut.

"Excellent." Clasping a handkerchief to her face, she took a small, putty-like ball from her reticule. "Then you might wish to hold your breath."

"Hold my…?" He looked up, eyes widening.

She threw the ball into the melee. It exploded in a cloud of thick, rose-colored smoke, obscuring the men.

Mr. Sterling stumbled from the gas, sleeve pressed to his face.

Picking his hat off the floor, she grasped his arm and steered him to the door. "The stinging in your eyes shall not last long. Or the other side effects."

He coughed, squinting. "Other side effects? Besides temporary blindness?" Tears streamed down his sunburnt face.

"Not everyone experiences incontinence." She guided him down the steps to the street. "Careful!"

He banged his hip on a hitching post.

"Sorry." Sensibility's lips twitched.

"You're hilarious." He coughed. "What did that gas do to them?"

"The men who attacked you will be unconscious for fifteen to twenty minutes, depending on their weight. Did you find anything of interest in the room?"

"Just that gorilla. He was searching for something. You are joking about the side effects?"

Smiling thinly, she guided him onto a wide, wood plank walkway. It jounced beneath their footsteps. "You'll find out soon enough. Who was the man you found in the room? Did you recognize him?"

He draped his arm over her shoulders, rubbing his streaming eyes with his free hand. "I take it you didn't."

"Should I have?" Her heart thudded, his arm hard and careful around her. He was too close for comfort, and if someone saw them her reputation would be… Oh, the devil with her reputation. This was San Francisco, and she was a lady tinkerer, and Mrs. Watson was in danger.

"He was one of the men beneath your window, in that crew that sent a bullet through it."

"He was a Hound? He must have been at the scene of the murder to have known the victim's room was empty and available to ransack. Which means—"

"He might be involved in – or a witness to – your Mrs. Watson's disappearance."

"Could the murdered man have been a Hound as well?" she asked.

They passed a cluster of tents, lit like lanterns from within. Their canvas sides billowed in the wind.

"Good question, but if the victim was a Hound, it wouldn't explain why he was killed."

"No." She gnawed at her bottom lip. "No, I suppose it would not. The Hounds have a base of sorts, a meeting house. Well, in actuality it's little more than a shack."

"You're thinking that's where they took Mrs. Watson."

"The Hounds are not known for deep thinking. And they are just the sort of low-minded scoundrels who would think it funny to pack a lady into a barrel."

"Mr. Crane and I will investigate the meeting house. And I'll take my hat now."

"How do you know I've got your…" Cheeks burning, she shrugged from beneath his arm. "Ah. You can see again."

He grinned. "I've been able to see for quite some time."

Her cheeks tingled. "You— And yet you allowed me to run you into that hitching post?"

"I knew you did that on purpose!"

"You deserved it. Mrs. Watson is missing, in danger, and you play silly games."

"There was nothing silly about that thug in the victim's hotel room, or about those bones. I'll escort you back to the boarding house."

"If Mrs. Watson is indeed a prisoner of the Hounds, we should go to their meeting place directly."

"I'll go. As soon as you're safely returned to the boarding house."

"Or we could learn if Mrs. Watson is indeed captive of the Hounds and rescue her." They turned up a darkened street. The figures of two men passed, bearlike masses in the thick fog.

"You and I are not going to storm the Hounds' headquarters," Mr. Sterling said.

"Certainly not alone if we are to be successful. We need to collect Miss Algrave and the equipment in my workshop. Mr. Night would be helpful as well, but it will take too long to find him."

"We're going to the boarding house."

The plank walkway ended, and she stepped into the street. Ahead, lights from the boarding house glowed, setting droplets of mist sparkling on its eaves and windowsills. She pressed a hand to her stays, releasing her breath. "I have no objection."

"No objection? Really? What changed your mind?"

"Miss Algrave is at Mrs. Watson's, waiting."

"How do you know?"

"Because a light shines in the kitchen. Either she has found Mrs. Watson, who is working off her frustrations in the kitchen, or she has not and is waiting there to tell me what she's learned. Miss Algrave dislikes the parlor and is one of the few people Mrs. Watson allows inside her kitchen."

"Miss Algrave does not report to you."

"Does she report to you?"

"Here we are." He stopped beside the steps, smiling. "Safe and sound at your boarding house."

Rolling her eyes, she stomped up the steps. The front door flew open.

Jane grasped her arm and yanked her inside, slamming the door on Mr. Sterling. "Where have you been? What are you doing hanging around outside?"

"Did you find Mrs. Watson?"

The door swung open, jostling Sensibility from behind.

"I stand corrected." Mr. Sterling stepped through. "You were right about Miss Algrave."

Mr. Crane walked in from the dining room, rubbing bits of glue from his face. "Ah, you're back. The Alcade was less than helpful, but what's left of the body is in the hands of the authorities — such as they are. And we have an identity, Mr. Peter Howe. Came to California to seek gold and never managed to find his way out of the San Francisco brothels. Oh. Pardon me, Miss Grey." He inclined his head.

"But Mrs. Watson?" Sensibility asked.

"Will be recovered." Jane tightened her grip on Sensibility's arm. "The most important issue right now is your safety. Come with me. Let the men find Mrs. Watson."

Sensibility's lips vanished in a thin line, and she shook Jane off. "Mrs. Watson might be in the hands of the Hounds. Or worse, the monster who killed those other scientists. Did you know they were also reduced to piles of bones?"

Jane's expression tightened. "No. I did not."

"I agree that Mrs. Watson is probably with the Hounds," Mr. Sterling said. "Don't worry, we'll find your landlady."

"How?" Sensibility asked.

A vein throbbed in Jane's forehead. "They know what they're doing." Jane lowered her voice. "Trust me."

"But—"

"Trust me." Jane steered her up the stairs.

"I may be able to trust you, but how can I trust them?" Sensibility hissed when they reached the top. "They have been withholding vital information from us both from the start. It must be a habit in your agency. What did you learn?"

"Patience is a virtue." Jane hustled Sensibility down the long hall and into Sensibility's bedroom.

On her desk, the oil lamp shimmered, wick low. Shadows lay deep over the crisp blue bedspread, the bureau opposite the bed, the ornate, mirrored wardrobe in the corner.

Sensibility stepped backward. "Jane—"

The door slammed behind them.

Her uncle, tall, lean, mustached, a revolver holstered at his hip, leaned against the door. Dressed head to toe in black, with only a shock of white at his collar, he looked like an elegant undertaker, hat tipped back on his head. "Is that any way to welcome your dearly departed uncle?"

Sensibility laughed shakily. "Uncle Corbin!" She glanced at Jane. "I told you he was not dead."

He quirked a dark brow. "It was a near thing and a useful ruse. Now quick, Sensibility, take only what you need. We have to get out of town."

"Perhaps you do, but I will not." Sensibility's nostrils flared. How typical. He assumed she would turn her life upside down at his behest. "Your timing is awful."

"But interesting," Jane said. In a flash, her revolver appeared in her hand, aimed at his chest. "What do you know about this, Grey?"

His eyes widened with innocence. "About what?"

"We don't have time." Sensibility ground her teeth.

Jane stepped forward, pistol steady. "I think we should make time. You're involved in this somehow, Grey. Now tell us what you know and quickly. Starting with where and how you stole Miss Grey's designs. Two men tried to throttle her over that little scam."

He made a moue of sympathy. "Did they? Gold miners can be somewhat excitable."

"Why?" Jane snarled.

Sensibility folded her arms over her chest. "We are wasting time."

He glanced at Jane. "It's a family matter."

"And Miss Algrave has been more family to me than…" Sensibility trailed off. Jane had been more like family than he had been, but she needn't rub his nose in the fact.

"Than I?" He smiled, rueful. "That's likely true."

"You've put Miss Grey in serious danger more than once." Jane's aim did not waver. "I reckon I'll stay."

He shrugged, a graceful gesture, than winced. "It's a long story."

"Shorten it," Jane said.

"Two months ago I was in San Francisco, come to borrow some of your ideas, niece."

Sensibility's lip curled. "Borrow?"

"For a good cause. Your father."

"My father?" Her heartbeat stumbled, an ache blossoming beneath her stays. Please to God, let him tell her that his death had also been a ruse. Sensibility reached for her watch, remembered it was gone, and smoothed the front of her waistcoat.

"There was a card game in Monterey," he said. "Exclusive. Which usually isn't a problem for me, but in this instance, no matter how I wheedled I could neither bribe nor beg my way in. You can imagine how aggravating that was. They play for money, but they play for other things as well – property, investments, power."

Sensibility brushed past him and knelt beside the bed, dragging out a small trunk from beneath it. She was a fool. Of course her father was gone – she had been the one to find the body. But for that moment, for that one mad, wild hope… "We have no time for tales of your adventures in gambling."

"You'll want to hear this one, niece."

"I don't need to. I can guess what happened. You thought to use one of my designs to get you inside the game." Sensibility unlatched the trunk and drew out an aether gun, handed it to Jane. "Really, how could you!"

"Exactly. But thanks to your notoriety, I was having a deuced time getting past the men lounging around your warehouse. Mr. Night should marry you before—"

"My notoriety is clearly a poor security measure. I will take steps in the future to prevent intruders, and I warn you not to test them."

His brow lifted. "While I was loitering outside, developing a plan, a woman approached me—"

"Not a lady?" Jane asked. "Who was she? What did she look like?"

"Definitely not a lady. Dark haired and fair complexioned, brown eyes a man could get lost in. One of our, em, fallen sisters."

"Oh, please." From the chest, Sensibility drew out a reticule and opened it. Five of her little gas balls lay inside.

They would have to be enough. She tightened the drawstrings.

"You did ask," he said.

"So you were approached by a prostitute." Jane sighted down the barrel of the aether gun and handed it back to Sensibility. "You keep the aether thing."

"I've got two. There's no reason you should not have one."

"Keep it. Call me old fashioned, but I'll put my trust in lead and blue steel." She turned her gaze on Sensibility's uncle. "And what then, Grey?"

"I realized that she could be of help getting me past those men, and she proved remarkably adept."

"Good gad. You mean she, er, diverted the men?" Sensibility's temperature rose. So that was how someone had gotten inside.

Jane shook her head. "So all you needed was a common—"

"Nothing common about that girl," Sensibility's uncle said. "She has a remarkable memory. Whatever she sees, she instantly remembers and records. Which gave me a better idea: rather than inconveniencing you by removing the plans, she simply had to glance at them and copy them for me."

"And then?" Sensibility leaned forward, her neck rigid.

"She looked, copied out the plans for me at her leisure, and I left."

"You picked my locks?"

He smiled modestly.

"And?" Jane prompted.

"I made it safely to Monterey and got to work. Which is when my bait finally hooked the fish I wanted."

"What fish?" Sensibility cried. "Certainly not all the players. Who were you really after?"

"Unfortunately," he continued, "things did not go as planned. They were quite intrigued by the designs and invited me to their next game. But I was followed on the way back to my hotel, assaulted, and left for dead by three rowdies. Needless to say, they took the plans."

"Naturally," Jane said. "So far, this sounds more like a confession than a revelation. What do you want? More of her schematics? Because it's a good bet you're not here to beg forgiveness."

"Forgiveness for what? I didn't actually steal anything."

"And then you found a body and talked a lady of your acquaintance into identifying it as your own," Sensibility said. "You did *find* the corpse rather than cause the man's demise?"

"Niece! I prefer to avoid violence where possible."

"Is that a 'no'?"

"I found the body behind a saloon."

Sensibility slammed shut the chest. "What do you want, uncle?"

"As the men who attacked me were leaving, they said something."

With her booted foot, Sensibility shoved the trunk beneath her bed. She clutched the aether weapon to her midsection. "And what did they say?"

"That they killed your father."

CHAPTER 15

The bedroom tilted beneath Sensibility's feet. The stab was quick, leaving a chasm in the center of her ribs. "What?" she asked.

"I quote: 'That's two Grey's I've killed, one more to go. Never killed a whole family before. Makes me proud.'" Her uncle rubbed the back of her neck. "That may not be an exact quote, but it is close enough. Sorry, niece. But you're a sensible girl, and I can't think of a way to soften the blow."

Sensibility rose. Fumbling behind her, she sat upon the bed, heedless of propriety.

"Are you sure?" Jane asked.

He canted his head. "You don't look terribly surprised, Miss Algrave."

"We know people are interested in the aether technology." Jane lowered the revolver, and it vanished in a tumble of lace at her sleeve. "I always suspected last year's troubles weren't the end of the matter."

"Sensibility, they killed your father, and you may be next," he said. "And would you be so kind as to point that device away from me?"

"Apologies." Sensibility lowered the weapon to her lap. The air thickened, her lungs laboring to draw breath. Her father – murdered? Ever since the unfortunate events of last year, she'd wondered if his death had been natural. But the confirmation sent her spinning in a confusion of shock and anger.

She had found him in his laboratory. If there had been evidence of foul play, she had not observed it. But at the time she had not been looking for signs, overwhelmed by the sight of her father sprawled on the chemical-stained floor.

"And why are you arming yourself?" her uncle asked. "Not that I'm opposed to it, but it seems a bit unnecessary inside Mrs. Watson's boarding house."

"You got in," Jane pointed out.

"We don't have time for these pettifogging arguments." Bolting to her feet, Sensibility pocketed the aether weapon. "Thank you for your concern. You have alerted me to the danger, and I shall act accordingly. And now if you will excuse us—"

He tipped back his black hat. "What are you two planning?"

"Do you care?" Jane asked.

He shrugged, the fabric of his long coat whispering against the wall behind him. "Just curious."

"You can show yourself out the same way you got in," Sensibility said. "Now if you will excuse us, we must depart."

"Then good evening, ladies." He bowed from the waist, his hat falling from his head. Catching it one-handed, he replaced it at a jaunty angle. He opened the window behind her desk and lifted one well-clad leg through.

Jane took Sensibility's elbow and steered her into the corridor. "You need to install better locks. Do you have any more of those gas bombs?"

"Here." She thrust the reticule into Jane's hands. "I made them for you after all. I can think of no better opportunity for you to test them."

"For me?" Eyes glowing, Jane touched her fingers to her collarbone.

"While you are the best markswoman I know, there are occasions when stealth and subtlety is necessary. I thought they would be useful for your work."

"Sensibility. I'm…" She placed a hand on her arm. "Thank you."

"It is the least I can do." Sensibility turned and locked the bedroom door behind her.

Walking down the stairs, Jane dug into the reticule. "Only six?"

"Let's hope that their entire membership is not in residence when we attack. However, these also produce a great deal of smoke, which should prove disorienting."

"That's good to know. I don't remember much about what happened the first time I set one of these off. I'll have to send the designs for these to Washington."

"Formulas," Sensibility corrected.

They made a tight turn on the stairs, their skirts brushing the walls, and descended to the first floor.

"All right," Jane said in a low voice. "Let's go out the back. I've got a feeling—"

"Miss Algrave, Miss Grey." Mr. Crane stepped from the parlor.

Dash it, they had not even made it out the door! Sensibility clasped her hands behind her back.

He bowed, his lanky frame loose. "Going somewhere?"

"Yes," Jane said. "Good evening, Mr. Crane." She wove around him.

He stepped into Sensibility's path. "This is what they want, Miss Grey. You, unprotected, out in the open."

"They are Hounds," Sensibility said, "witless bullies who've got nothing to do with the Mark. We cannot leave our friend in their hands."

"And we won't. Mr. Sterling is on their trail."

Jane gave a bark of laughter. "Mr. Sterling! What does he know of San Francisco?"

"Don't discount him. There's no one I trust more."

"He is but one man," Sensibility said. "The Hounds are many."

"Which is why you two ladies thought you could go up against them? I expected better of you, at least, Miss Algrave."

Jane's eyes narrowed to slits. She stepped closer to him, and he took a hasty step back. "Nervous, Mr. Crane?"

"Wary. I'm well aware of your… talents." He adjusted his thin necktie. "I do not wish to use violence against a lady, but be warned – I will defend myself."

"You mean you'll try."

The front door banged open, and Mrs. Watson staggered inside, her graying hair mussed, her skin pale. The lace at the cuffs of her blue silk gown dangled, limp and torn. Sensibility barely registered the familiar figure of her best client, looming behind her landlady.

"Mrs. Watson!" Sensibility raced to her, hastily jamming the aether weapon into the pocket of her skirt. "Are you well? What happened? Did they hurt you?"

Mrs. Watson lifted the silver chain about her neck and examined her cracked spectacles. Her hands trembled. "I need a brandy. And yes, I'm safe and sound, thanks to this gentleman."

Sweeping his hat from his head, Mr. Durand bowed. "Not at all, my dear lady."

Mrs. Watson waddled into the parlor. Stepping upon a stool, she unlocked and opened the liquor cupboard. Inside, crystal decanters gleamed. She clutched a tumbler to her chest and grasped a bottle filled with amber liquid. "Anyone care to join me?" she asked, gaze fixed on the cabinet.

"I wouldn't mind a tot." The mine owner ran a broad hand through his graying hair.

"Nor I," Jane said. "Mrs. Watson, what happened? Sensibility told us she'd left you guarding the body. When we returned, you were gone."

Mrs. Watson poured, splashing liquor on the sideboard.

"Allow me." Mr. Crane sprang forward. Taking the decanter from her hand, he poured drinks for Mrs. Watson, Jane, and Mr. Durand.

Shooting the drink back, Mrs. Watson descended from the stool. She lumbered onto the settee, her eyes dull. "No sooner had you left when someone grabbed me, stuffed me in a barrel, and bounced me across San Francisco. Imagine the joke!" Her lips stretched tight enough to snap.

"Someone?" Jane asked. "You didn't see them?"

Mrs. Watson shook her head and extended her glass toward Mr. Crane.

He poured another shot.

"It was dark, and he grabbed me from behind," she said. "And once I was in that barrel, I couldn't see a thing."

"Did you hear anything?" Mr. Crane looked thoughtfully at the decanter. Pouring a shot for himself, he slugged it down, his Adam's apple bobbing.

"Just street sounds and men laughing. Made me right angry. I kicked and shouted, but the street was loud, and I didn't think anyone heard me."

"Fortunately, I did," Mr. Durand said.

"And what did you see, Mr. Durand?" Jane asked.

His shoulders lifted. "They looked like a bunch of drunk sailors to me."

"A bunch?" Sensibility sat beside her.

He nodded. "When I passed them on the street there were three, and then a few more joined the group. I didn't recognize them, but I'll be sure to give a description to the Alcade. I was outnumbered, and I confess, my brawling days are long behind me. So I followed them, waiting for a chance. When we were down by the docks, they dumped the barrel and stepped away for a moment, and that's when I got Mrs. Watson out of there. Of course, I didn't know it was Mrs. Watson at the time." His graying brows drew together. "Thought it was a child."

Sensibility pressed a hand to her breast. "Good gad." Was that what the sailors had thought as well? It was monstrous.

"Well," Durand said, "the men were pretty drunk. It was an uncomfortable time for Mrs. Watson, but I suspect she was never in any real danger. Just high spirits."

"High spirits! This is outrageous." Sensibility paced the room, turning to avoid a low table littered with doilies. "If a lady can't guard a corpse without being assaulted and shoved into a barrel, I do not know what sort of place San Francisco has become."

"Aye, I miss the old San Francisco, such a sleepy village it used to be." Mrs. Watson clutched the empty tumbler to her breast. "But there were other hardships then. Once this gold fever is over, I suspect things will smooth themselves out."

"Er, did you say she was guarding a corpse?" Mr. Durand asked.

"A vagrant miner," Jane said. "Miss Sensibility had gone to get help from the hotelier, while Mrs. Watson remained to make sure the poor man's body was left alone."

"Tragic," Mr. Durand murmured.

"And I thought I'd be the second tragedy of the night. If it weren't for Mr. Durand…" Mrs. Watson covered her eyes with one hand. "I don't know how I'll ever be able to thank you, sir."

"No thanks are necessary. Anyone would have done the same."

"Oh, I doubt that," Mr. Crane said. "These sailors, do you think you can show me where they took Mrs. Watson?"

"Of course. Would you like to go now?"

"If you don't mind." Mr. Crane bowed to the women. "I assume you ladies will be spending the remainder of the evening in?"

"I'm not going nowhere." Mrs. Watson rested her head on the back of the settee.

Sensibility looked to Jane and nodded.

Mr. Crane bowed to Mr. Durand. "Then if you're ready, lead on MacDuff."

Mr. Durand removed his hat from the stand, and Mr. Crane followed him out.

Jane sat across from Mrs. Watson on a spongy, chintz-patterned chair. "Tell us everything. All the details. What really happened?"

"Perhaps Mrs. Watson would prefer to tell us tomorrow," Sensibility said, not liking the shadows beneath Mrs. Watson's eyes or the pallor of her skin.

Mrs. Watson fisted her hands. "Best to get it out of the way. I told you, I was grabbed and shoved into that blasted barrel. Someone lifted me up, and off we bounced down the road. I don't think it was more than five or ten minutes – though it seemed forever – and then I was put down. Thank heavens they set me down right-side up! It got real quiet, and there I sat, trying to beat my way to freedom, but the lid was stuck fast. Then someone picked me up again, and off we went, down to the docks."

"How do you know it was the docks?" Jane asked.

"Because that's where I was when Mr. Durand rescued me. I owe that man a debt." Mrs. Watson rose. "And now if you two will excuse me, I'm tuckered out."

"Of course," Sensibility murmured.

They watched the lady leave, and Jane shut the parlor door behind her. "Well, drunk sailors might have taken her, but we know the Hounds are somehow involved. That skeleton belonged to a Hound."

"I didn't get a chance to tell you – Mr. Sterling and I went to the victim's hotel. He found another man – a Hound – searching his room."

"That's that then. The Hounds have got to be a part of this. But stripping the man to the bones, that's not really the Hounds' style. The Mark must somehow be involved."

"Pulling the Hounds' strings?" Sensibility asked.

"But why would the Mark kill one of the Hounds?"

"Punishment for a failed assignment? A day ago, I would have told you the Hounds had no interests outside of bullying foreigners and harassing ladies on the street. I seem to have been very wrong."

"Maybe," Jane said. "I don't like the way things are connecting, especially after your uncle's story."

"Yes, it was surprisingly good of him to alert me, especially since it forced him to confess his perfidy."

"Practically out of character."

The two women looked at each other.

Jane's mouth made an O, and she sucked in her breath. "Damn it all!" Turning, she flew from the room.

Sensibility followed, dashing up the stairs, hems lifted.

Jane rattled the handle of Sensibility's door. "Open it."

Sensibility unlocked it.

Jane barreled inside, head turning. "What's missing?"

Her bedroom appeared as she'd left it. A current of damp, salty air flowed through the open window. A fold creased the blue bedspread, where the trunk protruded from beneath the bed.

"Oh, curse it." Sensibility knelt and pulled out the chest. "I'm quite certain I pushed my trunk completely beneath the bed." She unlatched it, lifted the lid.

"What did he take?"

"The other aether gun." Dash it, dash it, dash it! Roughly, she shoved the chest beneath the bed. It caught the hem of the spread, and the coverlet cascaded to the polished floor.

"If someone else doesn't kill that man, I will." Jane paced the short length between the mirrored wardrobe and the desk, skirts whirling. "He's going to sell that prototype, mark my words."

"We don't know that he intends to sell the weapon. He may wish to use it himself."

"Hardly. He was wearing a revolver, and bullets are one thing that are not in short supply in this territory. He'll stick to what he knows. It's the smart thing in a fight."

"But the aether gun has several advantages over a common revolver."

Jane made a dismissive sound. "Yes, yes. I've read and rewritten your reports for the government."

"You rewrote them? Why?"

"Because not everyone understands your scientific lingo. And don't get me off track. The question is, was your uncle spinning us a tall tale, or was there any truth to it?"

"Someone did try to kill him," Sensibility said. "Mr. Sterling and Mr. Crane were quite certain the killers had succeeded."

"Unless your uncle set the whole thing up, like you suggested earlier. I don't know what to believe."

"The answer to that is simple. Do not believe anything unless we can prove it with evidence we ourselves uncover. These so-called agents have misled us once about the murders of the scientists. Why should we believe anything they say?"

"We shouldn't," Jane said. "But at least I know they're who they say they are. I've met Sterling before."

"But can we trust them?"

Jane hesitated. "I want to. But under the circumstances, you're the only one I trust. You and Mrs. Watson. It's too bad Mr. Night is in Monterey. He's a good man in a tight spot."

"He's not in Monterey," Sensibility said. "He's in San Francisco, at the Presidio."

"He is? Well that's good news! Why didn't you tell me?"

Sensibility jerked the hem of her waistcoat into place. "I only learned of it tonight. He's been there for three days."

"Oh."

"Precisely." After an absence of months, those three extra days still burned. What did she really mean to him?

"You know Night. He probably had some duty that kept him away."

"Yes, that is what he said."

"You sound like you don't believe him."

"I do believe him," Sensibility said in a low voice. And still, his absence grated.

"Well then, there's no problem." Jane went to the window and slammed it shut, jiggling the lock. "The Presidio, eh? Sterling and Crane should have informed the

Army by now of what's happening. It would be interesting if the story they told the Army is any different from what those two gave us."

"I doubt Mr. Night will be able to help with that question."

"No, no, not Night. I've got another contact in the Army. Never mind, just thinking aloud. Now let us get this lock fixed."

Sighing, Sensibility opened one of the desk drawers. By "us," Jane meant "Sensibility." Pulling out a leather-wrapped set of tools, she set to work.

Jane sat on the bed, feet swinging, keeping up a running commentary on the séance. "I can't believe anyone believes his patter," she finished. "What an old fraud."

"Mm." Sensibility blew wood dust from the window sill.

Jane sat up straighter on the bed. "Mm? I know what that means. You disagree with me, but you don't want to say so."

Sensibility jiggled the new latch. "Very well, I disagree with you."

"Don't tell me you've been taken in by that charlatan?"

"I used my dark-seeing goggles during the séance. I did not observe any person manipulating the instruments."

"Maybe he used strings?"

"I would have detected them."

"Well, you can't believe in spirits!"

"I've seen no evidence to suggest spirits, but I have also seen no evidence to suggest fraud. It's an interesting puzzle."

"So you're going to go again?" Jane asked.

"If I have another opportunity. Mr. Hermeticus wishes to hire me to prove he is no fraud. I admit, I'm curious."

"This is an all-fired inconvenient time to get curious."

"Who knows? Perhaps we'll get lucky, and he'll attempt to induct me into the Mark. You know how the public face of that organization has dabbled with the occult. And like other Mark agents we've known, Mr. Hermeticus is charismatic, clever—"

"How do you know he's clever?"

"If he did commit a fraud at that séance, he accomplished it quite ably."

"But you don't think it was a fraud."

Sensibility pitched her toolkit onto the bed, barely missing the agent. "Oh, for heaven's sake, Jane! What do you wish me to say?"

"I don't know. Something sensible?" Jane crossed her arms. "Don't leave the boarding house without an escort. One of us will come by tomorrow morning."

"One of you? Jane, Mr. Sterling told me you were—"

"Reassigned. But this is where bad communications with the States works in our favor. I'll stick with you until this mess is resolved."

"And after that?"

"Washington."

"Good gad."

CHAPTER 16

Moonlight streamed through the laboratory windows. Turning slowly, Flora trailed her hands through the reflected light, her arms moving in an exotic dance. A laboratory. A real laboratory! It had been months since she'd played in one.

But this laboratory wasn't hers. She froze, blood thrumming in her head. It wasn't fair, wasn't right. They'd taken her precious laboratory, taken her father's secrets. Now, ignorant tinkerers like Sensibility Grey used those secrets to make their own fortunes.

A wheeled mechanical with a broom for a skirt bumped against her.

She leapt backwards, hand to her chest, heart thudding.

It turned and rattled away.

She quirked a brow, drawing a slow breath. So Miss Grey also understood the benefits of miniature devices. Who had she stolen that idea from?

Hands trembling, she strapped her dark-seeing goggles to her head. She strode to the closet and yanked open the door, smiled. The hidden door behind the cot and the trigger mechanism were obvious when viewed through her goggles.

Scraping the cot back, she pressed the knothole. The door popped open, revealing a shelf of books and a work table scattered with gears and one leather-bound journal – Miss Grey's. She flipped open the cover.

A furrow appeared between her fine brows. An aether gun? Interesting. According to the girl's notes, after a few abortive attempts she'd successfully created a working model.

Well, well. It appeared Miss Grey had some talent of her own. But it was also clear she didn't understand the way aether worked. If she had, she wouldn't have made her futile attempts to replicate the stolen distance control. Her father's distance control. Rage, hot and tight, flared in her breast.

She pressed her eyelids shut, mastering herself. No, she must not let fury possess her. Not yet. She must be fair. Perhaps she was wrong about Miss Grey. Perhaps Miss Grey had found her own way to the theory of aether control. One must not convict without evidence.

Lowering herself onto a round stool, Flora lit a lamp on the table and bent her head to read.

Two hours had passed when she roused herself, lips pressed tight.

The aether control work was not original.

Miss Grey was a thief.

And thieves deserved punishment.

But it was a *very* nice laboratory. If she killed the Grey girl now, scavengers would strip the lab clean within a day. And she had devices to alter. Her father's own, very special, very secret devices, and made with her help.

And then the thief would be punished.

CHAPTER 17

"I am perfectly capable of escorting Miss Grey to her lab." Flecking an invisible speck from the sleeve of her delft-blue gown, Jane turned to the parlor mirror. She adjusted her straw hat, tucking a chestnut-colored curl behind her ear.

Mr. Crane jammed his bony hands on his hips, his clothing hanging loose upon his frame. "Don't you have better things to do?" he asked. "If I recall, your assignment—"

"Oh, that?" Jane glanced at him, eyes wide with innocence. "I finished that yesterday."

Wavering beside the open parlor door, Sensibility fiddled with the plain brown cuffs of her blouse. She shifted her weight. Sensibility had an appointment with Mr. Hermeticus and did not wish to be late. And yet she had a strange aversion to stepping into the fog pressing against the windows of the boarding house. Her sleep had been restless, filled with dreams of dissolving flesh and gnawing teeth.

"Miss Grey is no longer your responsibility," Mr. Crane said.

Miss Algrave stepped closer. "That's what you think."

"That's what your orders say."

"So you *did* read my orders!"

"Well, if you're looking for sainthood among government agents—"

"Ha!"

"For heaven's sake," Sensibility muttered, wanting nothing more than to throw one of Mrs. Watson's lace-covered sofa cushions at the two.

Unusually, Mrs. Watson had been absent this morning. The breakfast lay cooling on the table, but the proprietress had not appeared. If the watery light streaming through the curtained windows seemed menacing to Sensibility, how must Mrs. Watson feel after her ordeal? She wanted to find her, to assure herself Mrs. Watson was well, but sensed that her landlady would seek her company in her own time.

Mr. Crane lowered his head, bullish. "Your orders—"

"Yes," Jane said, "*my* orders, and they did not originate from you. *I* choose how best to execute them."

"Children, children." Mr. Sterling clattered down the stairs and into the foyer. Lifting his hat, he bowed to her, his muscles straining at the navy-blue shoulders of his frock coat, its brass buttons gleaming. His trousers were an elegant blue plaid. It was almost as if he and Mr. Crane had switched clothing – Sterling's too tight, Crane's too loose. "Miss Grey. Miss Algrave. There's a simple solution. I'll escort Miss Grey to her laboratory."

Jane and Mr. Crane made noises of protest.

Mr. Sterling extended her an arm. "Miss Grey?"

She rested her hand on his sleeve, shooting Jane a silent plea for understanding. Mr. Hermeticus would be waiting. And if she were to face the newly disquieting streets of San Francisco, there was something comforting in the set of the arrogant Mr. Sterling's broad shoulders. "Thank you, sir."

He escorted her outside, and she paused on the porch. The sun shone flat and harsh through the fog. She winced in its light, the air cold and salty and stagnant. The scent of something rotting rose from the street. A wagon slogged through the mud, its driver plodding alongside his mule, both heads bent.

Mr. Sterling herded her onto one of the wood-plank walkways. "Mr. Crane told me you had an aether weapon in hand last night," the agent said. "Did you bring it with you?"

An image of the denuded skeleton rose before her, and the space between her shoulder blades tightened. "Yes. Under the circumstances, I thought it wise."

"May I see it?"

Releasing his arm, she drew it from the pocket of her brown skirt and handed it to him. Its brass fittings gleamed in the slanting sun.

He sighted down the barrel. "And it works?"

"It would do me little good if it did not."

"You'll have to give me a demonstration when we reach your laboratory." He tucked it beneath his gold brocade waistcoat, where it formed an awkward lump.

"May I have it back?"

"I'm sorry, no."

Blood heating, Sensibility spluttered. "What?"

"This is exactly the sort of weapon the Mark would like to steal."

"And exactly the sort of weapon that could prevent them from stealing anything." She nodded to a merchant she knew, sweeping the porch of his mercantile shop. Spades and tins for gold washing gleamed in the window.

"You won't need a weapon as long as I'm around."

Sensibility quickened her pace. "Good gad, you do have a high opinion of yourself."

He grinned. "I've got some experience in these matters."

"As do I. As does Miss Algrave."

The walkway ended. Lifting her skirts, she stepped from it, her boots squelching ankle-deep in the mud. She stifled a curse and wrenched herself free.

Eyes crinkling, he offered his arm. "May I be of assistance?"

"No."

He pressed a broad hand to his chest. "Ouch. I think I've been cut."

"At last you comprehend my meaning." Slipping in the mud, she grasped the side of an empty wagon to steady herself.

"Miss Grey…"

"Oh, for heaven's sake, will you stop attempting to ingratiate yourself with me? You have confiscated my device, insulted my friend, will not leave me in peace—"

"I won't leave you in peace because you're in danger. I'm here to protect you."

"So *you* say. So far, I've faced no attempted assassinations."

"Not lately. And you saw the bones. The man who killed those scientists is here in San Francisco."

She subsided. The bones. They'd been taken to the Presidio, but where would they finally come to rest? She forced herself not to reach into her pocket, to finger the bit of metal she'd taken from the alley.

"Trust me," he said, "I wouldn't have come all this way just to harass you, charming as you may be."

She stormed off, an effect marred by the mud slowing her steps. "And your false flattery has become as grating as Mr. Crane's rude remarks about my mechanicals."

A trio of men in heavy, miners' trousers, rough shirts and battered hats leaned against a hitching post, beside a saloon. One nudged the other, jerking his chin toward her.

Sensibility met their gazes, nodded, and looked away. She'd learned that modestly ignoring men such as these often led to more trouble.

"What makes you think the compliments are false?" Mr. Sterling asked.

"Their constant flow." She stopped in the street and glared. "If you must follow me about, can you not at least do so in silence?"

"Hey." One of the miners sloshed across the street to them and raised his hand. "Hey."

A corner of Mr. Sterling's mouth curled upward. "But we have so much to talk about."

The other two miners straightened off the hitching post.

"Hey," the first said.

"Can I help you, sir?" Mr. Sterling put his fists on his hips, squinting up at the miner.

"You bothering this lady?" The miner scratched his grizzled cheek, his breath stinking of garlic and sausage.

Sensibility's gaze flicked skyward. How she longed to say: *yes!* But she shook her head and smiled. "No, sir, he is not. But I thank you for your concern."

Mr. Sterling shrugged. "There you have it, friend." He made to move past, and the miner laid a meaty hand on Sterling's chest.

"I ain't your friend. And I say you're bothering the lady." His two companions came to stand behind him.

Sensibility cleared her throat. "Truly, sir, this is a simple misunderstanding."

Mr. Sterling punched him in the jaw.

Sensibility gasped. "Oh, good gad! Can't you go one day without striking someone?"

The miner staggered backward, and the other two men pounced. Sterling pivoted, sending one man into the wagon wheel. He elbowed the other in the jaw, and a flurry of punching and counter-punching commenced.

A crowd of men gathered, cheering. Sensibility staggered out of the way of the combatants and into the circle of men.

One grasped her forearm, keeping her from falling. "Careful, ma'am."

Sterling slipped and went down on one knee. Two of the miners grabbed him from behind, hauling him upright. The third stood before him, cocked back his arm.

Sterling kicked him in the stomach.

The man who'd righted her whooped.

Sensibility winced, torn between worry, guilt, and annoyance. "Can't you stop this?" she asked him.

"Why'd I want to?"

Entertainment! Sensibility ground her teeth, her chest tightening. This was mere sport for the men. But she couldn't leave. She had to stay, to watch, as distasteful as the spectacle was. Must Mr. Sterling beat his way out of every hint of conflict? Granted, beating things seemed to be his strong point. Crane appeared to be the brains of the partnership. And Sterling did look to be winning this battle. Two of his opponents lay still in the street.

Sterling punched the third. He went down, spattering mud across the trousers of the gathered miners.

Picking up his hat, the agent brushed off a bit of muck and picked his way to her. "Miss Grey? Shall we?"

Sensibility pressed her lips together. "I am late for my appointment." Turning, she minced to the warehouse, a block away.

She was late, Mr. Hermeticus was not waiting in the yard, and there was no note. Had he come and gone? She jammed her key into the padlock on the small warehouse door. The door was set within a massive rolling panel that allowed egress for her larger pieces of equipment and supplies.

Mr. Sterling stopped at the water pump in the warehouse yard. Grasping the handle, he thrust his head beneath the running water and rose, gasping, shaking his head like a dog. "Keeping you safe is messy work."

She raised a brow. "Is that what you were doing?"

"You recognize those men?" He washed his hands.

"No." She wrenched the padlock free and swung open the door. "There are so many miners streaming through San Francisco on their way to the gold fields, it has become impossible to keep track. If you'll excuse me, I'll just go upstairs to my lab."

"We wouldn't want to keep Mr. Hermeticus waiting."

"Unless he can pick locks too, he won't be waiting upstairs."

"Too?"

Silently, she berated herself. She hadn't told Mr. Sterling about her uncle's confession. "In addition to his occult talents."

They passed through the high-ceilinged warehouse. Sensibility cast an eye toward a great, oval shape, tented beneath a ship's sail she'd scavenged. In spite of the recent interruptions, she intended to finish Mr. Durand's excavating device before schedule, even if it meant working all night.

Lifting her hems, Sensibility hurried up the stairs. She unlocked the door to her laboratory, stepped inside, and halted, her skin prickling.

"What's wrong?" Sterling asked from behind her.

"I'm not certain." She edged deeper into the laboratory. Morning sun slanted through the windows, illuminating swirls of dust motes. She stopped beside a table littered with gears. "Someone has been in here," she said in a low voice. "These gears are not as I left them."

"But the door was locked?"

"Yes."

Mr. Sterling drew the revolver from his holster. "Wait here."

He prowled the laboratory, peering beneath tables, behind crates. At the door to Sensibility's sleeping area he paused, edged to one side, and kicked it open.

Sensibility bit back a cry of protest as he rushed inside. There were more important matters at stake than her door, now swinging out of kilter. Even from this distance she could see the splintered wood, the broken latch. But the latch, at least, would be easy to repair.

"It's empty," he called, and she walked to the closet door. He stood beside her cot, looking around. "You spend the night here often?"

"My work keeps me busy." The cot sat beside the wall, which meant that no one hid in the secret room behind it. She frowned. But the crude bed was out of place, at a gentle angle rather than jammed flat against the rough wall. Had the intruder moved it during a search of her laboratory?

Sensibility reached for her pocket watch. Remembering its loss, she dropped her hands to her sides. She daren't check the secret room now, not with Sterling there. If she did, he would insist on looking at the papers within, or showing them to Mr. Crane.

"Is anything missing?" he asked.

"I'll check." Returning to her workshop, Sensibility rummaged through file cabinets, bins and boxes.

Mr. Sterling tossed his hat upon a work table. At the front door, he knelt, examining the lock.

"No documents appear missing," she said, "but I have lost some supplies."

"There are scratch marks on your lock." He joined her at the cabinet. "It looks like someone picked it to get inside, someone who knew what they were doing. Were the supplies valuable?"

Sweeping a strand of hair from her brow, she leaned one hip against the table. "Everything is valuable, simply because everything is scarce, but particularly metal."

"Why metal?"

"The miners. If they cannot buy a spade, they will make one themselves. The contraptions they've built for extracting gold from the earth and rivers are ingenious."

"But not as ingenious as your excavator. Assuming it works." He crossed his arms over his chest.

"Of course it works. Why wouldn't it?"

"Funny thing about your designs. The models you've sent to Washington all work fine. But none of our scientists have succeeded in replicating them."

"Then perhaps your government should employ tinkerers and inventors rather than scientists. My designs are perfectly clear."

He angled his head. "Are they?"

"If you are accusing me of inserting flaws into the designs then that's, that's... It's ridiculous. Your government has the models. You yourself have admitted they work. Any tinkerer worth his salt could take them apart and build one for himself."

"Yet so far, no one has been able to. Have you got any ideas why?" Drawing the aether gun from inside his waistcoat, he sighted down the barrel at a limp mechanical dangling on the wall.

"No. In Dr. Mathers's letter to me, he admitted to having some difficulty and asked about the quality of the quartz crystal required. I explained that I use the clearest quartz available, and with the fewest inclusions. Perhaps the quartz was the issue."

He pulled a tattered envelope from inside his waistcoat pocket. "Is this the letter you sent?"

Her breath caught.

He handed it to her, and she opened the envelope, drew out the letter. "Yes, it is."

"Mathers never got a chance to read it."

"Oh," she said in a small voice. "I am sorry. I never asked…. Did he have a family?"

"Yes, a wife and three children."

Head drooping, she handed back the letter. Others had died as well, and she did not want to know if they too had families. She feared she knew the answer. This business had made too many orphans.

Her own father had died in penury. It was a miracle of fate that she had landed in San Francisco, among people who would pay for her mechanicals, too desperate to care if they were designed by a lady.

"I will help in any way I can to stop the man who took these lives," she said. "Short of returning to Washington."

"You're stubborn."

"And if you're right, the killer will come to me."

"Speaking of which, where is your Mr. Hermeticus?"

A furrow appeared between her brows. "He is not my Mr. Hermeticus, and I have no idea where he is or why he is late for our appointment."

"Be careful around him. He fits the profile of a Mark agent. He's not only newly arrived, but he's also begun setting up an occult society."

"I would hardly call a single séance an occult society," she said, mulish. She wanted to argue with him. And she wanted her aether weapon back.

"But it's a good start. Mr. Crane says he's got an idea about how Hermeticus is creating his ghosts."

"Does he?" She sniffed. "I look forward to hearing his theory." Mr. Crane had not witnessed what she had seen through her goggles. *Something* had been at that séance, and that something was not of human origin.

"Don't tell me you believe in ghosts?"

She shivered and went to the window. Behind the masts of abandoned ships, the bay heaved a dull gray. "The more I work with aether, the more I realize I do not understand."

"There are more things in heaven and earth, Horatio, than are dreamt of in your philosophy," he quoted. Correctly.

She touched her throat. "True."

"But that doesn't mean I have to believe in everything."

"No one is requiring you to."

There was a knock at the door. Sterling's hand moved toward the revolver at his hip.

"Yes?" she called out. "The door is open."

Krieg walked inside, smiling. He stopped short, plucking free a loose button from his cocoa-colored waistcoat. Pocketing the button in his brown coat, he ran a hand through his tangle of cinnamon-colored hair. "I didn't know you had company, Miss Grey. Mr. Sterling, isn't it?"

"Mr. Night." He nodded. "Miss Grey was about to demonstrate one of her devices."

Mr. Night strode into the room and laid his hat beside a set of test tubes and vials. "Then you are considering a purchase after all?"

"Her work is extraordinary."

Sensibility slipped her hands into her skirt pockets, her cheeks warming as Mr. Sterling expounded on his lie. As a government agent, of course he wished to remain anonymous. But her silence made her complicit in the falsehood, and she could not lie to Krieg.

"Mr. Sterling," she said, "Mr. Night is a particular friend of mine. I believe it would be in our best interests if you told him everything."

His brows rose.

"Or I will," she said.

"Very well." Sterling walked to her and caught her hands. "Miss Grey and I have an understanding."

Krieg paled.

"We do not!" She pulled away. "He's a government agent sent to protect me."

Krieg's coppery eyes hardened. Jaw set, he strode toward them.

Sterling dropped her hands. "Miss Grey, I wish you wouldn't have said that."

"Mr. Night knows of the Mark." She stepped between the two men, turning to Krieg. "He has worked with Miss Algrave before and is someone we may trust."

"Why didn't you tell me this last night?" Krieg asked.

Her hands fell to her sides. She should have told him. But she'd been tired and hurt and angry. "I didn't get a chance before we were interrupted, and then you left."

"And why," he said, his voice iceberg-calm, "do you need protecting?"

Mr. Sterling sat against the window sill. "You might as well tell him. He seems to know everything else."

"Hardly everything," Krieg said. "Why, Miss Grey?"

"Because all the other government scientists working on aether technology have been murdered." She stepped back. "They think I may be next."

"In any case," Mr. Sterling said, "we can't afford to lose Miss Grey. Not when there are still so many unanswered questions about her technology."

"Not as long as she is useful to you, you mean."

"Whatever he means," Sensibility said, "I have no desire to have my throat cut." *Or be shredded to the bone.*

Krieg's shoulders twitched. "Is that how they died?"

"Why?" Mr. Sterling asked. "Does that mean something to you?"

"A knife is a personal form of attack. It's close, messy."

"You believe it may say something about the killer's relationship to his victims?" Sensibility asked.

Krieg shook his head. "If the killer was a professional assassin, then he had no real relationship with the victims. But it does say something about the man. You mentioned the Mark. Do you believe they're involved?"

Sterling shrugged. "It's possible. They knew of the aether technology and of Miss Grey's work."

"And what are your plans to protect Miss Grey?"

"To stay with her until the killer shows his hand."

A pulse beat in Krieg's jaw. "And capture him?"

"A capture is preferable to a kill. Then we can learn who hired him."

"You're aided by Miss Algrave?"

"She seems competent."

"She is." Krieg nodded, stalked to the table, and clapped his hat on his head. "It appears you are in good hands, Miss Grey. I'll leave you to your work."

Sensibility's stomach plummeted. He was leaving? Now? "Wait." She followed him out the door, down the stairs. "Mr. Night!"

He stopped at the bottom of the steps and glanced past her, upward. Mr. Sterling stood on the landing above them, watching.

"I have business at the Presidio," Krieg said. "I must go."

"But…why did you come? Was there something you wished to tell me?"

"No. I was passing and just thought to stop in. I'm glad I did." Squaring his shoulders, he walked out.

Throat tight, she mounted the steps. She had thought they were… well, they'd never had an official understanding, but at the very least she had thought they were friends. Now she was uncertain what lay between them, if anything, and an ache pierced her chest.

"The more people who know who I am and what I'm doing here," Sterling said, "the greater the odds our enemy will also know."

She glared, squeezing past him into her laboratory. "Mr. Night will not betray us."

"What's his business at the Presidio?"

"I suppose it has something to do with the statehood question." She busied herself straightening a row of vials that were already in military order. "He has been working towards a constitutional convention for some months, but much is in the hands of the military."

"You suppose? You don't know?"

Sucking in her cheeks, she took her microscope from a shelf. "He has no reason to tell me everything about his work." But as she considered the question, she realized she knew next to nothing. She knew he was passionate about statehood, believing it to be the key to ending the territory's current anarchy. But she had seen little of him in the past months, and the details of his work evaded her.

Slowly she drew in her breath, released it. "Mr. Hermeticus is late, and I have work to do. Excuse me, sir." She bustled about, gathering her work tools, the watchful gaze of Mr. Sterling burning twin holes in her back.

CHAPTER 18

"And you're sure Sterling didn't notice?" Durand patted the pearl-colored flank of his quarter horse. It whickered and tossed its head.

The Hound handed him the key. "Nah. He strutted away from the fight like he was some pumpkins, all full of himself, like." He rubbed his bruised and fleshy jaw, his hand scraping across stubble. "You want one of us to go with you when you search his room?"

He untied the animal from the hitching post, careful not to look at the Hound. It wouldn't do for people to associate them, and the street was thick with miners and merchants. A fat grocer emerged from his store, broom in hand, and regarded them from his porch. "No," Durand said. "I have reason to visit the boarding house. You do not."

Durand pocketed the key, warmth spreading through his body in spite of the chill and fog. He'd succeeded in diverting suspicion. And while he hadn't quite gotten a hero's welcome, the Mark's plans for new operations in the territory hadn't been upset. California would remain a territory for now, and the slave and free states in stalemate. And with the Mark running things, when California did try to enter the Union, it would be as a slave state, further postponing the war.

"What do you expect to find in his room?" the Hound asked.

Durand swung into the saddle. "He's a foreign spy." He'd always been a good liar, but the Hounds were such simpletons he took no pleasure in the skill. "I expect to learn for whom he works and his goal." He expected to learn what the U.S. government knew about the Mark's operations.

"He works for the English, I'll bet," the Hound said. "The Russians were sniffing around here years ago. But that girl's English, so that's where my money is. The both of 'em are traitors."

Durand clenched his jaw. They might be simpletons, but they could be difficult to control. He couldn't afford for one of them to lose his head and harm Miss Grey, not yet at least. "Maybe she is, maybe she isn't. Maybe she's just a pawn in his game."

"Still, she's a foreigner, and she's building those freakish devices. She ain't right."

"As long as she's building those freakish devices for me, she's all right in my book. And she needs protecting."

The Hound wet his thick lips. "Okay, okay. We'll keep watching her, like you asked."

The horse shifted beneath his weight. "Watch only, until I say otherwise. She's important. We can't let the other side interfere."

CHAPTER 19

The clash of the hammer lulled Sensibility, a rhythm of metal on metal. Heated brass glowed on the forge, each blow she struck crafting the hot iron to her vision. The work yard vanished from her awareness. Her worries dropped away – Krieg's abrupt departure with so much unsaid, the dead scientists and their mourning families, her failures with aether, Jane's impending removal.

Sparks shot into the air. Unnoticed, sweat poured from her brow. Her limbs moved like well-oiled gears, as if she were a part of the fire and the thinning metal.

The music of the forge was all she needed, the forge and her breath and the swing of her hammer.

She plunged the red-hot piece into the water bucket, clouds of steam roaring upward, hissing. The metal crackled.

"Miss Grey?"

She started, glancing over her shoulder at him. With her tongs she drew the metal from the bucket. Examining the piece for cracks, she smiled. There were none. Satisfied, she set it aside.

Mr. Hermeticus bowed, sweeping his top hat from his head, exposing his shock of platinum hair. He swept his ebony cloak behind him with his free hand. "Please forgive my tardiness, my dear lady. I was unavoidably detained." His broad smile exposed his teeth, gleaming and straight and predatory.

Unease rippled Sensibility's spine. *Ridiculous*. She was simply unnerved by last night's events, events that had occurred outside the man's hotel.

"Were you standing there long?" She wiped her hands on her leather apron. Gulls cawed above them, invisible in the fog.

"A minute, perhaps two. I must say your work is mesmerizing." He glanced to the side, where Mr. Sterling lounged against a sawhorse, his hat low. "And I was not the only one entranced."

"Oh. Him. A client interested in the process." She tossed the tongs into the coals, and sparks flew. Her gaze tracked their upward movement, and she arched, pressing her hands into the low curve of her back, releasing the tension. The sky was unremitting gray, the sun obscured. How much time had passed since she'd begun her work? She'd been oblivious to all but the forge, and vulnerable.

"What are you thinking?" Hermeticus asked.

A man carrying a bale of hay walked past them on the street. Wary, she smiled. "It must be past noon, but it seems like I only began work a short time ago. Come. I have sketched some designs for your device. They are upstairs in my laboratory."

He followed her through the yard, and his gaze flicked to Sterling, lounging beside the open door. "It is a meditation for you, is it not?" he asked her.

"Pardon?"

Sterling peeled himself off the doorframe and trailed after them into the warehouse. The windows were dusty, sinking it into gloom.

"Your work," Hermeticus said. "The forge. Your focus was so intense that for you, time stopped. It is a form of meditation."

"I suppose one could say that. It is certainly engrossing." She rolled her shoulders, warm and sore and loose.

"I understand obsession well."

"For the spirits, you mean? How did you come to your work?"

"A loss. My wife." He fingered a gold chain that looped into the pocket of his embroidered waistcoat.

"Oh. I'm terribly sorry." She wended around the hydraulic mining machine, its tarp rippling in the breeze from the open door.

"Thank you. After she passed, I wanted to believe there was more than this earthly existence. That is what the church says. But today, we live in an era of science. We can prove the existence of other worlds. Who needs faith?" He chuckled, running his hand along the brim of his hat. "Sadly, my natural inclinations are more philosophical than scientific."

"Philosophical?"

"I studied the mystics, alchemy, the teachings of the Rose Cross, and learned to change my perception of reality. But alas, I cannot share my perception and so prove what I see. Meditation and incantations will do little to help my case before the public."

"You use incantations?" Sensibility paused at the base of the stairs, her pulse quickening. The incantations in her father's book made no sense to her, having nothing to do with science. Could Hermeticus provide some answers? "How?"

"As I understand it – and I do not pretend to understand all – there are three beliefs regarding incantations. The first has to do with mystics, though they consider them chants rather than incantations. By repeating the words over and over, mystics seek to change their inner landscape and therefore change their perception of the world. Magicians also use these incantations to change themselves, but they believe this change enables them to change the outer world. And then, of course, there is the more simplistic use of incantations, for summoning angels and demons to do one's work in the world. The latter may sound ridiculous, but there are people who believe such nonsense."

And what had her father believed? He certainly hadn't summoned demons to power his mechanicals. But she thought of the strange creature at the séance, and a shiver rippled her skin.

She made her way up the steps. "And you? You use incantations to change your perception?"

"They provide a focus point for my mind. And if I can change my own mind, there is much I can change about myself and what I see. All I can say is that the incantations have worked. I do not see spirits, so much as hear and feel their presence, but I have touched another plane." He flashed a quicksilver smile. "Now all I must do is prove it to the world. And you, what do you think of all this?"

"I think I would like my pocket watch back. Have you been able to locate it?"

His weight creaked on the treads behind her. "Alas, it has not reappeared. But I have every confidence it will."

"Why?"

"Because it is important to you, and the spirits are not cruel. You said it had sentimental value?"

"It was a gift from my father."

"Ah. And he is no longer on this plane of existence?"

Her throat thickened. "No. He passed away last year."

"Then your loss is still fresh." His voice dropped, and he hesitated. "My condolences, dear lady. Was he an inventor as well?"

"Yes. He taught me, though unfortunately not everything he knew. He was a genius, a dreamer."

The occultist glanced at the federal agent, behind them on the steps, and lowered his voice. "And you are made of more practical stuff."

"When one is alone in the world, one must be practical." She stopped at the door to her laboratory, retrieving the keys from the pocket of her leather apron.

"Yet it would be a shame to neglect the fanciful, especially for one so young. And you saw last night. You believe."

"I believe further inquiry is necessary."

Mr. Sterling cleared his throat behind them. "As long as my mining machine is completed on time."

Her brow wrinkled. She'd nearly forgotten the fiction that he was a client.

"Ah, yes," Hermeticus said. "I'd heard your mining contraptions are quite popular, Miss Grey. And costly." He turned at the top of the stairs, his cloak descending like a cloud, and extended his hand to Mr. Sterling. "I am Hermeticus."

They shook hands.

"Sterling."

The occultist scanned Sterling's dashing blue suit, gold brocade waistcoat, black hat. "Have you been long in the mining industry, Mr. Sterling?"

Sensibility fumbled with the new padlock on the door.

"A new enterprise," Sterling said. "I've come recently through Monterey. There are great things happening there."

"Ah yes," Hermeticus said. "I traveled that way en route to San Francisco. Lovely village. The ocean has a certain wildness there that stirs the soul."

"And you, sir? What has brought you to Miss Grey's door?"

"I am engaged in a very old enterprise," Mr. Hermeticus said. "Some might say ancient. I explore mankind's greatest question: what lies beyond?"

"Beyond?" Mr. Sterling asked.

"Beyond death."

Pocketing the keys, Sensibility shoved the door open and entered her workshop. If Mr. Hermeticus was a charlatan, he put on a bold face. Mr. Sterling was one of the most earthy men she'd met, deeply rooted in the physical. She could not imagine discussing such metaphysical ideas with him without squirming.

Mr. Night would listen to her musings without laughing. Like her, he had once seen and wondered. But Mr. Night was not here. She scrubbed a hand over her face, a feeling of heaviness stealing over her.

It did not matter. The scientific method was her armor and her blade. Sensibility would reveal nothing of her father's supernatural research until she could provide evidence.

"I suppose we'll all learn the answer to what comes after eventually," Sterling said. A clockwork sweep bumped against his booted foot, turned, and rolled away.

"But would you not rather know now?" the occultist asked. "I believe it is possible to pierce that veil. Indeed, I have pierced it. And now that we are fortunate enough to live in an era of science, my goal is to scientifically prove my discoveries."

Sensibility tossed the padlock on a worktable. It thunked and rattled on the wood, threatening to upend an alembic. "An admiral goal. And now, Mr. Sterling, I am about to discuss my designs with Mr. Hermeticus."

"May I see them?" Sterling asked. "I find this scientific investigation fascinating."

"I have no objections if you do not, Miss Grey." Hermeticus inclined his head.

She forced a smile. "Of course not."

Sensibility unrolled Hermeticus's drawings, planting iron weights on their edges to keep them from rolling in on themselves like Egyptian papyri. Beside his drawings, she laid out her own designs. "As I understand it," she said, "there are two issues at hand. The first is whether the medium is cheating. I can create a chair and table for you and set it with a pulley and clockwork system. It will alert watchers to any untoward motion you might make."

Hermeticus stroked his thick moustache. "I applaud the concept. But I confess, I am always shifting about in my seat. My aged bones cannot maintain a still posture for long."

"I can build a degree of tolerance into the design so a simple shift of weight will not set off any alarums. The motion of your limbs will be of the most interest to spectators in any case."

"Agreed," Hermeticus said. "And the second issue?"

"To prove the existence of spirits independent of the medium," she said. "You mentioned a shift in temperature when the spirits are present?"

"A drop in temperature," the occultist corrected.

"I can modify one of my smaller clockwork mechanisms to orient on the coldest region of the room. If the temperature drops, it shall move toward it. It would be clear soon enough if the mechanical is following a draught from an open window or orienting on something less easy to explain."

"You can do that?" Sterling's brows drew together.

"If I could not, I would not have suggested it."

Hermeticus stroked his moustache more quickly. "But that is brilliant! If this clockwork mechanism moves when I sense the presence of a spirit, it shall be confirmation of its existence!"

"It depends, as I said, upon where it moves. And it does not rule out the possibility of an accomplice, perhaps dragging blocks of ice beneath the floor or opening windows."

"My dear lady." The occultist pressed a hand to his chest. "I would never engage in such a cruel deception."

"Of course not," Sensibility said, "but I suspect other mediums are not as scrupulous."

"Indeed, such a device would distinguish me from the charlatans."

"And could you create its opposite?" Sterling asked. "An automaton drawn to heat?"

"Certainly." Sensibility curled one finger in her denuded watch chain. No doubt he had some idea to militarize the concept. Ah, well. She was not naïve.

"I wonder if such a device could be used for fighting fires." Sterling's eyes grew thoughtful. "The New York City fire of forty-five was…" He shook himself. "It could save lives."

"I had not considered that." In San Francisco, where most buildings were of wood, a fire would leap from street to street, consuming everything in its path. She shuddered. "Combined with the water pump technology I've been using for gold extraction, perhaps something could be developed. But I know little about how fire moves. Would it be truly beneficial to attack the hottest part of a blaze, or would energy be better spent elsewhere?"

"Good question," Mr. Sterling said. "Perhaps I can find out."

"You are civic-minded, sir." Hermeticus clapped him on the shoulder. "I congratulate you. But there is more to this world than what we can see and touch, and that is why we are here today. Miss Grey knows this, do you not?"

"Er, yes." She toyed with the thin watch chain. "Science is uncovering much about our universe."

Hermeticus scanned the plans. "I do not see a drawing for this cold-seeking automaton."

She grimaced. "The idea only came to me as we were speaking. But I can draw one up by tonight."

"And may I return this evening to see it?"

"I had rather hoped to bring it to you in your hotel parlor," Sensibility said. "I confess, I am eager to look again for my father's watch and…the séance has left me intrigued."

He looked pleased. "Has it? Has it indeed? Well, I am afraid I had no séance planned for tonight, but it matters not. Spirits are everywhere. If you wish, we can attempt to communicate here, in your laboratory."

Sensibility nodded, her smile tight. She did not wish. She wanted a pretext to prowl through that hotel. A séance, a murder, a missing watch. They all had occurred within its vicinity. "I'll revise the plans by evening, and then we can discuss my fees."

Hermeticus waved his hand negligently. "Money is no object, dear lady."

"Sir, prices in San Francisco are quite high," she said, "and none more so than for any metal that can be used in mining equipment."

He laughed. "Of that I have been made brutally aware, my dear lady. But at what cost science?" He tipped his hat. "Until we meet again." He left, his swirling cape vanishing through the door, his footsteps receding on the stairs.

"I've seen the prices of your mining equipment," Sterling said. "Where does he get his money?"

"From the Mark, you suspect?"

He shrugged, smiled. "I suspect everyone."

CHAPTER 20

Durand stood in the shade of a warehouse and lowered his head, studying the departing occultist. He was a fraud and could be useful. But Durand shifted, uneasy, the shoulders of his great coat leaden with damp. They'd bumped shoulders in the street, and there was something in the magician's glittering eyes that had unsettled him. They were the eyes of a true believer, piercing, unforgiving.

Durand wasn't a man to be unnerved. He'd been a small-time thug before the Mark had found him, a bone breaker with ambition. The Mark had encouraged his aspirations, taught him to tame his rage, given him focus, a family, wealth. Aside from the Mark itself, not much scared him. But those eyes…

He clapped his hat on his head. Whatever schemes Hermeticus was plotting, they wouldn't affect his plans.

Until they did.

Damnation. He would have to learn more about the magician. Then he would decide if he were a potential ally or foe.

A more direct problem was the so-called Mr. Sterling. His inspection of Sterling's room in the boarding house had turned up nothing valuable. Still, the man was a government agent, and he and his fine young muscles were spending far too much time around Miss Grey. Even now, the man lurked in her laboratory. He and his partner would have to be gotten rid of.

Fortunately, this was San Francisco. Incidents happened, and were quietly ignored.

He smiled.

The Hounds would run tonight.

CHAPTER 21

Sensibility peered through the microscope, and the brass wire expanded in the lens. "Remarkable," she muttered, her voice tinged with envy. She hadn't the tools to fashion anything so delicate. The equipment required...

Raising her head, she gazed sightlessly at a jumble of quartz crystals on her rickety, wooden table. Was it the work of the Mark? They had the funds to equip a significant manufacturing endeavor or a highly skilled artisan – either could have worked this bit of metal. Or perhaps the wire had come from one of the larger northeastern cities? She could not imagine anything like it being made in the California Territory, even if the Mark was involved.

All the wire really told her was that it was created by someone with access to better equipment than she. Sensibility sighed. Was there anyone with *worse* equipment than she? It was a miracle she'd acquired the microscope (from a biologist who had traded it for a pickaxe and shovel).

Absently, she picked up a crystal and ran her fingers along its rough edges. Raising it to her eyes, she gazed into its depths. "If I polished you into a crystal ball, would you tell me anything?"

"Excuse me?" Mr. Sterling raised his head from his newspaper. He slouched in a chair, his booted feet on a table, his hat lying beside them.

"Nothing." She laid the crystal beside the microscope.

The wire on the glass bounced, quivered, and oriented toward the crystal.

Sterling stretched, fists clenched, yawning. His blue jacket slipped open, exposing more of his gold brocade waistcoat.

Frowning, Sensibility leaned forward, returning her attention to the crystal, and the three-legged stool wobbled with her shift in weight. She nudged the crystal to the left. The wire quivered in response and reoriented.

Unhooking her goggles from her belt, she clapped them to her eyes, slipping the aether lens into place. The wire glowed gold, tinged pink about the edges, seemed to shift beneath her vision.

Aether technology! The wire had at some time been in contact with aether, and remnants – or memories – of the aether appeared to remain. Could something powered by aether have been responsible for the death of that poor man whose skeleton they'd found?

She cleared her throat. "Mr. Sterling, I believe I've found something."

"Oh?" He leapt to his feet. Tossing the newspaper on his chair, he strode across the workshop.

"I found this bit of brass wire beside the skeleton of the murdered man."

"And didn't give it to Mr. Crane."

"I am giving it to you. It is fine work, requiring tools and equipment unavailable in this territory." She handed him the wire.

"If you came to Washington, my government would give you access to whatever equipment you wished."

"Yes," she said, rueful. But she had business here – both personal and professional. If she went to Washington, they'd likely keep her under lock and key, and most certainly under guard. With their other scientists gone, she was a valuable commodity. She would never be alone again.

He rolled the thin strip of metal before his eyes. "Interesting. It may be evidence. Or not. Until we know more—"

"It has been in contact with aether technology."

"How do you know?"

She took the wire from him, her fingertips brushing against his palm, and set it in the microscope. "See, how it orients on this quartz crystal like a compass?" She shifted the quartz and the brass bumped across the microscope's glass.

He blinked. "Huh. Mr. Crane needs to see this." He shot a quick look at the door, resting his hand on the revolver at his hip.

She saw that he wanted to go, but did not want to leave her unguarded. "I assure you, I will be safe inside my laboratory. I shall lock the door if you wish to take this to him."

"No, I'm not abandoning you, not after someone got through your locks last night. Mr. Crane will be along soon enough."

And arguing with Jane, no doubt. Sensibility's jaw tightened. Blast! Would she never be free of these agents?

There was a firm rap on the door, and they glanced at each other. Mr. Sterling strode to the door, opened it.

Mr. Durand's broad form filled the doorway. His graying brows rose. "Mr. Sterling! This is a surprise."

"Durand."

The two men shook hands.

"Miss Grey was just showing me some designs for my project," Mr. Sterling said.

"Mining equipment, is it not?" Durand removed his hat. "Miss Grey should have that well in hand."

Brushing off her leather apron, Sensibility rose from the stool, her coffee-colored skirts rustling. "And you no doubt wish to see the progress on your excavator."

"I am quite eager to test it in the gold fields." Durand ducked his head apologetically.

Mr. Sterling cleared his throat. "I'm curious to see it. Would you mind—"

"I'm afraid I prefer to keep this device under wraps," Durand said. "I know that once it is working, others shall be clamoring for it. And there is nothing I can do to prevent you building more, Miss Grey. But as I am incurring the expense of developing this device, allow me to enjoy its exclusivity while I may."

"The cost will guarantee exclusivity for some time," she said. "Mr. Sterling, would you mind waiting here?"

His smile did not light his eyes. "Not at all."

She led Durand downstairs into the warehouse and to a tarp-covered, bullet-like shape. Unknotting the canvas sail, she tugged on a rope. The tarp cascaded to the dirt floor. Dim light filtered through the low windows and glinted off the steam-powered excavator, shaped like a monstrous clockwork badger.

"Good heavens." Durand circled it, jaw slack. "It looks like an animal, with limbs and claws."

"I modeled it after a badger. They are excellent excavators. But you saw the plans."

"Yes, but the designs cannot compare with the reality. How does it work?"

She walked around the mechanical, pointing out the space for the steam compressor, the water cannons that would carve the earth, and the shovel-shaped claws for digging in loose soil. "But you will wish to see inside." Hitching her skirts, she clambered up a metal ladder that ran along its back and to the top of the mechanical.

"Careful, Miss Grey!"

She looked down at Durand. A bald spot was making inroads on his graying scalp. "I have climbed this many times in the course of construction."

He colored. "Of course you have." With a nimbleness that belied his age and girth, he ascended the ladder.

She pointed to the circular hatch. "I believe the honor should be yours. You unlock it by—"

"Ingenious!" He knelt and unlatched the metal door, peering inside.

"The interior is quite finished. You may go in."

He squinted. "Have you a lantern?"

In answer, she knelt at the edge of the device and leaned over, unhooking a lantern from a niche in its side. Lighting it, she handed the lamp to Mr. Durand.

He hesitated, crouching over the hatch, shining the lantern light into its depths. "To be so close. It is truly finished?"

"The water pumps for hydraulic mining are completed and only need be attached. The limbs will be capable of excavation and traveling once the compressor is complete and installed. And I have an idea to quiet the noise of the steam engine, so it does not rattle the teeth of the men inside. It shall be finished within the next day or two."

"You said it would take a week."

"A steamship arrived yesterday, and I was able to acquire the needed equipment." By now all of San Francisco knew what could be sold to whom, and she had a contingent of rough but amiable scavengers at the ready.

"Marvelous." He slithered inside. "How does it work?" His voice echoed within the metal beast.

Grinning, she followed him down the ladder and settled herself on a chair bolted to the floor in the snug compartment. Durand had found the hook for the lantern above the control panel. She led him through the pulleys and levers of the control system, and was pleased to see he was a quick study. "I have documented the processes," she finished, "but I confess my handwriting can be rather difficult to decipher."

"That is not a problem. The operation of the mechanical is simplicity in itself. My men should have no trouble."

"Still, the documentation—"

"Yes, yes. I shall have one of my men copy out your instructions."

She pressed a latch and a hidden drawer popped out. "The documentation may be stored here."

"How many cubic feet can your machine move through in a minute?"

"It depends on the material it moves through, and if you are using the hydraulic pump or its claws to excavate."

"Assume we are using the claws and digging through the soil in this area, for example?"

"The soil in San Francisco is exceedingly loose. I would imagine it could excavate twenty to thirty feet per minute. But of course, you will be mining for gold in much more solid material. That should reduce the speed to four to six feet per minute."

"Perfect." He ran his hand across the control panel, tracing the path of a lever, his blue eyes gleaming. "This will revolutionize my work. And save lives, of course. You said the compression device will be finished in two days?"

"I plan to install it tonight, but I will need to test it to ensure you do not run into any difficulties."

"But you have built steam compression devices before. This should be no problem."

"None as compact as this one." If she had the equipment that had forged that bit of wire, could she have made the device smaller? She shook her head. It was not worth becoming a ward of the American government to find out.

"What is wrong?"

"Just imagining what might have been." But she was proud of this device. She had never built a mechanical so large, so sleek.

"You should take pleasure in your success," he said, echoing her thoughts.

He smiled, and her throat tightened. Her father would have loved this. Perhaps he would not have been as enamored with its prosaic use – digging metals from the ground – but he would have appreciated the design. Tears burned the back of her eyes, and she looked away. It had been a year, and painful memories still struck her at odd moments. But her father had been far from perfect, and while she missed him, she would no longer idealize him. Forcing herself to think of the hunger they'd endured while he'd poured money into his laboratory, she hardened her heart.

"I must remind you of our agreement," she said. "Payment is due upon delivery of the prototype."

He laughed. "I have not forgotten, Miss Grey." He leaned closer. "And Mr. Sterling, is he your new enforcer?"

"Merely a persistent client." Rising from her seat inside the cramped excavator, she climbed the ladder onto the roof.

Durand's head and shoulders emerged from the mechanical. "More persistent than I?"

"You have no idea," she said dryly.

"If you will pardon me, he does not look like a gold hunter."

"I am uncertain what a gold miner looks like when nearly everyone is a gold hunter these days. I have heard there are even ladies working the gold fields."

Mr. Durand grimaced. "That, I regret to inform you, is true." Standing on the mechanical's back, he stretched, slipped. Catching himself, he grimaced. "Well, it's got more room than I expected, but I wouldn't want to spend hours inside it. Still, I am impressed, Miss Grey." He bowed over her hand and helped her down the ladder to the dirt warehouse floor. "I look forward to the demonstration of your prototype."

"Our prototype." He had, after all, paid for it. Or he would when the prototype was delivered, she silently amended. And though she knew not to count her chickens before they hatched, the thought of future gold in her safe filled her with a warm glow.

CHAPTER 22

Stomach straining against her stays, Sensibility leaned back in her chair. Her shoulder brushed against the fringed, velvet curtain. She eyed Mr. Sterling across the small, circular table. The brass buttons on his frock coat glinted in the lamplight. "My dinner pail at the workshop will be wasted." There were few dining establishments in San Francisco, and all were costly. In spite of that, the room was filled with hopeful miners.

"But Mrs. Watson didn't pack a dinner for me, and I needed to eat, and I couldn't leave you alone." He forked the last bite of apple pie into his mouth and groaned. "It's true."

"What is?"

"Hunger really is the best sauce."

Sensibility smiled, grim. She'd a lifetime's proof of that. How her circumstances had changed in one short year.

"Now tell me more about yourself," he said. "How did you become an inventor?"

"Through my father, but I suspect you already knew that."

"What was your life like in Lima?"

"Is this for one of your reports?"

His forehead creased. "For me. I'd like to know who I'm protecting."

"Very well. I had no idea my father was working for the Mark in Lima. And I wonder if he truly understood who paid for his work. He never bothered much with details. I hope, at least, he did not know." But she feared he had known. He'd been single-minded when he was creating, and if he did not know who he worked for, it was only through willful ignorance. "I did meet some of his clients, of course—"

"That wasn't what I meant. Though that would be interesting for a report, I suspect Miss Algrave has already collected that information. I've never been to Lima. What's it like?"

"Oh. Lima?" she asked, unsettled.

"Lima."

She hesitated, unsure of what he wished to hear. "Lima is elegant. Sophisticated. Crowded. The air had a different quality there, and the light seemed softer somehow."

"You've got the eye of an artist. But I guessed that when I saw your mechanicals."

"They are hardly art."

"A miniature sweeper that looks like a maid? They're clever. And how did the young ladies of Lima spend their time?"

"I'm not the one to ask. I spent mine in my father's laboratory."

"No parties? No dances?"

"We were not of that set," she said stiffly.

"And now you're a lady of means."

She tipped her head.

"Mr. Crane told me," he said. "The names of your clients weren't the only items of interest in your account books."

"I see."

"So why hasn't someone – the good Mr. Night? – made an honest woman of you?"

She folded her arms. "That is none of your affair, sir."

His eyes twinkled. "Now that I've seen that account book, I might throw my hat into the ring."

"Mr. Sterling!"

He gave her a hangdog look, blue eyes wide. "I don't suppose you'd have me."

She burst into laughter. "I've received so many proposals, your utter lack of sincerity is a balm. I suppose you would insist I continue working?"

"How else shall we pay for the luxury I'd like to become accustomed to?"

"And you? Shall you give up the life of a... traveling man?"

"Alas, no. I'm happy with my life."

She sobered. Was this what lay between her and Krieg? Were they too engrossed in their own passions to tend to a passion for each other?

"What's wrong?" Mr. Sterling asked.

"Nothing." She ran her thumb along a chip in her blue and white plate. "Nothing."

"Well, something's bothering you."

"I feel watched all the time now," she said in a rush. It was true, but not what had disturbed her. "Of course, you and Mr. Crane and Miss Algrave are constantly at my heels, and I thought at first that was the source of the feeling. But now—"

"I feel it too."

She leaned forward. "You do?"

A man across the restaurant leapt from his chair, and it fell back with a clatter. He stomped the floor, setting the plates and saucers on his table rattling. "A rat!"

"Perhaps we should return to my workshop." She reached for her pocket watch, recalled that it was gone, and shoved the chain more deeply into her shallow, waistcoat pocket. "I do not wish to be late."

"Hermeticus can wait."

"It would be impolite to make him do so."

"But interesting." He braced his jaw on his fist, elbow on the table. "What do you think he'd do if he arrived at the lab and you weren't there? Try to break in? How long would he wait for you?"

"As long as he wished and no longer. If we miss him at my workshop, we will be forced to go to his hotel to make our apologies." Which, she realized, was not such a bad idea. "But if you insist—"

"No, no. You've convinced me. You and that rat." He signaled to the waiter.

"And how shall we explain your presence to Mr. Hermeticus this evening?" Sensibility asked. "Not even he will believe you are merely a customer."

"I doubt we'll need to explain anything. People will assume I'm squiring you about town for the usual reasons and leave it at that."

"The usual reasons?"

"As a beau. I'm not so unappealing, am I?"

Her forehead creased. "All joking aside, that is hardly the point."

"Then what is the point? Unless you're worried Mr. Night will get jealous."

"He's far too sensible." But would he be jealous? Things had become so muddled – she needed to speak with him soon. "But your constant presence is unseemly."

"You don't really care what people think, do you?"

"Of course I do. One would be a fool not to. Someday this mad rush for gold will end, and San Francisco will settle into respectability."

"And you plan to settle with it as a lady inventor?"

"I have noticed that in the Territory, money goes a long way toward purchasing respectability. In any case, I would rather be well-off and disreputable than respectably poor." She folded her remaining biscuit into a clean handkerchief.

Mr. Sterling raised a brow.

Defiant, she tucked the biscuit into her reticule. Yes, she was comfortably situated and could afford food whenever she wished. But she could not bring herself to leave food behind, and she would not change for one government agent.

"If you came to Washington, no one would have to know your profession. In fact, I suspect the government would prefer it be kept secret. You could pursue your passions and your respectability."

"At the cost of my independence? No thank you, Mr. Sterling."

"No one is truly independent. We all answer to someone." He handed the waiter some silver coins and escorted her to the door.

CHAPTER 23

Flora squinted at the gears and smooth metal fittings. She'd kept the flame low so as not to attract attention, and the brass gears glowed on the rough table. Miss Grey was most certainly gone for the night, but someone might notice the light and get curious. Her gaze darted to the door of the girl's laboratory.

New locks. They hadn't been any harder to penetrate than the old ones, but Miss Grey had realized someone had invaded her laboratory. Perhaps the girl was not quite as stupid as Flora suspected.

Well, Flora was forewarned. She would not take Miss Grey for granted, particularly not with so many deadly devices at hand. The unfinished aether weapon Miss Grey had left on the table would be lethal when completed.

Flora's brow furrowed, and she paused over her own mechanical creation. Could Miss Grey have designed the weapon herself? She shook her head. No, the design must have been developed elsewhere. Still, it was clever work. Flora would not have thought to concentrate the aether flow, to use the energy as a weapon itself. But aether power was not her talent.

Smiling grimly, she fit a gear into place. As much as she loved her little mechanical friends, it was time for them to advance.

Her elbow nudged a jar filled with yellow liquid, and she grasped it, steadying, her heart skipping a beat at the near disaster. It would not do for *that* to crash to the floor. Miss Grey had a rather astonishing selection of chemicals for such a backwards locale. All the warnings Flora's father had dinned into her head about which chemicals not to combine were now useful for the opposite reasons. He had feared a laboratory fire. But fire was just what she wanted. It was cleansing. Final. Excruciating.

It had been too long since she'd played in a real laboratory. Her muscles bunched, a dragging sensation beneath her stays. Flora's laboratory had been stolen, and Miss Grey had acquired hers on the back of that crime. Her jaw tightened. She must not think of it. Not now, when there was work to be done.

She bent her head to her mechanical. It was delicate work – *Come lend me your fine hands*, her father's voice echoed, distant, in her ears.

She swallowed. She must not think of him now either. Narrowing her focus to the metal parts before her, she shut out his voice, the sounds of Miss Grey's laboratory. Unheeded, black smoke rose from the old wick, blackening the lantern glass.

The door banged open. Her hand jerked, knocking her creation to the floor. Tiny gears pinged, scattered. She froze, her chest tightening.

A man advanced into the room, revolver aimed at her midsection. Miss Grey's watcher, Mr. Sterling.

Miss Grey stepped into the laboratory, her head tilted, lips pursed.

Elbows pressed to her sides, Flora's gaze darted around the laboratory, seeking escape. How could she have been so careless?

"What are you doing in here?" the man barked.

Flora edged backwards, her black skirts brushing a worktable. There was no innocent explanation for her presence. Something disreputable then? "I... I... was looking for something to scavenge." She raised her chin.

"To steal, you mean," Sterling said.

Miss Grey's gaze raked her, and Flora straightened, feeling her regard even in this dim light.

Something in the girl's expression softened. "You have not eaten much today, I think?" Miss Grey asked.

At the suggestion of food, Flora's stomach gurgled. She ducked her head. The fool might actually take pity on her! But she *was* hungry. When had been the last time she'd eaten? There'd been little time for food today, and she should have assuaged that need. Now she was glad she had not.

Miss Grey stepped forward.

Sterling stretched out a warning hand, and his revolver did not waiver. "Just a minute," he said. "How did you get past that lock? Who are you?"

A wave of dizziness swept over her. What name had she given to Miss Grey's uncle? Not her own, never her own. "Jenny," she said. "Jenny Arnold." She was fairly certain she'd never used Jenny before.

"What are you doing here, Miss Arnold?" the government agent asked.

Flora looked to the bottle on the table – *too volatile* – then to the row of chemicals on a low shelf. If she could pull down the shelf, they would mix, a toxic stew, and she might escape. *If* she could get to the shelf before he shot her. *If* she didn't succumb to the fumes herself. Rage sparked through her. How dare they treat her like a criminal, when they were the thieves! She'd see them both dead. "I heard there were things I could sell in here. Everyone knows she keeps metals."

"Put your hands on the table in front of you," Sterling said.

Shaking with rage, Flora laid her palms flat.

Sterling strode to her and ran his free hand over her skirts, checking her pockets.

The Grey girl made a sound of distress, and Flora ground her teeth. Now, she must play the helpless waif. Later, her little friends would gnaw these two fiends down to the bones.

CHAPTER 24

"Is she armed?" Sensibility asked. There was something painfully intimate in Mr. Sterling's search of the girl, Miss Arnold.

Sensibility shook her head. No, she was not a girl. There was a hardness about her dark eyes that spoke of challenges overcome. She was likely as old as Sensibility and slim to the point of emaciation. Her skin was smooth and olive-toned. Belgian lace adorned her raven-colored gown. Despite the low light from the single lantern, Sensibility detected the signs of careful mending, of better days.

Sensibility stared at the mechanicals hanging limp on one wall, unwilling to observe the search, to be a part of this violation. And yet, the lady had broken into her workshop, gotten past her new locks. She was no simple thief, and Mr. Sterling was right to take precautions. Could Miss Arnold have been the lady who'd aided her uncle when he'd stolen the plans for the excavator?

"No, she doesn't have any weapons on her." Sterling holstered his revolver and tossed a wrapped leather pouch on the work table. The pouch fell open, revealing a set of tools. "Is this yours?" he asked Sensibility.

"They are not." She walked closer and gazed on the implements without touching them. "So that is how you defeated my new locks."

Looking daggers at Mr. Sterling, the lady scooped up her tools and clutched them to her chest. "They are mine."

Sterling pushed his hat further back upon his head. "And who did they belong to before you acquired them?"

"They are mine." She raised her chin.

Reaching into her reticule, Sensibility laid the wrapped biscuit on the table. It was still warm, and Miss Arnold's nostrils twitched. "For you," Sensibility said, "if you'd like it. It is quite fresh."

She made no move toward it. "May I go?"

"You can come with me," Sterling said.

"Where?" Sensibility and Miss Arnold asked in unison.

"To the Presidio for questioning."

Sensibility frowned. It had taken a good deal of cleverness to get past her new locks, and that sparked both admiration and a measure of wariness. But the lady was gaunt, and her loose clothing reminded Sensibility all too forcibly of the dismal, mourning gowns she herself had worn not long ago.

Miss Arnold paled. "They'll hang me!"

"I doubt it," he said. "Unless you're wanted for something other than breaking into Miss Grey's laboratory?"

"I just..." Miss Arnold gulped, eyes wild. "No, I never!"

Sensibility stepped closer. "Mr. Sterling—"

"No, Miss Grey. Miss Arnold's made herself a suspect. We need to learn the truth."

"Good evening!" Mr. Hermeticus boomed from the doorway, top hat in hands.

Miss Arnold made a swift motion and a cloud of pink smoke erupted from the floor.

Sensibility buried her face in her inner elbow. Grasping Mr. Sterling's sleeve, she tugged him, coughing, away from the gas.

Miss Arnold darted past Hermeticus, rustling his cape.

"Stop her," Mr. Sterling croaked out, eyes watering.

"What?" Hermeticus asked.

Sterling stumbled from the room.

"I say, what's happening here?" Hermeticus ran a hand through his shock of silvery hair.

Sensibility threw open a window, then ran to the opposite side of the laboratory and opened another. Fresh, salt-scented air flowed into the room.

"We interrupted an intruder." She raised the wick on the lantern, and the light flared. An intruder who not only had gotten past her locks, but who also seemed to understand the use of her gas devices. Sterling had been correct – there was more to Miss Arnold than met the eye. But that did not necessarily make her a threat.

She paced the room, searching for signs of things gone missing. Her nearly completed aether weapon remained hidden on a worktable, beneath an oily rag. The quartz crystals lay beside it, undisturbed. If Miss Arnold had absconded with any bits of metal, they were too small to note. The biscuit, however, had vanished. She should have offered her Mrs. Watson's dinner pail, dash it all.

"That young lady? A thief? I find it hard to credit."

"She broke into my workshop. Hardship drives many of us to do things we could not have imagined in better days." It had driven her to become a professional tinkerer. Others were not so fortunate.

"Indeed. We are like stones beneath a flowing river, are we not? Time moves inexorably past us, wearing us down to our true natures."

Had she come to her true nature? Had Miss Arnold? Sensibility shook herself. "But you have come to see the new designs." She opened a file cabinet. "Here, let me show them to you." Sensibility spread the revised plans on a wide table. Moving the lantern closer, she lit a second and planted them at opposite ends of the papers. She pointed out the alterations, and they discussed fees.

Hermeticus did not blanch at the price she proposed. "Of course, normally I charge a fee to participate in my séances," he said.

She smiled. "Then let us deduct the price of our next séance from the bill, shall we?"

Mr. Sterling pounded up the stairs, panting. "I lost her. Was anything taken?"

"Not that I noticed," she said, "but I only had time for a cursory inspection."

"Will you be joining us for the séance?" Hermeticus asked the agent.

"I'd be delighted," Sterling said. "Thank you."

The occultist's expression pinched. He nodded. "Then shall we begin? We will need three chairs and a round table, if you have one."

"I'm afraid I do not," Sensibility said.

"Ah, well." Casting his gaze about the room, Hermeticus found a small, square table.

Mr. Sterling collected the chairs.

"A single lantern will be admirable." Hermeticus extinguished one of the lamps. Lowering the wick on the second, he centered it on the table. Long shadows flickered across the laboratory.

Sterling pulled out a chair for Sensibility, and the three clasped hands around the table. Her stomach fluttered, and she was unsure if the impending séance or the firm grasp of Sterling's hand quickened her pulse.

There was a long silence, and Hermeticus bowed his head. "Spirits of the past, we invite you to move among us. Be guided by the light of this world. Spirits hear us."

The lantern light flickered.

Hair prickled the back of her neck, her lungs tightening as if she was being watched.

The occultist's breath rasped, then silence blanketed them, a suffocating shroud. His palm in hers was warm, damp. Mr. Sterling released his grasp.

Sensibility swallowed, the sound loud in her ears. A sudden urge to get up, to shout, to run, seized her. The silence, the atmosphere, was uncanny. For an instant she thought she was the shade, insubstantial, unreal. She shuddered, unhooked her goggles with her free hand, and pressed a lens to her eye.

Metal clattered on her left, and she sucked in her breath. She looked toward the sound, eyes straining in the dim light. Flecks of sparkling aether drifted through the room, flowed toward a spot on the floor. A shadow flitted at the corner of her gaze. She whipped toward it. The silhouettes of vials and alembics, tubing and pipes stood in their rows, unmoving.

Mr. Hermeticus sagged against the table.

Sterling stood, grabbed the wobbling lantern. "Hermeticus!" Grasping the occultist's shoulder, he pushed the man back in his chair.

Sensibility reattached the goggles to her belt.

The occultist shook his head. "What? What happened?"

"You fainted," Sterling said.

"I did not faint! I was in a trance."

"And what did you experience?" Sensibility asked.

"Er, nothing I can remember. My apologies, dear lady. Did anything happen?"

"I saw a movement in the corner of the room," she said, "and something sounded as if it was knocked over."

"I saw the movement as well," Sterling said. "Probably a rat." Returning to his chair, he straightened his waistcoat.

"Then I did not imagine it," she said. "And there are no rats in my laboratory." She hoped.

The occultist's white brows lowered. "This is the first time I've been accused of summoning a rodent." He stood, knocking into the table with his thigh, and gave Sterling a hard look. "The vibrations tonight are not convivial to a séance."

"Sorry." Sterling crossed his arms over his chest. "Did I scare the ghosts away?"

"It is no joke," he said hotly.

"No." Sensibility rose. "Something was here, and I don't believe it was a rat. I felt we were being watched." She had not imagined that flitting shadow. Had the creature from the first séance returned? "Mr. Hermeticus, I have not been wholly honest with you. At the first séance I attended with you, I saw something. A creature. It did not appear natural."

"Mechanical?" Sterling asked.

"No, it seemed to be of flesh and blood. When I say 'unnatural,' I mean it looked as if it was not of this world, with large, cat-like ears and slanting, golden eyes. It wore a top hat." The description sounded ridiculous, even to her. But she had seen it, and this was not the first bizarre being she'd witnessed. "What was it?"

"I summon human spirits, my dear girl, not demons. And though I can feel and hear and sometimes even smell them, I doubt you would be able to see one. I suspect the creature was of your imagination. Sometimes, in trance, people can be highly suggestible. Shadows become shades, and a breeze through a window the touch of the departed."

Her gaze fell. "Then you have never seen the creature." Mr. Hermeticus did not have the answers she sought. As startling as its appearance had been, the creature had not seemed demonic. Whatever it had been, it was connected to the aether. If she could learn how, perhaps she'd understand how to use aether as more than just an energy source. Others had succeeded at utilizing aether for distance control of mechanicals. Why did this technology elude her?

"A rat," Mr. Sterling said. "If the first séance was as dark as this one, you were probably just confused and startled so that it looked like something monstrous."

"There are no rats in my séances, sir!" The occultist pounded his fist on the table, rattling the oil lamp.

Muttering stiff farewells, Mr. Hermeticus departed, looking as dissatisfied as Sensibility felt.

She shut the door behind the occultist and bolted it. "A rat? How does goading the man suit our purpose?"

"My purpose is to figure out if he's a member of the Mark." He cocked a brow. "What's yours?"

"He's simply a client."

"That doesn't answer the question."

She didn't respond.

He shrugged. "What was that about a cat in a top hat?"

"It wasn't a cat! Oh, never mind. Perhaps I was seeing things." She scrubbed her palms across her face, hoping he wouldn't see the lie.

There was a soft rap at the door.

"I'll get it." Sterling drew his gun and prowled to the door.

"John?" A masculine voice whispered. "Are you in there?"

Sterling unbolted the door and threw it open. His partner, Mr. Crane, sidled into the workshop. Jane whisked inside behind him, her skirts rustling.

"See anything?" Sterling asked.

"If Hermeticus has a partner," Mr. Crane said, "we didn't catch him."

Jane yawned. "We've been following him all day. I thought occultists led more interesting lives."

"Did he meet with anyone?" Sterling asked.

"Not a soul," Mr. Crane said. "When he wasn't in the hotel parlor, reading and scribbling in his journal, he was at the beach, watching the waves."

Sensibility walked to the table where they'd found Miss Arnold. The aether concentration she'd seen through her goggles had been near here, on the floor. Aside from her recent aether gun, which was not yet completed, of late she had been working primarily with steam and clockwork. So the aether she'd seen was likely not due to any of her creations. Her boot crunched something metallic, and she bent, picked up a gear. Beneath a nearby table something the size of her palm glinted. She picked it up, running her hands across the smooth, brass surface. It reminded her of the excavator downstairs, as if one of its hind limbs had been miniaturized.

Turning the limb over, she traced the path of a wire, the curve of meshed gears. This was not her work. Miss Arnold had either brought it with her or had been in the process of building it.

Something rattled inside the brass limb, and she shook it gently. A tiny quartz crystal fell into her hands. So it *was* aether technology.

Rustling skirts alerted her to Jane's approach, and she stood.

"Is something wrong?" Jane asked.

"No, just cleaning up some scraps that were knocked to the floor. I'll be ready to leave in a few minutes."

Jane shrugged. "Don't hurry on my account. The boys are still arguing about how Hermeticus is pulling his magic act."

Lifting the rag off the table, Sensibility exposed the aether gun. "I'd like to finish this without it getting confiscated."

Jane winked. "So you need a diversion?" she asked in a soft voice. "I can help with that." She strolled to the men. "Miss Grey told you she thought she was being watched. What about those windows?"

Smothering a smile, Sensibility bent to complete her task while Jane and the men argued about the windows, their usefulness as means of entry, and the advisability of curtains.

She tightened the last gear. The weapon vibrated in her hand, and she turned it off, pocketed the gun. Catching Jane's eye, she nodded.

"All right," Jane said. "Nothing's going to get done tonight. May as well think about it tomorrow."

"Amen to that," Mr. Crane said. "I could eat a horse. While you two were dining in style, Miss Algrave and I were stuck trailing Hermeticus on the beach."

The three agents argued good-naturedly on the walk back to the boarding house. Sensibility walked ahead, lost in thought. Incantations and aether and strange creatures – how were they connected? If Miss Arnold was building an aether-based mechanical, it was evidence she might be part of the Mark. Sensibility shook her head. No self-respecting Mark employee would go that hungry. Something dreadful had happened to bring her low, and Sensibility was unwilling to accuse her just yet. She needed to learn more before revealing her suspicions.

If only Krieg were here! Her eyes grew damp, and she blinked. She couldn't think of him now. She needed to focus on the problem of Miss Arnold, for either she was an enemy or a fellow tinkerer in distress.

As if summoned by her thoughts, Miss Arnold slipped across the dark street and into a saloon.

Pointing at the saloon, mouth agape, Sensibility stopped on the side of the muddy road and looked back at the agents. They bickered, unseeing. Her hand dropped to her side. If they caught Miss Arnold, they would take her to the Presidio before Sensibility had a chance to speak with her. And she *must* speak with her.

Catching up to her, Jane tucked her arm inside Sensibility's. "I hope you're satisfied with my diversion."

She swallowed. "You have exceeded my expectations."

They strolled to Mrs. Watson's boarding house, and the four clomped inside the foyer, divesting themselves of coats, hats, gloves.

Sensibility smothered a yawn with her hand. "I suppose someone will escort me to my laboratory again tomorrow morning?"

"I will," Jane said.

"Someone will," Mr. Crane said.

"Then goodnight." Sensibility mounted the stairs.

"Goodnight, Miss Grey," Mr. Sterling said.

She did not look back. She had to find Miss Arnold, and she had to do it without one of the agents in tow. Sensibility smiled. It wouldn't be the first time she'd escaped out a window.

CHAPTER 25

There was a soft knock on the door.

Durand looked up from his desk, polished and broad, taken from a deserted rancho. It was a beautiful piece of craftsmanship, but he missed his old roll-top in the States. "Come."

The door swung open and a young Hound slipped inside, whipping off his hat. The youth's face was so spattered with freckles it appeared to be covered in dirt. His clothing hung loosely, as if he'd inherited them from an older relative. Or stolen them off a clothesline. Either was possible.

"Well?" Durand asked.

"Somethin' happened tonight. That agent, Sterling, chased a young lady out of the laboratory."

Durand lifted a brow. "Chased?"

"Out the laboratory and up the street. She's a right fast one."

"And?"

"And he lost her, but I didn't. She went up Signal Hill." He ducked his head. "And then I lost her. That place is a regular rabbit warren."

"And who is watching Miss Grey now?"

The youth shifted his weight. "Well, I figured you'd want to know about that girl."

Durand rose, leaning on a thick walking stick, fingers twitching. "Who is watching Miss Grey?" By God, the boy was thick.

"Well, no one. I was the only Hound on watch. I had to choose between Miss Grey and the girl, and we all know Miss Grey goes to only two places – that boarding house and her laboratory."

Durand's vision clouded. Whipping the stick, he cracked the boy on the side of the head.

The Hound groaned, knees buckling, and fell in a heap.

"You are not required to think!" Strength flooded his body. He raised the stick to deliver another blow, thought better of it, and grasped the boy by the collar, hauling him to his feet. "Nick!"

A man opened the door and stuck his ruddy-faced, fleshy head in. "Yeah, boss?"

"Set two Hounds to watch Miss Grey. This boy," he shook the youth, hoping his brain would rattle, "followed a woman from her laboratory to Signal Hill. Find the woman and bring her to me."

Nick grinned. "Signal Hill?"

"Yes." Durand pursed his lips. "This might be a job for all the Hounds, now I think on it. Another cleanup operation. And when I say all, I mean all but the two you'll set to watching Miss Grey."

Nick's eyes glittered. "Yes, sir. What about the magician? You want a watch on him?"

"No. We've watched enough. I'll take care of him myself. Tonight."

CHAPTER 26

In her room, Sensibility lit the lamp on her desk, locked the door behind her and threw open her wardrobe, digging out a pair of stained trousers. She paused, hand on the mirrored door, her pale reflection wavering in the deep shadows of the room.

She smoothed her skirts. While working at the forge, she preferred trousers. But Mr. Sterling's presence that morning had stifled the impulse, and she'd sufficed with a leather apron that day to protect her gown from stray sparks. Tonight, however, she would need trousers if she were to clamber out the window without tripping and crashing to the ground. Besides, if the Hounds caught a lady alone after dark, they would summarily escort her home.

Her lips pressed together. Did the Hounds really believe they were the safety committee they claimed to be?

Undressing, she slipped into the trousers and a simple navy blouse.

At the open window, she paused. The last time she'd escaped this way, dressed in trousers, San Francisco had been a nearly deserted village. No one had noticed her. Tonight would be different. She could not avoid men on the streets, and if they deduced she was a lady, her trousers would attract comment or worse. She needed a better disguise.

Knuckles whitening, she squirmed backwards out the window, feeling with her booted feet for the narrow ledge below. The windowsill was slick from the heavy mist, and she tightened her grip.

Her feet met air, and for a bad moment she wondered if she had shifted in the wrong direction or, irrationally, if the ledge had moved. Wriggling further, her right foot touched solid wood. She crouched on the ledge, grasped its edge, and swung down. One foot banged the stair banister beneath, and she winced. Balancing on the rail, she jumped to the soft earth of Mrs. Watson's backyard.

The mist stung her cheeks, and she sidled around the corner of the house, her heart thudding beneath her ribs. Tiptoeing up the porch steps, she paused beside the closed door, listening. Sensibility edged it open.

The entry was empty. Whipping inside, she grabbed a man's hat and greatcoat from the coat tree, thrust the hat on her head, and returned to the porch, softly shutting the door behind her.

She slipped into the thick coat and trotted down the steps. The shoulders hung too low, and the hem drifted well past her knees. Fortunately, ill-fitting, damaged clothing were something of a staple in San Francisco and would not attract attention.

Light from nearby buildings turned the fog a sickly amber. Tugging the hat low, she made her way to a plank walkway and strode down the street.

A man jostled her. Swallowing her indignation, she nodded, saying nothing, edging from his path.

Miss Arnold might have come and gone from the saloon in the time it had taken for her to return to the boarding house, change, and evade the federal agents. And if she did not find Miss Arnold there, perhaps it would be for the best. But the lady was a tinkerer, like Sensibility. Her recent impoverishment, her appearance in San Francisco, alone, all bespoke a young lady in need. Sensibility set her jaw. She had to find her.

Ahead, light, laughter and the plinking of an out-of-tune piano poured from the saloon's windows and swinging doors. Stepping off the plank walkway, she crossed the muddy street.

She leaned against the corner of a darkened mercantile store, willing herself invisible. And as if by magic, no one noticed her. Men hurried or stumbled past, depending on their degree of inebriation. No one bothered the slim youth, hat low, arms folded over "his" too-large great coat.

How long should she stand there? If she knew Miss Arnold was inside, she'd wait all night. But what if Miss Arnold had already left, and Sensibility watched a saloon with her quarry already fled? A spatter of raindrops struck her, and she shivered, pulling closer to the building.

She'd wait an hour.

Three miners stomped past, bellowing a bawdy song.

Sensibility ducked her head. At least the coat she'd borrowed was warm. Beads of water glittered on its sleeves, and she withdrew deeper into the shadows.

Miss Arnold emerged from the saloon. Without looking left or right, she flounced down the street.

Sensibility followed.

No other women walked the streets alone, and even in the swirling fog and darkness it was easy to keep her in sight. Once, Miss Arnold stopped and whipped her head around, as if she sensed she was being followed. Sensibility did not pause, walking on as if all was normal. The lady's shoulders relaxed, and she continued down the street.

Miss Arnold turned west, climbing a steep hill, and Sensibility hesitated. This was Signal Hill, a three-hundred foot mound named for the semaphore on its peak, alerting San Franciscans to the arrival of ships in the harbor. But today the hill was better known for its "Chileno" inhabitants – primarily fallen sisters. They clustered in rude tents and dilapidated shanties that threatened to tumble down the steep slope. It was rough, dangerous. Heaven help Miss Arnold if this was her home.

The acrid scents of wood smoke and human offal seared her nostrils, and Sensibility's resolve faltered. But she pressed onward, striding up the steep hill, avoiding the rivulets of dank liquid streaming down the center of the muddy alleys. Dark eyes stared at her from crude doors and windows – too many faces for such small dwellings. Refuse lay in piles along the road, an occasional rat slinking across her path. Sensibility stuffed her hands in her pockets, her throat thickening. Had she not a talent for tinkering, she might have found herself in similar circumstances.

Miss Arnold turned down a narrow alley lined with shacks.

Hurrying forward, Sensibility paused at its mouth. Miss Arnold's skirts brushed the walls of the narrow passage. Sensibility wavered, unsure. She shouldn't be here. It was a wonder she hadn't been challenged. If Miss Arnold knew she was being followed and was leading her into a trap, there would be no one to aid her.

She would be on her own.

Nodding curtly, Sensibility entered the passage, her muscles rigid.

At the end of the alley clustered a ring of tents. Raising a canvas flap, Miss Arnold ducked inside one, vanishing into its depths. A light flickered on within.

Drawing a deep breath, Sensibility pushed aside the flap. "Miss Arnold?"

The lady lounged on a cot, her arms folded at her side. A central, wooden pole propped up the canvas, and from the pole extruded a lantern on a rusty hook. The only other item inside was a battered carpetbag.

Miss Arnold's eyes widened, accentuating the angularity of her face. "Miss Grey?" She rose, her black gown fading into the flickering shadows, and something thudded to the earthen floor. "What unusual fashions one encounters in San Francisco." She stared pointedly at her trousers.

Sensibility ducked inside, her throat dry. She let the canvas drop behind her and rubbed her forearms, feeling suddenly inadequate. "Please forgive the intrusion. I saw the partially-built mechanical you left in my workshop. I'm afraid it was damaged in the confusion, or I would have brought it to you. But if you would like to complete it, you are welcome to use my laboratory."

"How uncommonly kind of you."

"Not really. When I arrived in San Francisco, I was quite on my own. Were it not for the strangers who aided me, I would have—"

"Ended up in these palatial surroundings?" Miss Arnold circled, a cat stalking its prey.

"Things were different a year ago. I am very pleased to make the acquaintance of a fellow tinkerer."

"Inventor."

"Excuse me, inventor." Sensibilities cheeks warmed. "Most of my creations are my own design, but I'm unused to calling myself an inventor. Your invention… I saw that it utilized aether but could not fathom its purpose. I've corresponded with other scientists who used aether technology. However, the pace of the mail is so slow, no more than one or two letters have been exchanged. I've been using aether as a power source for my devices, but I've encountered other devices which used aether as a sort of, er, distance control. Though I have been seemingly able to replicate the mechanics of these devices, they fail to operate. I confess, I am utterly stymied." Shoving her hands in the coat pockets, she stammered to a halt.

Miss Arnold rolled her eyes. "That's because you are a power mage. You could no more create distance control technology than I could create an aether-powered device."

"Power mage?"

Miss Arnold stomped her foot. "How can you presume to work with aether and remain so ignorant of its properties? It is a wonder you have come as far as you have. I can only presume someone has helped you with the designs."

"I am building off my late father's work," she said stiffly.

"That explains it."

"Unfortunately, he passed before he could give me a better explanation of the science. What do you mean by 'power mage?'"

"Aether doesn't merely interact with our technology, it also interacts with the person working with it. You connect with aether on an energetic level, so you are able to successfully build devices powered by aether. My research indicates these abilities are genetic. Your father likely had the same sort of connection to aether."

Sensibility grasped the tent pole, steadying herself. "But that is extraordinary." It would explain why the scientists in the States were unable to replicate her designs. "How did you discover this? As I mentioned, I have been corresponding with other scientists—"

"Fools."

"—and they had no inkling of this personal connection between builder and aether."

"Likely because they relied on the discoveries of others rather than blazing a trail for themselves."

Sensibility's shoulders curved inward. "As have I." She thought she had journeyed far in her investigations and experiments. But Miss Arnold was right. She had been fumbling in the dark, standing upon the shoulders of better scientists. Her face tightened, hot with shame. "Miss Arnold—"

The lady raised a warning hand and cocked her head.

A long scream rent the air.

Miss Arnold dove for the cot, knocking it sideways, and grabbed a bowie knife from the floor where it had fallen.

Brushing past Sensibility, the lady strode from the tent, dropping the flap in Sensibility's face as she followed, close on her heels.

Sensibility brushed the canvas aside.

Motionless, Miss Arnold stood in the alley. Another scream pierced the night.

Glancing at each other, the two hurried down the alley toward the cry, until they reached a wider road.

Men's shouting and coarse laughter drifted up the hill.

The shrieks and cries grew in volume and fear bloomed in Sensibility's core. Reaching into her pocket, she grasped the aether gun. Women stampeded past like animals running before a forest fire. They jostled Sensibility, their eyes wild and sightless.

A woman caromed into Sensibility, and she lost her footing, falling hard against the side of a shack. The fragile construction shuddered beneath her weight.

Miss Arnold shoved the women roughly aside. Grabbing another girl by the shoulder, she spun her about. "What is happening?" Miss Arnold demanded.

"It's the Hounds! The Hounds are attacking." The girl moaned. "They'll kill us all."

Miss Arnold released the girl and started forward, jaw set.

"Are you mad?" Sensibility asked. "We cannot...you cannot stop a band of men with a bowie knife. Can't you hear them? There are too many!"

Miss Arnold whirled, lips peeled in a snarl, eyes hard and flat. Sensibility stepped back, half-expecting to receive the sharp end of her knife.

Miss Arnold lowered the blade and trotted down an alley. "This way," she called over her shoulder.

They darted through the twisting and turning paths, struggling up the steep hill, then turning down. They barreled through winding alleys, slid down slopes slick with mud and waste.

Footsteps thudded behind them, but Sensibility dared not look, heat and terror at her back. The tents and shacks were an inferno, silhouettes of fleeing women darting before them. Fear and smoke choked Sensibility's throat. She ran on, the shrieks and cries fading behind her.

Rain came, pattering in the dirt, turning their paths into a river of mud, running off the brim of Sensibility's hat. She slipped on a pile of refuse and stumbled to the ground. Gasping, bracing herself on the grimy adobe wall next to her, she clambered to her feet and peered down the alley.

Miss Arnold had vanished.

A rough hand grabbed her, yanking her around. She raised her hand to strike, but a quicker hand grasped her wrists, raw from her earlier injuries. They blazed with pain, and she gasped.

"Sensibility!" Krieg released her, his face a valley of shadows. "So it was you, and I have not been on a fool's errand."

"Krieg!" She resisted the urge to hurl herself into his arms. "Miss Arnold, did you see her?"

"Who? I saw you were with another lady, but I lost sight of both of you in the chaos. I thought…" He smiled crookedly. Lifting his hat, he raked a hand through his tangle of coppery hair. "I saw you lurking in men's clothing and thought you were up to no good, so I followed you." He set the hat more firmly on his head, casting his hawkish profile into darkness.

"But you did not attempt to stop me. Thank you." She exhaled a shaky breath.

"I see you eluded your minders."

"But not you. Krieg, the fire—"

"Is dying." He pointed up the hill. The smoke indeed appeared to have lessened. It swept low along the hill, pressed against it by the rolling damp. "We were fortunate in the weather."

"Good gad." She pressed a hand to her heart.

"Now, why have I been chasing you through the worst part of San Francisco?"

"So much has happened, I barely know where to begin."

They turned and picked their way down the slick road.

"Start with why you're dressed as a man."

Rain streamed from the brim of her borrowed hat and down her neck. She turned up her coat collar. "It's deucedly difficult to climb out a window in skirts. Besides, any lady caught alone on the streets by the Hounds' 'safety committee' is summarily escorted home. If Sterling or Mr.

Crane weren't escorting me hither and yon, one of those fool Hounds would. I dressed as a man and was ignored."

"Fortunately. So you climbed out your window to evade the government agents. But where is Miss Algrave? If there's trouble to be had, I'd expect to find her with you, in the thick of it."

"Yes, well. Her loyalty lies first with her government. I thought it best to investigate on my own. Did you know an assassin made an attempt on my life last month?"

"What?"

"Neither did I. Miss Algrave only just informed me. I confess, I am still put out that she kept me in the dark. If she does not trust me, then how can I—"

"Perhaps she erred, but you can trust her to do her job and protect you."

She slipped on a loose rock, and Krieg grasped her elbow, steadying her.

She did trust Jane to do her job. But Sensibility had thought she was more than a job. She'd thought they were friends. Her lungs constricted.

"So you escaped the agents," Krieg said. "Why?"

"A young lady inventor broke into my laboratory. Krieg, she works with aether! She escaped Mr. Sterling, but I saw her entering a saloon and returned to the spot in the hopes I could find and speak with her. She led me to Signal Hill."

"Then the lady is in dire straits. Do you know her name?"

They turned onto California Street, a broad boulevard thronged with men hurrying to escape the rain. Her muscles slackened. "She told us she was a Miss Jenny Arnold, but the name could be false. Mr. Sterling suspects her of being part of the Mark."

"As should you. You can't trust strangers, particularly one that broke into your workshop."

"The agents are determined to drag her to the Presidio for questioning or to interrogate her themselves. But don't you see? She understands aether! I must speak with her. Our brief conversation was a revelation."

"A revelation that will do you little good if you're dead. You should not have gone alone."

"I don't trust the agents, and Miss Algrave apparently does not trust me, and you were nowhere to be found." *As usual*, she silently added. "But what of you? Your disappearances and secrecy are beginning to make me wonder if you are also involved in some outré adventure."

He did not respond for a long moment. "The ground is drier beside the buildings."

"That is all you have to say to me?" But she edged beneath an overhang, where the mud was not so deep.

"I'm afraid that's all I can say for now. I have a... client, and this must be confidential."

Something in his eyes shifted, and she knew he was lying. He did not trust her either. Her shoulders sagged. His opinion of her had changed. Or had her belief in her friendship with him – and with Jane – always been a delusion?

CHAPTER 27

The magician stood on the bluff and stared into the lowering fog. The lantern dangling in his hand did little to penetrate the dense mist. Waves, heard but not seen, lapped at the northern shoreline. "I confess, Mr. Durand, I am surprised by your interest in the spirit world."

"Why?" Durand examined his cigar. Its smoke coiled upward, disappearing into the mist. The fog dampened his great coat, and inwardly, he cursed the occultist's habit of an after-dinner walk. Who walked about in the blasted wet? "We all must die, must we not? Who has not wondered what comes after?"

"You are not satisfied with the explanation in the Good Book?"

"We are both men of science," he lied. Hermeticus was a charlatan, and Durand didn't give a fig about science beyond how it could advance the Mark's plans. "You explore the philosophical, searching the aether, and I the geological, excavating beneath. We are both digging for answers," he said, waiting for a reaction to his mention of aether.

Hermeticus chuckled. "As above, so below, eh?" He turned to the south, and hope flared in Durand's chest that he'd given up the walk, and they would head for shelter. "Good heavens, what is that?" The magician stared, brow furrowed, at an orange glow streaking the fog, high on a hill.

"It looks like a fire." Perhaps that would get the man moving.

"Do you think it will spread?"

The orange blush faded, plunging the town into darkness.

"It does not appear likely," Durand said. "Not in this damp weather."

The man did not take the hint, staring, mouth agape, at the now-dark hill.

Durand cleared his throat. "I noticed you leaving Miss Grey's workshop."

Hermeticus turned to him and raised his brows.

"I am a client of the lady's as well," Durand said. "Though I cannot imagine what device someone with your philosophical interests might require."

The man stood on the wet sand as if he'd been planted there. "Sadly, many people believe my séances to be cheap fakery. Initially, I approached Miss Grey to build a device which would prove I was not moving – pulling wires or knocking tables to create the effect of spirits at work. But Miss Grey believes she can create a mechanical which will detect the presence of ghosts – or more specifically, the temperature variations that occur where spirits manifest."

"A thermometer? That is not new."

The occultist's eyes gleamed. "A very sensitive thermometer mounted upon a mechanical that will move toward the coldest spot in the room."

"Hm…" It sounded innocent enough. Foolish, but innocent. "How lucky that you found a talented inventor in the wilds of the California Territory."

"And for you as well," the magician said. "The lady has developed quite a reputation. News of her mining contraptions has spread as far east as Kansas City."

"I wonder which your clients will find more marvelous – you or Miss Grey's contraption?"

"The true marvel is the spirit world. We swim in it, but do not notice." Hermeticus rambled on.

Durand pretended to attend, nodding and grunting at random moments in the occultist's monologue. It seemed the magician was no threat. The Mark might even find a use for him. They'd lured the wealthy and gullible into their net before through occult fraternities. Why not use Hermeticus as a front?

Durand smiled. With the Hounds on one side and Hermeticus and his high-society marks on the other, Durand would be well on his way to fulfilling the Mark's goals. Then he could return home. A sudden longing filled him, and he beat it back.

The mist turned to rain.

"We shall catch pneumonia if we stand here," Durand said. "Shall we return?"

Hermeticus did not respond.

"Hermeticus?"

The occultist's eyes glazed, his expression slack, his mouth moving silently.

Durand waved one hand in front of the occultist's face. What new hell was this? "Hermeticus?"

"The aether…" Hermeticus made a gurgling noise.

A chill shuddered through Durand. "What about the aether?"

"The incantations… change… the inventor."

What utter nonsense. Incantations? The man knew nothing of aether and was blathering gibberish. It was difficult to believe people were taken in by this bunkum. But he'd long given up on being surprised when people turned out to be fools. The trait was far too common.

"Sensibility… danger." Hermeticus slumped forward, gasping.

Durand stifled a sigh. "You all right, old fellow?"

"A vision. I've never had one so clear." He stood, staggered, his lantern swinging. He braced one hand against Durand's shoulder. "Miss Grey is in danger. And there's something else I must tell her."

"In danger? What sort of danger?" He pried the hand free of his great coat. So the occultist did know something. What game was he playing?

"I'm not sure. A threat from a client, I think." He tugged on his mass of white hair. "The message from her father is fading. I must find her immediately!" He strode off, toward lights, civilization, Durand at his heels.

Hermeticus stopped suddenly in the street, his boots sinking ankle-deep into the mud. "Her father – did you know he was an inventor as well? He kept speaking of aether. But was he calling to me from the aether or about the aether?" Water streamed down the magician's top hat, dripping off its brim to the shoulders of his cloak. "No matter. I must deliver the message he gave, and Miss Grey can attempt to interpret it. It is not my business…"

He squelched down the road.

"Her father?" Durand asked sharply.

"I've never seen a vision so clearly. I do believe the man was murdered. Yes, I definitely got a sense of a death unavenged."

He knew. Hermeticus knew! But how? Never mind, it did not matter how. The man knew too much of the Mark's business. The fact that he'd mentioned aether, even if wrongly, was enough. And if Miss Grey suspected her father had been murdered, it would make her more difficult to manage. "Surely it is rather late to disturb the lady with such a fantastic story."

"No. She will want to hear this. Miss Grey needs to know."

And now was he trying to shake him, to blackmail the Mark? Heat cascaded through his body. Either the man was telling the truth – a truth about her father Miss Grey should not hear – or Hermeticus was bluffing, trying to jolt him into saying something he should not say.

They neared the boarding house. Rain had emptied the dark road, and they were alone. He must decide now.

In a swift motion, he drew his blade and plunged it into the occultist's neck.

CHAPTER 28

"You're displeased with me," Krieg said.

Vision blurred by the driving rain, she could not penetrate the shadows beneath his hat, could not fathom his expression. "You have a right to your privacy." She pressed her lips together.

"But you grow weary of secrets."

"Oh, what does it matter? You cannot or will not…" Cocking her head, she stared at a heaped mass of fabric near the steps to the boarding house. "What is that?"

"Someone's hurt." Krieg went to kneel beside the crumpled form. He reached forward, than drew back. "Go inside. Get one of your agents."

Not a doctor, an agent. Then the person was dead.

She walked to Krieg, her footsteps dragging. The pile of clothing resolved into a pair of boots, a cloak, an outstretched hand. Her insides twisted. "Oh, no. Mr. Hermeticus."

"You know him?"

"A client. I spoke to you of him."

"Ah, yes. The occultist, and he is at your doorstep. Why would he come here so late at night?"

"I don't know. Are you certain he's… gone?"

He drew his hand across the occultist's eyes, closing them forever. "I'm sorry. There's a deep wound in his neck. A knife, I'd guess."

"Murder? But who would kill him?" She'd found another man dead, and this time one she knew. This could not be happening. But it was, and she must be sensible, gather her thoughts. "We thought… we suspected he was part of the Mark." Clearly, they had been mistaken. Poor Hermeticus. He had harmed no one. Rain blurred her vision, and she dashed the back of her hand across her eyes.

Something tugged at the hem of her great coat, and she gasped, jumped backward. One foot slipped in the mud, shooting forward, and she landed on her opposite knee.

"Are you all right?" Krieg stood, extending his hand.

The creature from the séance crouched in a puddle. A monocle dangled from its cream, linen vest, undarkened by the rain. Its cat ears twitched, its gold eyes wide with sorrow.

Her heart thundered in her ears. It wasn't possible, wasn't real. Her head spun. "What… What are you?"

"Sensibility?" Krieg stepped closer.

The golden eyes seemed to deepen, drawing her, stopping her pulse. Krieg, the rain, the world, fell away. It was just she and the creature, and she was no longer certain if she existed. It held out one closed, gnarled fist.

Dizzy, unthinking, she reached forward, and the fist opened. Something smooth and metallic cascaded into her palm. "My pocket watch," she whispered. "You had it all along."

"You found your pocket watch?" Krieg's brow furrowed, and the world snapped back into place. "The man must have come to return it."

She clasped the watch to her chest and stared at the creature. It was no phantom. It was here. Now. There was so much she should ask it, but she could not think, and so she fell back upon her manners. "Thank you."

It shook its head, ears flapping. Pointing to the fallen man, it bounded away.

Sensibility struggled to her feet. It was of the aether. It understood her. She must know more. "Quick. After him."

"After who?"

"Him, it, whatever it was."

He grasped her arm. "Whatever what was?"

"The creature! Didn't you see it?"

"Sensibility, you're shaking with cold and shock. Come inside. Let me deal with Mr. Hermeticus."

"But… I saw it." She swayed. And she'd seen the creature without the aid of her aether lens. Was she going mad? Something bit into the palm of her hand, and she unclenched her fist. Her copper pocket watch glinted in her palm. It was real. The creature had given it to her. It had been here, and it had not been her imagination.

Unresisting, she allowed Krieg to guide her up the porch steps and inside the boarding house, to light and warmth.

A gangly miner with stringy blond hair stood in the entry hall. He gulped, Adam's apple bobbing, and pointed at Sensibility. "That's my hat!"

"Thank you for lending it to me." She lifted it from her head and handed it, dripping, to him.

"I didn't lend—"

"Go to the parlor," Krieg said.

"Are you ordering me?" Sensibility shrugged out of the damp coat and hung it on the tree.

"Not you." Krieg jerked his thumb toward the other boarder. "Him."

"What are you bossing me for?" The man's bulging eyes widened.

"Where's Sterling?" Krieg asked her.

"I'm going to my room," the boarder said.

"You do that," Sensibility snapped.

Sterling emerged from the dining room, rolling down his sleeves. "What's—" His gaze scorched a trail from her boots to the top of her head. "Why are you dressed in men's trousers?"

"Hermeticus is outside," Krieg said. "Murdered."

Jane and Mr. Crane strode from the parlor, their faces flushed. Mr. Crane and Mr. Sterling nodded to each other then dashed out the front door.

Jane folded her arms across her chest, her bell sleeves cascading down the front of her Delft-blue bodice. "Dare I ask?"

"No," Sensibility said.

Jane sighed. "You're not still mad about that assassin?"

"No. Well, yes." She shook her head. "But that's not the issue! A man lies out—"

Mrs. Watson ambled down the hall, rubbing her eyes. "What's all this then? This is supposed to be a nice, quiet boarding house, and you two are arguing like fishwives."

"I apologize, Mrs. Watson," Sensibility said.

"Well, go into the dining room, and tell me what's happened. Something's happened, because I know Mr. Night wouldn't be bothering a lady at this hour without good reason."

They followed her into the dining room, and she clambered into the chair at the end of the long table. The poppy centerpiece drooped, already fading. "Well?" Mrs. Watson asked.

"I'm afraid a man was killed outside your front porch." Krieg scraped the bench across the floor and sat.

Mrs. Watson's eyes bulged. "Not one of my boarders?"

"No. Mr. Hermeticus," Sensibility said.

Her landlady sank back in her chair. "Well, that's all right then. Not that the poor man deserved it, but when you take people's money pretending to talk to their departed loved ones, you walk a dangerous path."

"I'm not certain he was pretending," Sensibility said.

"Don't tell me you believed his twaddle!"

Sensibility pocketed the watch.

The front door bammed open, and the two federal agents lurched into the dining room, lugging Hermeticus's still form between them. A darkened lantern hung from the crook of one of Mr. Crane's fingers.

"I'll need to examine the body in better lighting." Mr. Crane nodded toward the dining table.

Mrs. Watson hopped from her chair, scowling. "Not in my dining room, you won't! And you're dripping mud all over the floor."

"We can hardly leave the man lying in the street." Mr. Crane shifted the body in his arms, setting the lantern on the table.

"Where did you find that lantern?" Sensibility asked.

"Near the body," Mr. Sterling said. "It had rolled beneath one of the boarding house steps. He must have dropped it during the attack."

Mrs. Watson shook her head. "Come with me, boys. There's a shed out back with a good, solid lock and a table big enough for the poor scalawag. You can examine him there." She disappeared into the kitchen, muttering.

"The shed might work, if there's light enough," Mr. Crane said. Carrying their burden, the agents followed Mrs. Watson.

"Is Mr. Crane a doctor?" Krieg asked.

The back door slammed.

Jane's smile was lopsided. "Mr. Crane is many things, a too-smart scientist among them. If there is anything to be learned from what is left of Mr. Hermeticus, he'll find it."

"I'm afraid that won't do us much good," Sensibility said, "if Mr. Crane will not share what he's learned. I must go to Mr. Hermeticus's hotel room, now, before a maid has a chance to disturb it. It cannot be a coincidence that he was killed here."

Mr. Sterling returned to the dining room and dusted off his palms. "You will stay here. I'll check out the man's hotel."

"You have no authority over me." Sensibility removed the lantern from the table and lit it.

Mr. Sterling jammed his hands on his hips. "As a representative of your employer, I do."

"As a representative of my client you mean," Sensibility said. "A client I have just sacked. You may relay *that* to Washington."

"I could lock you in your room."

Krieg laughed. "You think a lock will keep Miss Grey where she does not want to be? You have been beaten, Sterling. Now, Miss Grey, shall we go to the hotel?"

Her jaw tightened. In spite of Krieg's defense, his presence spiraled hurt through her center. But she would be more likely to achieve her ends with him than without him. "we've no time for me to change into a gown," she said. "I shall need to once again borrow a coat and hat."

Mr. Sterling plunked his hat on his head. "Well you can't have mine," he said. "And that ridiculous coat—"

"Belongs to Mr. Watson," Sensibility said. "As he is still in the gold fields, neither he nor Mrs. Watson will mind if I borrow it."

"Fine," Mr. Sterling said. "You two come with me to the hotel. Mr. Crane will stay here and examine the corpse."

"I'll just stay here to observe Mr. Crane's, um, work," Jane said.

Grumbling, Mr. Sterling strode into the parlor and waited while Sensibility slipped into the purloined hat and great coat. Her aether weapon weighted its pocket.

Krieg offered her his arm.

"Not, I think, while dressed in trousers," she said.

The federal agent snorted, and Krieg's face darkened.

Outside, the rain had lessened to a fine drizzle. The lights in houses along the road had been extinguished, plunging the street deeper into blackness.

Raising the wick on the lantern, Sensibility slipped and grasped a vacant hitching post for support. What she needed to invent was a mechanical device to transport her across this blasted mud. Krieg grasped her arm, and gently took the lantern.

"Thank you," she said.

He grunted and did not remove his hand from her elbow until they reached a plank walkway.

Krieg lifted her bodily onto it. "Apologies," he said, "but we won't reach the hotel until morning at this rate."

Their booted feet echoed hollowly on the wood.

"Why do you think Hermeticus was outside your boarding house, Miss Grey?" Sterling asked.

"I don't know. We had set no appointment."

"To return her pocket watch, most likely," Krieg said. "She found it on him."

Sensibility shot him a look of annoyance. She'd told him Hermeticus hadn't brought the watch, but if Krieg did not believe her tale, who would? "Perhaps you are right."

"Your pocket watch? It's an odd time of night to return it," Sterling said.

"I was quite insistent about getting it back. Hermeticus knew it had personal meaning to me. Do you still think he could have been a member of the Mark?"

"We know its members have fallen out before," Sterling said. "And the Mark exerts strict discipline over those who go astray."

"Murders them, you mean," she said.

"Exactly."

Mr. Hermeticus had seemed sincere in his beliefs, excited by her plans to help him prove the existence of spirits. It was difficult for her now to believe he was a charlatan, particularly after having seen that creature. But it would not have been the first time she'd been gulled.

Arriving on the hotel porch, they shook off their hats and damp coats, scraping their boots before entering the lobby. The front desk was deserted, but men clustered around it, discussing something in low voices. Sensibility caught the words, "Signal Hill," and then they glanced at her and moved into the parlor.

Frowning, Sterling watched them close the door. "What's that about?"

"The Hounds attacked Signal Hill this evening," Krieg said, dimming the lantern. "There was a small fire, which thanks to the rain didn't spread."

Shaking his head, Mr. Sterling rang a bell on the desk. "The Army's in no position to deal with them."

"No, they're not," Krieg said.

Yawning, hair askew, the clerk emerged from a room and slumped behind the desk. He scratched his mutton chop whiskers. "Yes?"

Sterling leaned across the desk and said something in a low voice.

The clerk shook his head, his red-rimmed eyes widening.

Sterling clinked Spanish *reales* into his palm.

Closing his fist around the silver coins, the clerk handed Sterling the key, shook his head, and vanished into his hidey hole.

"Shall we?" Sterling bounded up the stairs.

Krieg and Sensibility followed him across the red-carpeted landing and along a narrow passageway lined with plain, numbered doors. The agent stopped before number thirteen, unlocked the door, and shoved it open. Ducking his head inside, he nodded to Krieg.

Krieg raised the lantern high, and the two men rushed into the room.

Searching the man's room had been her idea, but Sensibility hesitated in the doorway. The men peered inside the wardrobe, beneath the sagging bed, behind the faded, blue curtains.

Krieg placed the lantern on a narrow desk. "It's safe," he said to her. "We're alone in here."

She blew out her breath. If she were to bring Hermeticus justice, she would need to invade his privacy. Walking to the cheap, wooden desk, Sensibility opened one of the drawers. Empty. She pulled back another. A leather-bound journal lay inside. She ran her hand across the roughened, black cover. Saying a silent prayer for forgiveness, she opened the journal.

"What have you found?" Sterling rummaged through a leather satchel on the bed.

She heaved a sigh of relief. "His commonplace book." Less personal than a journal, a commonplace book contained scraps of found knowledge – his notes on séances and visions, quotations, and observations. She flipped to the final pages. They contained rough sketches of the plans Sensibility had drawn for the occultist. "He had a good memory for detail." She scanned the prior page, and the one before that. "There are some notes on our séance and my missing pocket watch. He seemed excited and baffled by the disappearance. But there is no mention of any appointments since he arrived in San Francisco, no names mentioned aside from my own. It's all a record of his thoughts on the spirit world."

Sterling looked up from the bed. "Keep it. Mr. Crane will take a look at it."

Sensibility clutched the book to her chest. The room was Spartan, lonely. "What will happen to him, to his things? There must be someone in the States who will miss him." At least there was a body to return to them. He had not been killed like the others, reduced to bones. Had they interrupted the killer before the process could be completed? Or had the murder been committed by someone else?

"Hermeticus is almost certainly a pseudonym," Krieg said. "Unless we can find some indication of who he really is and where he's from, it will take time to find his family. For now, we'll have to bury him here. But we can keep his things safe, if someone comes looking."

If. Sensibility's heart turned to lead. "He was a widower."

Mr. Sterling paused in the act of rummaging through a carpetbag and looked up. "Oh?"

"That's all I know," she said.

"Too bad." He returned to his search.

Thumbing through the book, her hand hovered above a page. A pair of slanting eyes peered up from one of the pages. The creature! He had seen it! Then why had he denied it? "I would like to take more time to read this."

"You may," Mr. Sterling said. "But I'd like Mr. Crane to get a chance at it too. If it's encoded, he'll be able to decipher it."

Nodding, she stuffed the journal into the empty pocket of her borrowed great coat. It was as much as she could hope for.

Krieg checked the pockets of the clothing in the wardrobe. "Empty. If nothing else, Hermeticus kept his things in order."

Sterling locked the door behind them, and they trooped downstairs. Laying the room key on the desk, Mr. Sterling rang for the clerk.

The man slunk from his room, gaze darting about as if he expected brigands to spring upon him at any moment.

"Did you see Mr. Hermeticus leave this evening?" Sterling leaned his elbow on the front desk.

The clerk squinted. "What's it to you?"

Sterling slid another coin across the desk.

"Yeah." The *reale* vanished into the clerk's pocket. "Around eight o'clock with another man."

"Another man?" Sterling asked.

"They ate dinner together, here in the hotel dining room, then left."

"Did you recognize the man he dined with?"

"That rich miner fellow. Older gentleman. What's his name?"

Sensibility pressed her palms onto the desk. "Not Mr. Durand?"

"Yeah. Durand. That's him."

"Did you see which way they went?" Sterling asked.

The clerk shook his head. "I can't see through closed doors now, can I?"

Sterling cocked a brow. "Thanks for your time."

They left the hotel, stopping upon its porch. A patch of clouds slid apart, revealing the stars.

"Do you think the clerk is hiding anything?" Sterling asked.

"No," Krieg said.

"Neither do I," Sterling said.

"I would not have imagined Mr. Durand had much in common with Mr. Hermeticus," Sensibility said.

"Aside from both being clients of yours?" Sterling asked. "No. But the body was still warm when we found it. Mr. Crane estimated that he was most likely killed after ten o'clock. That's only a two-hour gap between his departure with Durand from this hotel and his murder."

"Durand may know something," Krieg said. "And I'd like to know where he is now."

The blood drained from Sensibility's face. Could Durand have been attacked as well? Was the Mark targeting her clients?

"I know where he lives," Sterling said. "You two go back to the boarding house and let Mr. Crane know what we've discovered."

"At some point," Sensibility said to Krieg, "he will tire of giving orders that are ignored."

Sterling removed his hat, ruffling his hair. "Miss Grey—"

"—is coming with you, apparently," Krieg said. "As am I."

"Fine." Shoulders set, Sterling strode off and slipped in the mud, catching himself before he hit the ground.

"I begin to understand your suffering," Krieg said to her.

Stepping carefully into the street, they followed the agent.

"I cannot blame him," she said. "He does not wish his investigation to be saddled with me, and I do not wish my investigation to be clotted with federal agents."

Krieg grunted. "You found something in that commonplace book."

"Did I?"

"I saw your expression."

They stepped around an abandoned donkey cart.

"We have witnessed strange things in this Territory," Sensibility said. "I think Mr. Hermeticus knew stranger."

CHAPTER 29

The ship rocked beneath Flora, and the lantern overhead swayed, throwing shadows across the wood-plank walls.

She gazed into her copper hand mirror. The mirror itself had been replaced by a square of pink-colored aether glass. In it, Miss Grey, dressed as a man, slithered down the dark street with her guardians. The view jerked about, first to their boots, then to the tops of their heads, then to their boots again.

Miss Grey and her confederates stopped at a house, and the federal agent pounded on the door. It was a late hour for social calls, and Flora leaned closer, lips parted, wishing she could hear as well as see.

She should have killed Miss Grey when she'd had the chance. The little thief had actually come to her, and they'd been isolated on Signal Hill. She could have slit her throat, dumped her bones with the other shantytown waste, and none would have been the wiser.

And yet, something had stayed her hand. Had it been pity? Or worse, a form of self-pity? After all, they were both orphans of inventors. And they both had skills of their own, though Miss Grey was at heart a copyist.

But who had she copied the aether gun from? Flora had never seen its like, but it could not possibly be of Miss Grey's own invention.

Flora shrugged, the fabric of her mourning gown sliding loosely over her thin frame. Miss Grey was a copyist, a corrupt idea thief, and that was the end of it. After all, what had Miss Grey done when they'd met but press her for information, for Flora's secrets?

Her neck corded, and the image in the glass blurred. Grey didn't even know she was a power mage. It was the grossest ignorance! The metal bit into Flora's palm, and she drew a shuddering breath to calm herself.

She'd been weak, had seen something reflected in Miss Grey that had been in herself. But it was an illusion. She and Miss Grey were nothing alike. She was a true inventor. Miss Grey was nothing more than an opportunist, and the agent with her tonight was a killer. She did not know the hawk-nosed man – but if he was an associate of Miss Grey's, then that was his misfortune.

Fumbling in the pocket of her thin pelisse, her fingers found the distance-control device. Her thumb caressed the three levers.

In the aether glass, the door to the house opened. Sterling gestured. The door widened, and the three stepped inside.

She set the distance-control device on an overturned bucket. There might be children inside the house. And with all of her mechanicals activated, she could not order only one inside the dwelling to scout. Tonight her mechanicals would be forced to run in troops, and she could not send a troop into a house to spy. In such numbers, they would be seen. She would have to wait for Miss Grey to emerge.

She'd simply wait until they returned to the street, and then she'd loose her friends to strip their bones.

CHAPTER 30

The unpainted door swung open, and the barrel of a shotgun telescoped toward Sensibility. "You'd better have a good reason for beating on my door at this hour," a masculine voice growled.

"Mr. Durand?" Sensibility stepped forward, her boots squelching in the mud. "We apologize for calling so late, but there has been another murder."

The shotgun barrel dipped. Durand stuck his head out, his gray hair a wild tumble, his blue eyes streaked with red. One end of his gray shirt was untucked from his trousers, his suspenders hanging low around his wide hips. "And what's that to do with me?"

"It was Mr. Hermeticus." Sterling tilted back his black hat. "I believe you dined with him earlier."

Durand's eyes widened. "Hermeticus? The magician?" He stepped back. "Come in, before all the warm air escapes."

Scraping their boots on the steps, they filed inside.

Durand motioned to four chairs around a table. A single lantern, centered on a stained, blue tablecloth, lit the cramped room. Rumpled blankets lay atop a sofa, sunk deep in the shadows against a wall. "I don't have a parlor to invite you into," he said. "This place isn't much, but it's all I need for now. Most of my time is spent at the gold diggings anyway." He glanced at Sensibility's trousers and pursed his lips.

Sterling hung his hat on a peg by the door, and Krieg drew a chair for Sensibility.

"What's this about Hermeticus?" Durand asked.

"We found his body an hour ago outside Mrs. Watson's boarding house." Krieg put his lantern on the table. "He'd been stabbed."

Durand balanced his gun against the table and sat, sighing heavily. "Another killing. Sometimes I almost sympathize with the Hounds' safety committee."

"I believe you dined with Hermeticus this evening," Sterling said. "Why?"

Durand's eyes widened. "I was curious about the fellow and the contraption Miss Grey was building for him. It was an awful dinner, the steak tough as leather, but he was a considerable conversationalist."

"What happened after dinner?" Bracing his elbows on the table, Mr. Sterling interlaced his fingers.

"We parted not far outside the hotel," Durand said, "I to go to my home and I presumed Hermeticus to his hotel. He didn't tell me of any plans to visit you or your boarding house, Miss Grey."

"Can you tell us what you discussed?" Sensibility asked.

"Sure." Durand looked toward the ceiling. "Let's see, life in the States. Life here. We talked a bit about our work – I was curious, you understand. And…" He colored, glancing at Sensibility.

"And?" Sterling asked.

Durand shifted, his mouth twisting. "He had a sort of fit at one point, told me later it was a trance. But he said some odd things about Miss Grey."

Sensibility leaned forward. "What did he say? It might explain why he was outside my boarding house when he was killed."

Mr. Durand hesitated. "He said the incantation changes the inventor."

"The incantation changes the inventor?" Sterling glanced at Sensibility. "What does that mean?"

The phrase sounded familiar, but she shook her head. "I don't know. Did he say anything else?"

"Nothing I could make out," Durand said. "His performance gave me a bit of a turn, I admit. It was an interesting evening, but I was halfway glad when it was over."

Sensibility sagged. The occultist's riddle pricked at her. She'd heard something of the sort before… from Mr. Hermeticus? They had been discussing incantations…

"So after dinner, you returned straight here?" Krieg asked. "What time was that?"

"After eight," Durand said. "I did some reading and fell asleep on my couch."

The shotgun slid sideways against the table, and Sterling caught it by the barrel, handed it to Durand.

The miner nodded, stood, and laid the weapon on the sofa.

"Did you see or hear anything unusual?" Krieg asked.

"In my house?" Durand's bushy brows lifted. "Why should I?"

"The Hounds attacked Signal Hill tonight," Krieg said, "and started a fire. It is only thanks to the rain that it did not spread to the lower part of the town."

Durand muttered a curse. "Pardon me, Miss Grey. I'd overheard some talk on the streets of cleaning out the riff-raff but had no inkling that was what they intended. Did I say I sympathized with the Hounds? I was wrong. Fools like that will be the ruin of San Francisco."

The incantation changes the inventor. It changes the inventor. Changes her? Mr. Hermeticus had said something about mystics changing their perception of the world. She'd recorded their discussion in her journal, but she'd be deuced if she could remember it now.

"If something isn't done, the problem of the Hounds will only get worse," Krieg said. "To the Hounds, foreigners are the source of all San Francisco's ills. And more and more foreigners will continue to flood the city as long as this gold rush continues."

Durand pursed his lips. "Are you sure the men were Hounds?"

Krieg heaved a sigh of exasperation. "Who else?"

"Even if they were," Durand said, "how do you propose to stop them? Form another so-called safety committee? The sheriff is useless and at odds with the current Alcade. Would you sweep them both aside?"

"If we need to gather volunteers to assist in arresting the Hounds," Krieg said, "so be it. But ultimately, we must elect a new Alcade committed to creating a police department, as they now have in Philadelphia."

Durand smiled wryly. "Philadelphia is a long way away, and we shall not solve the problem of the Hounds tonight." He yawned. "Please let me know if there is anything I can do for Mr. Hermeticus. I wish I could tell you something that would lead to his killer, but aside from his so-called vision, nothing remarkable occurred when we dined this evening."

"You said you spoke of the States," Mr. Sterling said. "Did he mention where he was from?"

"New York, I believe."

Her brow furrowed. The incantation changes the inventor – what the devil did it mean? They'd discussed mystics and magicians but certainly not inventors.

"Er, Miss Grey," Durand said. "When will my excavator be complete?"

She jerked her head, remembering she was a part of this conversation. "It is ready now," she said. "You may test it tomorrow, if you like."

"I like very much. Thank you." Mr. Durand yawned and stood. "Now if you don't mind…" He looked toward the door.

Murmuring apologies, they left Mr. Durand and slogged toward Mrs. Watson's boarding house.

"He could be lying," Krieg said.

Mr. Sterling's smile was shark-like. "I work on the theory that everyone's lying."

"But why?" Sensibility asked. "Why should anyone wish to kill Hermeticus? He was not murdered like the others, stripped to the bones. We assume he was a villain because he was an occultist. But to many, my own creations must seem strange and nefarious. And my work with aether is—"

"A branch of science we are only now coming to understand," Krieg said.

"Of course, but to the unsophisticated or uneducated, it would appear magical," she said. "We cannot assume Mr. Hermeticus was a criminal simply because the man conducted séances."

"Can't we?" Krieg shook his head. "Asking people to hand over money to speak with their dearly departed is the lowest sort of confidence trick."

"If it was a trick," Sensibility said.

"I've seen this game before," Mr. Sterling said. "The first séance was just a taste. Once he identified a likely mark, someone desperate and wealthy enough, he'd have offered private séances and charged San Francisco prices."

"Perhaps you're right." Sensibility touched the lump in her waistcoat pocket where her pocket watch now lay. The men had suggested the most logical scenario. But she wanted to believe in Hermeticus. Because he was dead, and she swamped by guilt and pity?

A metallic whisper of sound raised hairs on the back of her neck. She stopped, listening. In the distance, an out-of-tune piano plinked and far-off waves hushed. Something else, faint and unidentifiable, tickled the edge of her awareness. Where had she heard that sound before, light, musical, menacing? Her pocket watch ticked faintly in her waistcoat, and she touched it, frowning.

"Is something wrong, Miss Grey?" Sterling asked.

"Do you hear that?" she asked.

"Hear what?" Krieg walked to her, the lantern swinging loose in his fingers, his long shadow rippling.

She closed her eyes. The noise was louder now. "Clockwork. The sound of thousands of tiny gears turning. It seems to be getting closer. Don't you hear it?"

Sterling cocked his head. "All I hear are the waves."

"And that blasted piano," Krieg said.

She turned in place, ears straining. "It's coming from over there." She pointed to the yawning mouth of an alley, much like the one she'd found the bones in, and her blood chilled. "I heard it before, when we found the skeleton of that unfortunate man."

"Unfortunate cutthroat, you mean," Sterling said.

Krieg raised his lantern. "I don't see—"

A shadow pooled about the alley mouth and flooded toward them. Sensibility backed away, her steps quick, jerky. Sparks flickered in the shadows, glints of reflected lantern light.

Sensibility gasped. "It's mechanical."

"Not it, they." Sterling snarled. "Run!"

She turned and fled, her booted feet slapping in the mud. The muck grasped at her ankles, threatening to wrench her boots from her limbs.

Grabbing her elbow, Krieg hauled her forward.

"Inside," Sterling shouted, pointing at a neat, square-shaped house. Light from its lace-curtained windows flooded the low porch, welcoming.

Leaping up the two steps, Sensibility banged on the door. "Hello!" Sensibility shouted. "Help!"

"No time." Krieg seized her elbow, and she glanced over her shoulder.

Mechanical rats swarmed up the steps, their metallic whiskers quivering, bolts gleaming. Krieg lifted Sensibility over one of the porch rails and vaulted after her into the street. Sterling hurtled after them. A rat lunged, its eyes glowing pink, and snapped off a bit of the porch railing.

Sensibility yelped, and a broad hand shoved her forward, down an alley. They pounded onward, Sensibility's lungs tight, her heart thundering beneath her stays.

"Inside's no good," Krieg panted. "Did you see how that thing chewed right through the wood?"

Drawing his revolver, Sterling turned, running backwards, and shot one rat, then another. Metal bodies flipped sideways, lay still, and were swarmed by more. Dozens? Hundreds? "We need to stay off the main roads, keep them away from other people." Sterling turned and ran, holstering his gun. "What are they?"

"Mechanicals," Sensibility said. "They must be distance-controlled using aether."

They skidded around a corner onto a quiet street scented with brine.

"How do we stop them?" Krieg shouted.

Sensibility's mind fumbled. They could either damage the physical devices or interfere with the aether-based distance control. But she had never understood how to build an aether control, much less how to disrupt such a device. They needed something which would wreck the mechanical or disrupt the aether. They ran blindly, the waves growing grew louder, the tang of salt heavy in the air.

"Salt water!" She veered left and slipped, falling forward. Her fingertips pushed off the ground, and she righted herself. "This way!"

Charging down a slope, they crossed a wide, empty street and raced through a stretch sand into icy bay water. Sensibility walked backward, watching the mechanicals, until the bay reached her knees. She dragged her hands in the water, washing them of mud. The bay clutched and tugged at her limbs, at the borrowed great coat.

Krieg grasped her hand. "They're not following."

Mechanical rats massed on the shoreline, their pink eyes malevolent.

Sensibility drew a shuddering breath. "These must be the tool used on the scientists and the man in the alley. It would account for the tiny bite marks we found on the bones, the rapidity with which the bodies were reduced to skeletons." The mechanicals had to be destroyed. But if they were distance controlled using aether, where was their controller hiding? How did he or she – *she* – see where to direct the rats? Were there other ways to use aether – perhaps to view things remotely as well as control them remotely? But that would imply two varieties of aether in one creation, and Miss Arnold had indicated that was not possible.

"Are you sure it's the salt stopping them and not just the water?" Mr. Sterling asked. "The metal would sink, wouldn't it?"

She bent and splashed water at the rats. Three pairs of eyes darkened. The other rats scattered backward.

"All right, you've proved your point." Mr. Sterling sloshed through the water. "The salt water does disrupt them."

The rats spread along the beach, some following him, others staying to watch Krieg and Sensibility.

"But we can't stay in the bay forever," Mr. Sterling said, "and I don't have enough bullets to finish them off."

"You won't need bullets. Try this." She reached into her coat pocket and tossed him the aether gun.

It flew over his head. He jumped, the weapon grazing his fingertips, and gun and man splashed into the bay.

Ears burning, Sensibility cursed her bad aim, her impulse to throw rather than hand it to him.

Dripping, Sterling glared at her. He wrenched off his hat and slapped it on his thigh. "And you said salt water—"

"Disrupts aether. The weapon is dead."

He aimed the aether gun and pulled the trigger. The gun fizzed, smoke coiling from its barrel. "So much for that idea."

Sensibility shivered, damp seeping up her trousers. She pressed her fingers to her temples. "All right. We need to disable the mechanicals, but whoever is controlling them is not foolish enough to send them into the water."

"How does the salt water disrupt the aether?" Krieg asked.

"It's not the water," she said, "it's the salt. There is some property in salt which appears to ground the aether energy. I surmised it might do the same for an aether control."

"So they're aether," Krieg said, "but they're also machines. How do they work?"

"Not by steam or they'd have some sort of chimneys for the vapor to escape," Sensibility said. "And they cannot be powered by aether, because I do not believe a single inventor can create a mechanical with multiple aether forces at work. Besides, I can hear the clicking of their gears. They must be clockwork automatons."

"So we wait for them to run down," Sterling said.

"If what I've seen is any indication, that could take hours," Sensibility said. "We need to get rid of these things before daybreak and some other poor soul stumbles upon them."

"A boat," Krieg said. "If we can find one, we can row out of range, land somewhere the rats can't find us."

Sterling kicked water at the mechanicals. They scuttled back, then surged forward like a tide. "Have you got any other ideas?"

"A moment, please," she snapped. "It is not every night one gets chased into the bay by a hoard of clockwork rats." Her head spun, thinking up possibilities and discarding them as impossible. She snapped her fingers. "The hydraulic mining pump. We must return to the warehouse beneath my laboratory."

"Why?" Sterling asked.

"There's a hydraulic mining pump inside. If one of us can get past the mechanicals and get the hose into the bay, the others can stoke the boiler. When there's enough of a head of steam, we can pump the salt water from the bay to spray the rats."

"We'll need to get past the mechanicals on the beach first," Krieg said. "They'll outrun us."

"All right," Sterling said. "Miss Grey, stay here. Night, go north. I'll take south. Look for a boat that will give us a head start on the rats."

"Take the lantern," Krieg said to her.

She shook her head. "I'm not going anywhere. I don't need it. Take it."

He hesitated, nodded and waded off. A portion of the rats broke away, following his lantern light. Another third followed Mr. Sterling.

The two men vanished into the darkness. Eventually, the sound of their splashing faded too, leaving only the soft crush of waves, the far-off sounds of a saloon, and the gentle scuttling of tiny mechanical feet upon the sand. The night blanketed her, a freezing veil of damp.

Shivering, she focused on a faint light glowing over a far-off rooftop. It was too distant to illuminate the beach, but at least it existed, life went on, and she was not wholly alone.

A wave, higher than the others, splashed about her hips. Her teeth chattered.

Don't think about the cold. Think about something else. The incantation changes the inventor.

Magicians used incantations to change the world. That was what Mr. Hermeticus had said. Mystics used incantations to help them change themselves. But why would an inventor want to change herself?

Two types of aether usage in one mechanical… What if an inventor could change himself so that he could create with multiple forms of aether? What if she was not limited to being a power mage, as Miss Arnold had suggested? What if she could change herself and utilize aether for distance control, or for distance vision?

She shook her head. It was fascinating, but she had more pressing matters to attend to. It would take time to heat the boiler and create enough pressure to pump salt water from the bay. How many minutes would they have before the mechanicals chewed through her warehouse's walls?

She needed to organize her thoughts and actions. She'd light the boiler first. One of the men could escape out the back and run the hose through a window to the bay. Once the mechanical pump had a head of steam, one of the other men would have to operate the jet – they would not have time to fix the pump in place, and the force of water would be impossible for her to control.

Something shimmered white on the water, and she started. A gull bobbed past, its eyes shut, oblivious. She released her breath. Think, she must think.

The mechanical rats were diabolical, but a part of her admired their creator's ingenuity. Their creator had been clever, pitiless. En masse they could do tremendous damage, but they were small enough to slip into narrow spaces.

Oars splashed to her right, and she oriented on the sound. There was another splash.

"Hello?" she called out.

"Miss Grey!" Mr. Sterling shouted, his voice eerie, lifeless across the water.

A dark shape glided into view, resolved into the silhouette of a small rowboat. Mr. Sterling held out his hand.

Half-climbing, half-falling inside, she landed in a puddle that stank of rotting fish. She crawled onto a bench, and the boat rocked violently.

"No Mr. Night?" Sterling asked.

"No, but he has a lantern. He shouldn't be difficult to find."

Mr. Sterling's wet coat draped over the edge of the rowboat. His sleeves were rolled up, his arm muscles cording with each stroke of the oars. On the shore, a liquid shadow followed them.

"The rats?" he asked.

"They've fallen behind, but they're still following."

"Mr. Crane would appreciate the technology," Sterling said. "Too bad it's hell bent on killing us."

"Not the technology. The person using it."

He grunted. "I stand corrected."

A light flickered ahead of them.

"I think I see Mr. Night," Sensibility said.

He rowed harder, his muscles straining against the damp fabric of his white shirt.

"Halloo!" Krieg shouted.

Sterling turned the boat, and they glided beside him.

Handing Sensibility the lantern, Krieg lifted himself into the boat.

The swarm of rats massed on the shore, their pink eyes gleaming, malignant.

"We need to land as close as possible to your warehouse," Sterling said, "but I've lost track of it in the darkness."

"The abandoned ships block the shore around the laboratory," she said. "I'm afraid if we tried to dock at one of the piers—"

"The rats would have us trapped," Sterling finished. "Mr. Night – a hand?"

Krieg sat on the bench beside him and took an oar. Silently, they rowed, the boat skimming across the water. The masts of abandoned ships rose before them like a sea of crosses.

"They're falling further behind," she said.

"Good," Sterling said. "We're running out of shore."

"Turn," Krieg shouted.

The boat veered toward the beach, bumped over a wave, and ground to a halt on the sand. The men leapt from the boat, and Krieg swung Sensibility onto the shore. They raced up a hill, across damp sand, and onto a muddy road.

"Which way?" Sterling asked.

"To the right." Krieg grasped Sensibility's hand and tugged her forward.

She glanced back. A tide of glowing pink eyes followed, flowing like water across the mud that sucked at their boots, slowed them, sent them stumbling.

CHAPTER 31

Skidding around the corner, the three hurtled through Sensibility's work yard and past the cold forge.

She lifted the thin chain about her neck and bent to unlock the padlock, not trusting her shaking hands to maintain their grasp on the heavy key. Krieg held the lantern for her, illuminating the wooden door. The lock snicked open, and she freed it from its clasp.

Sterling shoved her inside, and Krieg slammed the door behind them.

There was a thunk, and the door rattled. The wood vibrated beneath a torrent of scrabbling, scraping, gnawing. Sensibility backed away.

Sterling shoved a table across the floor and overturned it, pushing its top against the door. "Where's that pump?"

She ran to a corner of the warehouse where a canvas covered a malformed lump. Whipping off the fabric, she exposed a cannon-like device mounted atop a steam pump on wheels. Canvas hose coiled beside the machine.

"Now what?" Sterling asked.

The warehouse filled with the sounds of thousands of crunching teeth and the whir of clockwork gears.

"Someone needs to take this end of the hose down to the bay," Sensibility shouted, "while I heat the boiler. When the mechanicals break through, we'll spray them with the salt water." She sprinted to a box of coal and dragged it toward the pump.

Sitting the lantern on the floor, Krieg snatched the box of coal off the ground and set it down beside the machine.

"I'll go," Sterling said. "You stay with Miss Grey."

Sensibility nodded toward the wall facing the bay and filled the coal hopper. "There's a window—"

"Which the rats will be able to crawl through if they find it," Sterling said. "They've proven they can climb. You'll need to block the window up after I go through."

"There's plenty of canvas for that here," Krieg said. "I'll take care of it. You go."

Mr. Sterling unlatched the low window and slipped through.

Krieg fed the limp, canvas hose to Mr. Sterling until it unfurled in a straight line from the pump to the window, across the dirt floor.

"Are you sure the hose can reach the bay?" Krieg asked her.

"It was designed for miners who needed to transfer water over long distances, from streams to hillside." Sensibility shut the lid on the glowing coals and looked to the agent, his torso framed in the open window. "Mr. Sterling, someone is controlling these devices."

He draped the coil of hose over his shoulder. "If I find him, I may be able to stop this at the source, you mean."

"Him," she said. "Or her."

"How could I forget?" His teeth flashed. He tilted his hat to her and disappeared into the night.

"The hose will need more slack," she said to Krieg.

"Sorry." Krieg reeled in a yard, then closed the window on the flat hose. "He's right about that window. If they can chew through wood—"

The door shuddered, the table against it scraping back, and he threw himself against it. "So much for the door. Don't you have anything metal we can jam against it?"

A window shattered. Mechanicals streamed through, gears whirring, whiskers twitching.

"Upstairs, quick!" Grasping the lantern, Sensibility bolted for the narrow stairwell. She leapt up the steps, two at a time, grateful for the freedom of movement the trousers provided.

"Sensibility! Wait!" Behind her, Krieg's boots thundered, and metallic feet clicked against wood.

She dared a look back, and her breathing stalled. Two steps beneath Krieg, the stairwell was thick with glittering clockwork rats.

"Sensibility!"

Unlocking the workshop door, she slid inside.

Krieg followed, slamming it shut. He looked about, eyes narrowed. "We're trapped up here."

"This is only a diversionary tactic."

"The windows you mean? All right. There must be something we can use to lower you through to the street."

"Forget the windows. In here." Tugging at him, she swung open the door to her sleeping cubby.

He glanced at the cot. "There's no way out. The windows are—"

"Yes, there is an exit." Handing Krieg the lantern, she dragged the cot from the wall and pressed the knothole. A section of paneled wood clicked open. "Through here." She ducked inside the secret room and sank to her knees beside the desk.

Krieg shut the closet door and stepped inside. His eyes widened at the papers sigils and clockwork diagrams lining the walls. He ran his fingers over a sigil to Mercury. "This is not a plan for a mechanical."

"No. I have many interests." Heart pounding in her ears, she inserted her fingers into a gap between two floorboards and tugged. A section of floor came up, revealing a tight staircase.

"Liar." His smile was summer lightning. "You have one interest, your work."

Her lips curved in response. "We're much alike in that regard."

Something crashed in her laboratory.

"At least we know now they are not motion activated," she said. "Someone is most definitely using a distance-control device. We must go."

Another crash, and something splintered.

She lowered herself through the hole in the floor, her shoulder brushing one side of the stairwell. "It's a bit tight."

"I'll fit." Slipping off his coat, he tossed it aside. "Barely," he muttered.

He stepped inside, arching his back to maneuver through the hole in the floor and around the first twist of stairs.

The trapdoor clunked shut above them.

"May as well buy us a bit more time," he said.

They wound down the stairs, the lantern lighting the narrow passage. At one point, Krieg nearly did get stuck, but he twisted sideways and pushed around a corner. "I didn't know your talents extended to architecture," he said. "Next time, make a bigger escape route."

"To keep this passage secret, I had to keep it small." She stopped before a solid wall. Feeling along the side, her fingers found a raised knothole. There was a click, and the wall cracked open. She pushed it wide and crouched, dropping the remaining three feet into the warehouse. Racing across the barren floor, she followed the thin, pale line of hose and lifted the window that trapped it fast.

Krieg hopped down and swung the hidden door shut behind him.

Hurrying to the hydraulic pump, Sensibility grasped a lever and eased it forward. The pump roared to life, rattling her teeth.

"We need to get out of here," Krieg bellowed over the machine. "They'll be on us any minute."

"Aim the nozzle at the stairs," she shouted. "I won't be able to control it."

"What?"

"The nozzle!"

"Sterling might not have made it to the bay. We need to run."

Mechanicals streamed down the stairwell. The hose remained flat, lifeless.

"Aim it," she shrieked.

The hose jerked, swelled.

Swiveling the machine on its wheeled base, Krieg grasped the cannon-like device beneath one arm.

Sensibility released another level. Water exploded from the hydraulic jet.

Krieg staggered, and water shot toward the ceiling.

Darting around one giant wheel, Sensibility grasped the end of the nozzle with both hands. She dropped. Her knees hit the dirt floor. The jet lurched downward, and water pounded into the ground, splattering them both.

"Less weight," Krieg yelled.

She raised herself to a crouch, her hands slippery on the brass.

The water cut a swathe through the mechanicals, flinging them aside, washing them into a muddy pool. They floated, limp, swirling around the canvas-draped excavator.

"That's done it," Krieg said.

Sensibility released her grasp on the hose and scuttled to the back of the machine, shutting the water valve, releasing the steam pressure. Gradually, the hose flattened.

Krieg and Sensibility stared at each other, chests heaving.

"Never a dull moment," Krieg said.

Sensibility burst into laughter, then clapped her hands to her mouth. "It's not funny." Her legs trembled, and she leaned heavily against one of the pump's spoked wheels. "We were nearly killed."

"I can scarcely believe it happened at all."

She pushed off the wheel. Sloshing through a puddle, she picked up one of the mechanical rats. Its limbs flopped in her grasp. Unhinging the jaw, she touched the tip of a metallic fang, drawing blood. She sucked in her breath and flapped her hand. "The teeth are nasty. I'll need to examine these in my laboratory."

"Are you certain they won't come back to life?"

"In my experiments, the effects of salt water on aether are fairly permanent. The mechanicals can be repaired, but they will not reactivate without some tinkering."

Sterling slid the window up and leaned in. "I see it worked." Clambering through, he picked up one of the mechanicals. "You ever see one of these before?"

"No," she said. "I'll need to examine them."

"Mr. Crane will want to as well."

"If he wishes to use my laboratory, there is plenty of space," Sensibility said.

Mr. Sterling nodded. "You'll stay here, Night?"

"Of course."

Shoving aside the table propped against the door, Mr. Sterling strode out, mechanical rat in hand.

"You said this woman you met, Miss Arnold, is an inventor," Krieg said. "Could she be responsible?"

"The person who controlled these devices may not be the same person who invented them. But she is the only person I know of in San Francisco who understands aether."

"You must tell the agents."

She trudged up the steps to her laboratory. "I know." Miss Arnold was the most likely culprit. She had to be part of the Mark. Sensibility swallowed her disappointment – at herself for wanting so badly to know another lady inventor, at Miss Arnold for having fallen so low.

Lighting the lamps in her workshop, she removed the great coat and settled herself before a long table. The disabled mechanical lay limp, dead. Running her fingers along its joints, she marveled at the semblance of life it had once had. The thing was a work of art. It even had whiskers.

She drew a sharp breath. The whiskers!

Sliding from the stool, she hurried to a tall apothecary cabinet with a multitude of tiny drawers. From one she extracted the thin wire she'd removed from the site of the skeleton by the hotel.

It was a whisker. So the rats had indeed been responsible for those tiny bite marks, for stripping the corpse to its bones. The confirmation filled her with a strange mixture of elation and dread.

Returning to her table, she unclasped the goggles from her belt and strapped them to her head, sliding the magnifying lenses into place. Fine scores in its brass and copper plating hinted at fur. She shook her head. Her creations were cave paintings to this inventor's Michelangelo. A part of her did not want to disassemble the mechanical – it was too beautiful to take apart.

Ah, well. She had plenty of rats to disassemble. She could live with damaging one. Unrolling her leather tool kit, she set to work.

She'd created her own miniature mechanicals, but nothing as elegantly designed as these rats. Still, she *had* made an overlarge mechanical fashioned after a badger. Why not smaller mechanicals modeled after animals? Why not clockwork butterflies or beetles or birds that could fly?

She smiled at the idea of flight. She might as well attempt to invent a basilisk. But if birds could fly, why not a mechanical bird? Perhaps the idea was not so mad. Even Leonardo had dreamed of flying.

An hour later, she sat frowning over two chips of polished quartz – one cut hexagonally, the other smooth and oval-shaped.

Krieg dropped two canvas sacks upon the floor with a crash, and she looked up.

"You notice me at last," he said. "And I think that's all of the rats."

A gray weight pressed her insides, and she leaned back on her stool. "Neither of us has given much notice to each other over the last six months, have we?"

"No." He looked toward the window, his craggy visage reflected in the black glass. "We have both been busy with other interests."

"But don't you think," she said, hesitant, "if we truly cared for each other, we would rank among each other's greatest interests?"

"Of course you rank."

"Do I?"

"Sensibility, I'm working toward statehood. Statehood! Can you imagine what that means? It's all I want…" He flinched.

"We have not seen each other in months, and yet when you returned to San Francisco, you went directly to the Presidio."

"It was statehood business."

She blew out her breath, her heart a lead weight. "I thought as much. Three days, Krieg. Could you not have spared a few hours to let me know you were here?"

"Is that why you are angry?"

"It is more than that. The time we've spent apart has been by choice. We should wish to be together. Now I feel I barely know you."

"That's ridiculous."

"Is it? How can we know each other when we spend so little time together? And if the territory does become a state, what then? Will you go to Monterey to work in the government you have spent so much time attempting to build?"

He frowned. "I had considered it. I'm sorry, Sensibility. I had not considered your feelings in the matter." He gave her a lingering, pained look and glanced away.

"Do not be." Her throat tightened. "I am equally guilty."

"That isn't true. You've been here all the time."

"Working like mad, as obsessed with my work as you with statehood."

There was a long, awkward silence. Deep down, she'd known this was coming. But her heart was shattering, splintering.

She raised her chin. "We have always been friends, and there's no reason for that to change."

A muscle spasmed in his jaw. "I should go," he said. "But—"

"But you promised Mr. Sterling you would stay with me. It's all right. Let us speak of other things."

He cleared his throat. "Other things then. What have you learned?"

She focused on the crystals, and they blurred beneath her stare. "Very little. The mechanicals are powered by a rather brilliant bit of clockwork and controlled remotely with this crystal." She nudged the hexagonal quartz with her fingertip. "But this tumbled quartz and the aether technology connected to it are new to me."

He came to her and motioned toward the quartz. "May I?"

"Of course." *Let him look away, see anything but my face.*

He picked up the stone and held it to the light. "Smooth as a river rock. It reminds me of a tiny eye."

"Actually, I found it behind the device's right eye. These mechanicals chased us through San Francisco, around corners and down long streets without so much as pausing. I wonder if this aether technology allows the controller to see through the device's eye via this bit of quartz?"

"Interesting theory," he said.

"Miss Arnold told me that the inventor connected energetically with the aether, and only certain inventors can make particular types of aether devices. She said she could no more build an aether-powered device than I could build an aether distance control. But if I'm right, aether is used two ways in this clockwork mechanical – for distance control and for remote seeing. So either there were two inventors collaborating on the rats, or Miss Arnold misled me and inventors can develop different types of aether devices."

"Well, at least you and Mr. Crane will not have to fight over these. There are plenty of rats for you both to dissect to your hearts' content."

"And for Mr. Crane to remove to Washington, if any scientists remain to study them. These must be the devices that gnawed the scientists down to their bones. But I do not understand the knife cut to the victims' throats."

"A cut throat is a kinder way to die than being eaten alive," he said, grim.

"We were given no such quarter."

"Perhaps because there were three of us. It is one thing to cut a man's throat from behind, quite another to take on three armed enemies."

"But Hermeticus's body was left intact, and we assume he was alone when he died – aside from his killer."

"That is not the only difference in the murders," Krieg said. "He was stabbed in the back of the neck, severing his spinal cord. His throat was not cut."

"Then we are dealing with two killers. If Miss Arnold is involved, she may have an accomplice."

"Miss Arnold?" Mr. Sterling entered the laboratory, and Jane and Mr. Crane filed in behind him, their faces taut. "You think she's behind this?"

Sensibility wove her fingers together. "After you chased her from the laboratory, I found she had been working on an aether device."

"An aether device!" Mr. Crane's lantern jaw fell open.

"Yes. When I confronted her later—"

Mr. Sterling's face darkened. "You confronted her?"

"This evening," Sensibility said. "She admitted to being an inventor and to understanding aether technology."

Pink spots bloomed in Jane's cheeks. "When? Why didn't you tell me?"

"For the same reason you did not inform me of the earlier attempt on my life," Sensibility said. But there had been an element of pettiness in Sensibility's withholding of information, and her face warmed. "Besides, one does not need to invent aether technology to use it. The evidence was not damning. However, these rats are most certainly the devices that cleaned the bones of the dead scientists in the States and of the poor man we found in the alley." She led them through her discoveries.

Mr. Sterling cursed and jammed his hat further back on his head. "We need to find Miss Arnold."

"You might look on Signal Hill," Sensibility said.

"Tell me you did not interview her there." Jane fumed.

Mr. Crane looked up from the mechanical rat hanging limp in his hands. "Not during the attack by the Hounds?"

Sensibility nodded. "I lost her in the confusion."

"That may have saved your life," Mr. Sterling said. "Where did you see her?"

Sensibility described the path, the tent.

"Signal Hill is as good a place as any to hide," Jane said. "The Chilenos might notice her, but they won't ask questions, and there are many, er, ladies on their own up there. I'm acquainted with several of the more prosperous ladies of business there. If they know where she is, I can get them to tell me of her whereabouts."

"You can't go up there alone," Mr. Crane said. "Not dressed in that get up. You'll stand out like a peacock."

Jane arched a brow. "Thank you."

"He's right." Mr. Sterling glanced at Sensibility.

"I'll stay here with Miss Grey," Krieg said. "Now that Miss Arnold's devices have been destroyed, I should be able to handle the lady if she's foolish enough to return."

"She may have an accomplice," Sensibility said.

"Lock the door." Mr. Sterling frowned at the hole gnawed at the base of the wooden door, where the rats had chewed through.

"I'll repair the door tomorrow," Sensibility said. "Tonight, I need to study these mechanicals."

Mr. Sterling nodded, and the three agents trooped from the room.

"I'll look for something to board up the holes in the door." Krieg vanished down the stairs after them.

Listening to their fading tread on the steps, Sensibility pulled out Hermeticus's journal from the pocket of the great coat, draped over a stool beside her. She had lied – she'd gone as far tonight as she could with the rats. But soon enough, Mr. Sterling would remember to confiscate the journal. She needed to learn what she could from it while she had the chance.

The occultist's penmanship was long and angled backwards, as if bracing against the vagaries of life. But the journal indicated a true fascination with the occult. Hermeticus found meaning in daily occurrences, his meeting with a startled coyote, a crow that had attacked a bit of brass ornament in his top hat, a twist of phantomlike fog. She flipped forward. Even his meeting with her was fraught with layered meanings. *She is an alchemist of the forge, a shamaness of technology.*

"No," she muttered. She was much simpler than those things. "I am but a tinkerer, no more, no less."

"Less," a woman said.

Pink clouds of smoke engulfed her, and Sensibility knew no more.

CHAPTER 32

It was time, and the Hounds were sleeping. Durand kicked the crude, wooden bedframe.

The sleeping Hound jerked awake. "What?"

"We're moving now, boys." Durand rubbed his hands together. The Hounds would run tonight. His body lightened, as if feeling the coming rise of the Mark. By tomorrow morning, he'd have completed his mission, and the territory would lose hope of achieving statehood. The Mark would be satisfied, and he would be secure.

Other men groaned, stumbled from their pallets.

His target waited, the excavator was ready, and the fog would obscure them, causing more confusion. No one would be able to stop him once he was inside his new weapon, but the excavator wasn't as fast as a swift horse, and at some point, he'd have to emerge. Then he would be vulnerable.

"You men, take your positions outside the Presidio." Durand pointed. "You three, come with me."

"Come where?" one Hound asked.

"To the foreigner's laboratory. It's time to collect our weapon. If the Army won't bring order to this territory, we will!"

The men whooped.

He checked his pocket watch. Miss Grey would not be at her workshop this late at night. At least he could avoid killing the girl. But an inventor of her caliber could not be allowed to work for the American government. The Mark needed her talents, and someday, there would come a reckoning. But not tonight, not by his hand.

"Some of those spies she's working with might have set guards," Durand said. "If anybody tries to stop you, kill 'em quick."

CHAPTER 33

Dry mouth. Pounding headache. Sensibility rolled to her side, hands bound behind her. She opened her eyes, one cheek pressed to rough floorboards. A miniature sweeper scuttled past, bumped into a workbench, turned, and raced away.

She was in her workshop, and that at least was something to be grateful for. But was there anything more humiliating than being disabled with your own weapon? A flush of embarrassment warmed her chest. She wriggled her hands, and the ropes bit into her raw wrists. Her own ropes, thick and strong.

She craned her neck, her breathing harsh. The workshop was still, silent, empty. Had Krieg been gassed as well, or worse? No, she would not think of worse. If someone wanted to incapacitate him, gas would be the safest mode of attack. And then… She swallowed. Krieg was alive. He had to be.

A latch snicked, and soft footsteps approached her from behind. "You're awake." Miss Arnold knelt before her, the lady's mourning skirts spreading upon the floor. Thick hanks of dark hair escaped her chignon, trailing down her shoulders. She rolled a gas ball in her hands. "Interesting little toy. Who made it?"

"You found it in my workshop, didn't you? Who do you think made it? What do you want? Why have you done this?"

Miss Arnold's narrow face twisted with rage, and she rose. "Why? Why? You took everything from me!"

"I barely know you. I only arrived in this territory a year ago. I have done nothing to you, Miss Arn—"

Miss Arnold kicked Sensibility in the ribs.

The pain stunned her, blossomed, became her world. She gasped, breathless.

"Don't call me that," Miss Arnold said.

Sensibility struggled to speak, gulping, but no words emerged.

"Pennyworth. My father's name was Pennyworth. You knew him. Say it!"

"I don't know any Pennyworth."

"He was a doctor, a scientist. Dr. Pennyworth."

"None of the inventors of my acquaintance were named Pennyworth," Sensibility said. "What have you done with Mr. Night?"

"Inventors of your acquaintance?" Miss Pennyworth's eyes glittered, wild, her voice shrill. "How dare you elevate yourself to their level! You do not create. You destroy. You are one of the locusts, devouring all before you and then claiming supremacy."

"Miss Pennyworth, I am sorry, but I do not take your meaning. You imply I have done terrible things, but all I have ever done is—"

The lady laughed, her voice brittle as thin ice. "You think you are not responsible? The Mark killed my father, stole his devices – the devices you have in your laboratory!" She gestured at the row of aether-control mechanicals hanging on the wall, the gaping barrels of volley guns protruding from their round mouths. "You are guilty by association!"

"Your father?" Sensibility swallowed. "Then the mechanical rats were built by two – you and your father. One of you had the talent for remote aether control and the other… created a way to see through your mechanicals using aether?"

"You have an uncanny knack for understanding the work of others, Miss Grey. No wonder the Mark recruited you, the perfect technology thief."

"I'm no friend to the Mark. They destroyed my father too. And I found those mechanicals in the basement of a rancho miles south of here. I took them to study, yes, but not on behalf of the Mark."

"And learned nothing." Miss Pennyworth's lip curled. "You have no power over aether control."

"Miss Pennyworth, we are both victims of the Mark."

"You and I have *nothing* in common."

Sensibility levered herself to a seated position. "If I thought you were part of the Mark, I would be your mortal enemy. So I can understand why you thought I was yours, though I never worked with the Mark or knew of your father. But why kill the other scientists in the States? Why kill Mr. Hermeticus?"

"The others? You pretend they are innocent as well, when they had my father's technology? When the same mechanicals hung in their laboratories? They were all thieves, and they called themselves his friends!"

"Oh, no." Her stomach plummeted. The technology Jane had sent to the U.S. government last year, the items from the battered rancho, had been given to other scientists to examine, the scientists who'd been murdered. "Wait, they were friends? Your father knew these men personally?"

"Their betrayal is what cut the deepest."

"But they were scientists working for the American government. They didn't betray your father. Like me, they were experimenting with found technology. They had no idea your father was its author."

"No idea? They knew he understood distance control. They asked his advice! Can you imagine how he felt, advising them on technology stolen from his very laboratory?"

"But they worked for the U.S. government, not the Mark!"

Flora shrugged. "They were copyists, like you. Whether they worked for the Mark or not, they profited from his work and deserved to die."

Sensibility struggled to her feet. Her wrists burned, chafing at their bonds. "Mr. Hermeticus was no scientist."

"Who?"

"The occultist. Why did you kill him?"

"You can't hold me responsible for every death in San Francisco. I am no murderer. I only kill with purpose. I have no idea who killed this Hermeticus."

"And my uncle? What was your connection to him?"

Miss Pennyworth laughed. "How delicious that was. Your Uncle thought he was taking advantage of me to steal your plans. In reality, he helped me get into your workshop. Men are such fools. And then when he faked his death, I was there as well, crying into my sleeve about poor, murdered Mr. Grey."

"You are the fool. If you followed him, you should have known he went to Monterey to track the Mark. It was likely Mark agents who tried to kill him. If you hate the Mark—"

"If?" She screamed with rage. "How dare you question me!"

Sensibility's legs shook, threatened to fail her. "What have you done with Mr. Night?"

"Your guard dog lies unconscious below. I had to dose him with gas twice to keep him down."

Sensibility walked toward her. "Miss Pennyworth—"

"You disgust me. Nothing you have created is original. You have not a unique thought in your head. You associate with killers—"

"You say the Mark stole your father's devices. How? Did he work for them?"

Miss Pennyworth's lips flattened.

"He did, didn't he? My father did as well. I'd like to think he didn't understand who he was designing for, but I suspect he simply chose not to look too closely. I, however, understand that organization perfectly. There is nothing that would induce me to work with them. We do not need to be enemies," she lied. Miss Pennyworth was clearly mad.

"Even if you did, as you say, *understand* the Mark, you do not understand the first thing about aether." She stalked to the table and picked up a lantern.

"I am learning!" Bile rose in her throat. Sensibility had decoded the mysteries left for her by other, smarter scientists like her father. But everyone learned from others, and she had made discoveries of her own, even if they had to remain secret.

"Learning? And who did you learn from? My father! My father who's death you facilitated! No longer. You are done, Miss Grey." Miss Pennyworth hurled the lantern against a wall. Flames raced up it, licking a shelf lined with chemical-filled jars.

Sensibility stared, horrorstruck. "Mr. Night! Wake up!"

"I'll make certain he does not, never fear. I am not cruel." Grasping another lantern, she threw it at the opposite wall. Flames roared across the splattered oil, colored the windows orange.

Sensibility's vision washed crimson. "Don't you touch him."

Something tugged at the hem of her trousers, and she looked down. The creature from the séance lifted its top hat to her. It smiled, slow, cold, revealing pointed teeth. Winking one of its slanted golden eyes, it straightened its green waistcoat.

Sensibility's lips parted. She swayed, dizzy. "You! What—"

The thing leapt at Miss Pennyworth.

Shrieking, she staggered backward and banged against the glass, flapping her hands at the gray and green blur of motion about her head. Streaks of blood colored her cheeks.

Sensibility gaped, disbelieving.

The creature slashed with its claws, drawing another line of crimson across Miss Pennyworth's forehead.

Sensibility shook herself. The creature was vicious but small, and would not succeed in disabling Miss Pennyworth.

Bending at her waist, Sensibility rushed forward, driving her shoulder into the madwoman's midsection.

Miss Pennyworth stumbled backwards, and glass shattered, fell tinkling to the floor. She screamed.

Crinolines brushed Sensibility's cheeks. A boot clipped her chin, and Sensibility tasted blood. She cried out, fear, rage, and confusion thrumming through her veins. Trembling, she straightened.

Miss Pennyworth was gone.

She peered through the broken window. The woman lay still on the street below, her legs canted at an odd angle.

Trembling, Sensibility drew back into the room. Her knees buckled, and she braced her hand on the wall, panting. She looked about.

The creature had vanished. Flames roared, engulfing a shelf of empty vials and alembics.

"Krieg." Sensibility ran to the door. Turning her back to it, she fumbled the door latch with her bound hands. It clicked open, and she yanked. The door did not budge.

"Dash it all!" Sensibility turned, fuming. The new deadbolt was shut fast. It was also set too high on the door for her to reach with hands bound behind her. *Think. Think!*

The escape hatch in her hidden room…? No, hands tied, it would take too long to open it. And even if she succeeded, how could she drag Krieg from the burning building? She needed to free herself. If only her wrists hadn't been so swollen, if only she'd worn her spring-loaded knife that night. She searched the laboratory for a file, a knife… Jagged teeth of glass glinted on the floor.

Hurrying to the window, she knelt, feeling behind her on the floor for the glass. Her fingers touched something sharp. Frantic, she grasped the shard and worked at the ropes.

The flames arced higher, swallowing the window frames.

"Krieg!"

Hurry, hurry, hurry. The glass stung her wrists, and warmth dripped down her fingers. It would never work. She didn't have time.

"Stop thinking about what you can't do and cut the bloody rope," she muttered.

The cords loosened. She tugged one wrist free, wrenched off the ties.

Someone pounded on the door. "Sensibility!" Krieg shouted.

"In here!" Racing to the door, she unlocked it.

Krieg burst into the room. "Let's get out of here." He grasped her wrist, slippery with blood.

"No." She tugged away. "There's no rain tonight. If the fire spreads, it will set the entire block ablaze and then all of San Francisco. I have fire extinguishers."

"You what?"

Opening a cabinet, she pulled out three heavy copper canisters and handed him one. "They contain a pearl ash solution contained within compressed… Oh, just aim it and depress the lever!"

They attacked the flames, billowing clouds of white ash colliding with the black smoke. The smoke was choking. Her eyes burned, tears streaming down her cheeks. She would not lose her precious workshop. Miss Pennyworth would not take it from her, not when she had worked so hard.

Krieg tossed aside his canister and picked up another. He trained his extinguisher on a blazing shelf. The flames subsided, died.

Her fire extinguisher spat a weak cloud of ash, then nothing. She shook it. It was finished. She whirled, looking for the water bucket, her last hope, but there were no more flames to attack.

Coughing, the two leaned against a table. Sensibility clunked the fire extinguisher onto the floor, and it rolled against a wall.

"Another of your inventions?" Krieg removed his cravat and rubbed the back of his neck with it.

"No. It was invented thirty years ago in Britain. I merely copied the idea." She raised her chin. And no, she was not merely a copyist. The aether gun was all hers, as was Mr.

Durand's excavator. Perhaps she did not understand everything about aether, but figuring things out had always been a great part of the fun. "Dash it all, I don't care what she said!"

"Pardon me?"

"Miss Pennyworth, the woman who attacked us and set the fire." The full horror of the night slammed into her, and she pressed a hand to her chest. "Oh, good gad. I pushed her through the window. She's lying injured in the street, possibly dead."

Wiping a smear of soot from his brow, Krieg went to the broken window. He leaned past the shards of glass. "I don't see anyone."

"Impossible!"

Lanterns in hand, they raced downstairs and into the dark street. Miss Pennyworth was nowhere to be found.

CHAPTER 34

Flora limped toward the docks, each step a head-spinning swirl of agony. She focused on the ships ahead. Their masts swayed in the fog, blurred.

Gritting her teeth, she struggled on. In this condition, her enemies would find her. Worse, they would find her work, and she must protect the work at all costs. That, at least, they would not take from her, as they'd stolen from her father. The work and Miss Grey and San Francisco would burn.

CHAPTER 35

"You let her escape?" Fists on his hips, Mr. Sterling lounged against one of the laboratory tables.

"The fire was a more pressing concern." Sensibility swept up the glass. Her miniature sweepers bustled around, ineffectual against the larger shards.

Jane shook her head. "We'll find Pennyworth. San Francisco's not so big that she can hide forever."

"Miss Pennyworth doesn't need forever," Krieg said. "Just long enough to finish the job."

"How could we have been so wrong?" Jane asked. "The killings had nothing to do with the Mark. It was all a personal vendetta."

"But they did," Sensibility said. "She claimed the Mark had killed her father and stolen his designs, the mechanicals we found on the rancho and sent to Washington last year. But I wonder if he'd really sold those mechanicals to the Mark?" Like her own father had sold his designs.

"When the scientists were murdered," Mr. Sterling said, "we did look into Pennyworth's death, but there didn't seem to be a connection."

"When did he die?" Krieg asked.

"Six months ago," Mr. Sterling said. "Weeks before the other murders."

"And after we found the mechanicals on the rancho and sent them to Washington," Sensibility said. "So if the Mark did take his designs, it was well before he died."

Mr. Sterling nodded. "His death looked like a suicide. When we get back to Washington, we'll reexamine the evidence."

"And I suspected the killings and Mrs. Watson's kidnapping were part of an attempt on the Presidio gold," Krieg said. "I was a fool."

Sensibility paused. "What gold?"

"Statehood costs money," Krieg said. "If the vote succeeds – and I believe it will – then the new government will need to prove itself and restore order. And that means people must be paid to do the new government's work. The local leaders have been storing gold at the Presidio in anticipation of that day. It's the safest place in San Francisco."

Jane cocked her head, frowning. "Do you hear something?"

"A gold shipment?" Sensibility tossed her broom in the corner, and it clattered to the floor. "That is why you have been spending so much time at the Presidio?" She was sick to death of these secrets!

"I didn't know of any gold," Mr. Sterling said.

"There's no reason why you would. It belongs to private citizens, not the U.S. Army." Krieg set his hat upon his head. "At any rate, it looks like my work here is done. I'll take my leave." Avoiding Sensibility's gaze, he hurried from her workshop.

She stared after him, half-relieved, half-hurt. His eagerness to go had been all too palpable.

Mr. Crane lifted his head from the study of one of the clockwork rats. "So it's over. Now maybe I can relax and figure out how these devices work."

"You don't hear that?" Jane asked.

"No." Sensibility took a bottle of alcohol from a cupboard and doused her damaged wrists. Her wounds burned, and she hissed, wincing. "Miss Pennyworth denied killing Mr. Hermeticus, and I don't see any reason why she would lie. She was certainly happy enough to take credit for the deaths of the scientists."

Retrieving a roll of gauze from the first aid cupboard, Jane lightly bound Sensibility's wrists. "That death may never be answered. San Francisco is a violent place, and most crimes today go unsolved. If statehood can put a stop to the Hounds and this lawlessness, I'm for it."

"But he was killed right outside Mrs. Watson's," Sensibility argued. "Surely that signifies a connection. The murder cannot have been random."

"Maybe not," Mr. Crane said. "I don't like the coincidence much either. But it's possible he just had the bad luck to be attacked when he was returning your pocket watch."

"He didn't—Never mind." Hermeticus had not come to return the watch. The strange, golden-eyed creature in the top hat and waistcoat had given it to her. Tonight, it had saved her from Flora – expecting she would help it gain revenge for the occultist's death? In any case, this was a story that would not go into any government report.

There was a roar of sound. The building trembled, lurching sideways.

Sensibility stumbled, her eyes widening. Vials and jars and bits of metal cascaded from the shelves, crashing to the floor.

Mr. Sterling grasped Sensibility's shoulders, forced her beneath a table. Wood groaned, glass splintered, as if the building were being wrenched apart.

Then, silence.

Hands shaking, Sensibility grasped the edge of the table and slid from beneath it. "Good gad."

"I told you I heard something." Jane emerged from beneath a table, her eyebrows an angry slash.

Mr. Crane brushed dust from his chocolate-colored trousers. "An earthquake?"

"Mr. Durand's excavator." Sensibility ran down the stairs. Where the rolling doors had once stood shut there was now a gaping hole. On the ground lay a crumpled canvas tarp. Two strange horses stamped, eyes wild, tied to the hydraulic pump. Deep tracks in the mud led to a crumpled, masculine form.

"Mr. Night!" Sensibility raced to him. Kneeling, she ran her hands lightly over his body and felt a lump on the back of his head. He groaned but did not stir, and she released a breath she hadn't realized she'd been holding. "He's alive."

A crash rang out down the street. Sensibility tensed. "Someone has stolen Mr. Durand's mechanical. Mr. Night must have interrupted them."

Mr. Sterling untied a horse and tossed his partner the reins. Untying the other, he swung into the saddle.

Jane knelt beside her, lifting her skirts from the mud. "He'll be okay. You go. I'll watch Mr. Night."

Mr. Sterling held out a hand to her. "You do know how to stop that machine?"

"Yes." She placed her hand in his, and he pulled her up behind him.

Mr. Crane grunted and clambered onto the second horse. "Nice of the thieves to leave us transport. Whoever stole that machine was in quite a hurry."

Sterling kicked the sides of his horse, and the animal leapt forward. Sensibility squeaked, flinging her arms tight around his waist.

Mud and water kicked up beneath the horses' hooves. They thundered down the dark road, following the sounds of splintering destruction.

Skidding around a corner, Sensibility was certain the animals would lose their footing, crash headlong into a building and end them all. She shut her eyes. The nighttime fog iced her skin, and she hid her head behind Mr. Sterling's back, sheltering from the stinging cold.

"There he is," Mr. Crane shouted.

She peeked around Mr. Sterling's shoulder.

In motion, the excavator looked even more like a monstrous badger. It lumbered down the road, its claws digging into the earth, its metal seams creaking. Screams and shouts followed in its wake. The mechanical stopped at a crossroads, then headed west, plowing through the corner of a saloon. Light and men, cursing and laughing, spilled from the torn building. Indifferent, the excavator trudged up a steep hill, away from the town.

Sterling drew his revolver, and a shot thundered in her ears. The bullet pinged off the side of the mechanical.

"It's headed toward the Presidio," Mr. Crane shouted.

"The gold," Sensibility said. Krieg had been right after all. "But who's inside the excavator? Certainly not Miss Pennyworth. She had to have been badly hurt by the fall – too badly to climb inside."

"Offhand," Mr. Sterling said over his shoulder, "I'd say your client."

Her heart bottomed. Of course, Mr. Durand. "He was the only person who knew the mechanical was complete, and I gave him rudimentary instructions on how to operate it." Her voice jigged with every step of the horse's hooves.

"Also, this is his horse," Sterling said.

The excavator sped forward, fading into the darkness.

Mr. Sterling swore and reined the horse to a trot.

"What's wrong?" Sensibility asked.

"I won't race when I can't see where we're going. If we lose the horse, we'll never catch up with that excavator."

The sound of a puttering steam engine floated down the hill to them, and there was a great crashing and scraping.

Mr. Crane drew his horse up beside them. "At least it won't be hard to track."

They followed the trail of crushed foliage and overturned earth to the top of a peak. A stand of oaks, bent and broken, clung to it like a tonsure.

Sensibility leaned sideways and scanned the hillside, a tangle of menacing silhouettes. In the dark and mist, she couldn't differentiate between stone and shrub, tree and tor.

The fog parted. Below, moving away from the base of the hill, moonlight glinted off metal. She pointed. "There!"

They maneuvered the horses down the steep slope, Sensibility leaning back in the saddle. She had never been comfortable on horseback, and less so on this wild night ride. At the base of the hill, the fog vanished, exposing the full moon sailing high in the sky.

Sterling urged his horse across a smooth field. The chug of the steam engine grew louder, and metallic grinding and scraping echoed across the plain. Edging down another incline thick with undergrowth, they halted at the edge of a ravine. The excavator swayed at the bottom of the channel, clawing at the far side of the cliff. A mountain of earth slid, rumbling, and landed atop the mechanical.

"He's buried," Mr. Crane said. "We've got him."

"Not if Mr. Durand read the manual." Sensibility swallowed hard. "The excavator was designed to move through earth." This was the second time in one night one of her own creations had been used against her. How could she not have known she was building a weapon?

Dirt and stones exploded from the gorge.

The horses reared, whinnying, and Sensibility's heart leapt into her throat. She clung to Mr. Sterling, all sense of propriety fleeing in the face of her terror.

"Whoa, boy." Mr. Sterling soothed his animal.

The earth in the gully shifted, and the excavator's snout emerged.

"This ravine opens up not far from here," Sensibility said, her voice shaky. "Mr. Durand will be able to emerge there and return on his path to the Presidio."

"Let's take advantage of his position." Mr. Sterling slid from the back of the horse and helped Sensibility down. "How do we stop it?"

"There's a hatch on top of the mechanical," she said. "If you can get me inside, I can stop it."

"You can't go down there." Mr. Crane slid from his mount and gestured toward the roiling earth and boulders, churned by the excavator. "You'll be crushed."

"Come on." Mr. Sterling ran along the edge of the ravine, hopping easily over large rocks and fallen tree trunks.

Sensibility followed unsteadily behind the men.

At a stretch of smooth ground, Sterling ran flat out. He leapt into the abyss.

Sensibility's throat closed. "Mr. Sterling!"

Swearing, Mr. Crane jumped after him.

Climbing over a tree root twisting from the side of the cliff, she peered over the edge.

The men clung to the back of the excavator. Its shoulder glanced the loose hillside. Dirt and rocks showered them.

"The hatch," Sensibility screamed, keeping pace with the mechanical below. "It's beneath the machine's neck."

Shaking himself like a dog, Mr. Sterling dislodged clumps of earth from his head and shoulders. He climbed awkwardly up the mechanical's back and grasped the hatch, his muscles straining.

The mouth of the ravine opened before them. Durand was nearly free of it, and then he would be able to push the excavator into a gallop. She had to get down there before that happened, but the excavator was so far below. *Jump.* She swallowed, eyeing the long drop.

The excavator angled toward her. *Now. Jump now.* Breath surging in and out, she leapt, elbows, torso, knees, crashing into the mechanical. Pain arced through her, driving the air from her lungs, and she was sliding, falling, scrabbling.

A hand grasped her wrist.

Her legs flailed, found purchase on the mechanical. She looked up into Mr. Sterling's blue eyes.

"The hatch is locked from the inside." He heaved her atop the mechanical.

"This way." Awkwardly, she scrambled to the circular opening, the excavator swaying and bumping beneath her. Kneeling beside Mr. Crane, she brushed a layer of dirt from the ring surrounding the hatch. Feeling her way around its edge, she depressed a latch.

The round door popped open. Something buzzed past her ear.

Mr. Sterling grasped her shoulder and yanked her backwards.

A Hound, beard scraggly, gun drawn, crawled from the mechanical.

Sterling kicked him in the knee.

Howling, the man went down on his bad leg. The excavator stumbled over a cluster of boulders, rocking sideways. The Hound shrieked and tumbled to the ground. A revolver emerged from the open hatch, and a meaty hand squeezed off three shots.

Sensibility ducked, clinging to the rungs, her ears ringing.

Mr. Crane slammed the hatch shut on the man's wrist once, twice. The revolver skittered down the back of the excavator. Mr. Crane opened the hatch, and Mr. Sterling reached inside, yanking the Hound out. He pitched him from the mechanical.

"How many men can fit down there?" Mr. Crane asked.

"It was designed for two," Sensibility shouted. "But who knows? There is at least one more person driving it."

Mr. Crane made a face, his chest heaving. "Once more, unto the breach."

Shoving him aside, Mr. Sterling dove headfirst into the excavator. Two shots rang out, the ricochets tinny exclamation points.

The excavator turned and plowed into the hillside, its front feet and claws tearing into the earth. Dirt and debris showered them. Sensibility shielded her head with her arm, edging away.

"It's clear." Mr. Sterling's voice echoed from the belly of the mechanical.

Mr. Crane handed her down the ladder. Sliding after her into the cramped space, he slammed shut the hatch.

A lantern swayed on a hook, revealing Mr. Durand slumped atop the control panel.

"Is he dead?" Crane asked.

"Unconscious." In the seat beside Durand, Mr. Sterling rubbed his knuckles.

"Too bad," Crane said. "How do we stop this thing?"

"Clear a space," Sensibility said.

The men shoved Durand over the top of his chair, dropping him into the narrow space behind it.

Sensibility clambered over him into the free seat. She released a valve, turned a flywheel, and reached above her, tugging on a cable. The excavator shuddered to a halt, rocking them forward.

Adjusting the viewing lens, she peered into it. "We appear to be deep in the hillside. I'll have to reverse us out."

She manipulated the levers on the panel, and the excavator lurched sideways with a horrible thudding and grinding sound.

Mr. Crane grasped a metal handle above him, steadying himself. "Do you know what you're doing?"

"This is my first test from within a hillside," Sensibility said. The excavator really was handling marvelously. "Mr. Durand was only paying for a prototype. He understood that the finished model—"

"She can do it," Mr. Sterling said.

Mr. Durand groaned.

"Can I hit him?" Mr. Crane cracked his knuckles.

Sensibility ground the gears. The excavator whumped and shifted backwards. The moon appeared on the horizon of her viewing lens. "Ha! We're clear."

"All right," Mr. Crane said. "Help me get Durand out of here. I'll take him to the Presidio on the back of one of the horses. You two can return the excavator to the warehouse."

"It's a deal." Mr. Sterling lifted himself from his seat.

Mr. Crane opened the hatch, and a gust of cool air ruffled Sensibility's hair.

The men dragged Durand from the mechanical, their booted feet clunking on the metal above. After some minutes, Mr. Sterling climbed down the ladder and rejoined her.

"Interesting piece of machinery," he said. "Could this have gone through the Presidio walls?"

"Through, beneath, possibly even over."

"If you mounted weapons on top, you could take it into combat."

"Only if your government paid me. Need I remind you this excavator was a private commission?"

He chuckled.

Ignoring him, she pressed her eyes to the viewing lens. She changed gears and aimed the excavator north, toward a stretch of beach that curved around the city. The beach was relatively flat and would make easier going than San Francisco's hills.

"I'll make the recommendation," he said. "What will you do with the excavator now that your buyer is under arrest?"

"I should have no trouble selling it to the next wealthy miner who comes along." If one ever did. Mr. Durand's promised money would have set her for the year. She should have known his offer had been too good to be true, and she gave a quick shake of her head. She was as bad as her father had been, so eager for the commission that she hadn't looked at who was offering the money. A surge of pity for her father welled inside her, and a weight shifted from her breast.

"What's wrong?" Mr. Sterling asked.

Sensibility smiled. "Foibles, frailties and family."

"What?"

"Nothing's wrong, not anymore."

They were soon on the beach, fog rolling across the water, and Sensibility increased their speed. Her first test of the excavator was a success! She wanted to dance, to embrace Mr. Sterling, to whoop like one of the Hounds. She had only run limited tests on the mechanical within the confines of the warehouse's hard-packed dirt. Tonight, it trotted easily across the sand, jouncing them up and down.

Mr. Sterling braced his hands on the dash. "The going's a bit rough."

"Isn't it wonderful? We're moving at fifteen miles per hour!" Her voice jigged with each step. "Let's see if I can reach twenty!"

"But where are we going? I can't see a thing."

"Oh." She half rose from her seat. "May I?"

"Please."

Leaning across him, she grasped a brass knob and slid back a narrow strip of exterior metal, unblocking a window.

"Look out," he said sharply. "We're headed for the water."

Cheeks warming, she sat hard and adjusted the controls, turning the mechanical. "Apologies. Perhaps I should slow."

"No, don't. Look up ahead."

Through the rectangular window, an orange glow lit the sky.

Her eyes widened. "Is that—?"

"Fire. And a big one. Hurry."

She wrenched the excavator northward, and they clambered over a sand hill. The town spread before them. Ships blazed, flames rolling across the road to the row of warehouses fronting the water. Her row. Her blood ran cold. The dock area was in flames, warehouse rooftops roiling with smoke, ship's masts turned to burning crosses. She strained to see her laboratory, but in the haze of flame and fog, she could not make out which building was hers.

"It will spread," Mr. Sterling said. As if at his command, another building exploded in flames. "The buildings are too close to each other. It's hopping from one to the next. Soon it will move from the docks into the town proper."

She raced the excavator across an open field, past a row of tents and onto the main road bordering the bay.

"That pump inside your warehouse," Sterling said, "Is it powerful enough to fight this blaze?"

"It was designed to cut through rock. Handled improperly, it could do as much damage as the fire. Mr. Night and I were barely able to control it against the mechanicals."

"And handled properly?"

"It should be able to douse the fire, but its boiler is cold by now. It will take time to build up a head of steam."

His jaw tightened. "Time is something we don't have."

They galloped down the road, fire filling their field of vision. Her building rose into view, intact, and Sensibility breathed a sigh. But the roof of the warehouse next door roared with angry flames. Sparks shot through the air, tossed by the wind toward the bay.

Her stomach twisted with guilt. Though her laboratory was undamaged, others had suffered. More buildings would fall if they did not stop the fire.

"If the wind shifts," Mr. Sterling said, "your warehouse will catch, and then the shops and houses after that. We need a firebreak."

Sensibility tugged her collar, heat from the fire penetrating the metal excavator. "A firebreak?"

"Knock down your building and those two beside it. Create a break, leaving the fire nowhere to go. That will give me time to get the pump going, and we can deal with what's left of the fire."

Numb, she watched a ship in flames tilt, sink beneath the water. Destroy her workshop? Not all her work, her notes, her beautiful building. *No!* She scrambled to think of an alternative. "But… What if it fails? The pump is inside my warehouse, it could be useful."

"I'll get the pump out to the street first. Once I'm clear, take down the building."

Her grip tightened on the levers. "But—"

Rising from his seat, he opened the hatch and disappeared up the ladder, shutting her inside with a clank.

She leaned against the control panel. Through the window, she watched him race into the gaping hole Mr.

Durand had left in her warehouse. Mr. Sterling leaned out and waved to a chain of men who'd formed a bucket brigade. Three broke from the line and followed him inside.

Her workshop, her warehouse, were everything she had. They were her present, her future. There must be an alternative!

The wind shifted, blowing clouds of black smoke towards her. An orange flicker danced atop the roof of her laboratory.

Mr. Sterling and two men rolled the pump into the street. A fourth, Mr. Night, carried a coil of hose over his shoulder.

Gritting her teeth, she shifted gears and turned the mechanical, ramming it into her building. The excavator barely acknowledged the obstacle. It sliced through the wood beams like a knife through warm water, and she cried out as if she were being cleaved in two. Objects clattered on the roof of the excavator, ringing her ears, and she shouted again.

Don't think. Don't think about it.

She breached the other side of the building, turned, and drove through it again. And again. Her building collapsed in a pile, and she turned on the one beside it. Heat built inside the excavator, her perspiration mixing with the tears snaking down her cheeks. She plowed through one building then the next. And when they were reduced to piles of broken beams, she rolled across them, determined to stamp out any remaining flames, to crush the wood to ash.

Mr. Sterling hurtled in front of the excavator, and she slammed on the brakes, raising herself to standing.

Idling the device, she engaged the brake and dashed the tears from her face. She unhooked the access latch and climbed the ladder then stopped, leaning her hips against the hatch rim. Where her warehouse had once stood was now a flattened pile of debris. She swayed, oblivious to the hot metal stinging her palms. What had she done?

"It's finished, Miss Grey." Soot darkened Mr. Sterling's face, and beads of sweat dotted his brow.

She stared, bereft, at the ruins of her life, just another pile of matchsticks in a block of the same. Everything she'd worked for was gone. "Yes. Quite finished." Her knees hitched, and she grasped the hatch, bracing herself. There would be no coming back from this destruction.

The fire brigade clustered around the excavator, muttering.

Legs leaden, she clambered out.

"What the devil?" One of the men pointed. "She's wearing trousers!"

CHAPTER 36

Sensibility dug through the ruins of her building, found a loose and soot-darkened bit of paper, and stuffed it into her carpetbag. The sun glittered off the water, taunting her, stinging her eyes. After all the fog and darkness, today had dawned revoltingly bright, the sky marred only by trails of smoke drifting from the ruined ships listing in the harbor.

Men walked past and shot her dark looks.

She turned away, ignoring their glances and wishing Krieg and Mr. Sterling had been able to remain. But they had received word that Mr. Crane had not only delivered Durand — now a confessed Mark agent – to the Presidio, but also a handful of accomplices who appeared to be Hounds. The two men had hurried off, Krieg to ensure the security of the gold, Mr. Sterling to learn more about the Hounds Mr. Crane had captured. She adjusted the torn apron-skirt around her waist. The skirt was one of the few recognizable personal items she'd located in the detritus.

"I found something." Jane slid down a pile of beams and handed her a leather-bound journal.

"My father's diary. You found it!" Clutching it to her bodice, she lowered her head. She had prayed it had survived the collapse of the building. But they had been searching for hours, and it was such a small thing.

"There's more stuff back there too," Jane said, "papers and things." She yawned, her chestnut-colored curls limp and smelling of smoke, her blue gown darkened by ash.

"Thank you." Sensibility scrambled up the mass of wood, and a splinter drove in her hand. Roughly, she wrenched boards away, tossed them aside. Her safe lay at an angle beneath a blackened piece of timber. She pulled more boards away and found a flattened cot, the remains of a desk, and the papers from her secret room. She sagged against Jane. "It's here. My work is still here."

"Even if it hadn't been, you would have pieced it together." Jane arched her back, massaging it.

Sensibility shook her head. "Perhaps. I'd like to think so. But this makes starting over much easier."

"Yes." Jane looked at the water.

"Starting over in Washington, I mean," Sensibility said.

"Washington?!" Jane grasped her shoulders, and Sensibility slipped on a loose board. "You're coming with me?"

"I can't very well stay here. The good citizens of San Francisco blame me for the fire." There had been a near riot after Sensibility had emerged from the excavator. Only the arguments of Krieg, Jane, and the federal agents had saved her from the mob. But the new day had brought with it a renewed desire to blame someone for the disaster.

Sensibility knew who the real culprit had been – Miss Pennyworth. Yes, the fire *could* have been an accident. But Miss Pennyworth was mad enough and capable enough to start the fire, and they still had not found the woman. Sensibility wondered if they ever would.

"It will be dangerous traveling across the country," Jane said. "There'll be deserts. Freezing snows. Hostile Indians."

"If you are concerned for your safety, I suppose we could travel by ship."

Jane's face fell.

"However," Sensibility said, "I would like to see something of this continent, and we will have Mr. Sterling and Mr. Crane for company. Mr. Sterling is quite determined to see me to Washington himself. I suspect his employers have given him a financial incentive to get me there."

Jane grinned. "More like a threat to demote him if he doesn't. But what about Mr. Night?"

"He is a good man and a good friend. But his life is here." Eyes gummy with weariness, she stared at her soot-covered hands. Time had only deepened the ache of that loss. But the loss had really occurred months ago. It was only last night that she had been forced to face its reality.

"Are you sure you want to leave?" Jane asked.

Sensibility was unsure where her place in the world was, where she belonged. But where she could work, she would be happy. And there was much to do. Mr. Hermeticus had opened up a new world of possibilities. She thought she understood what the incantations meant now. If she was right, the ramifications were staggering.

Sensibility cleared her throat. "I'm more certain about this journey than when I first traveled to San Francisco, and that is something."

"Is it enough?"

It would have to be. "In any case, I have made it clear to Mr. Sterling that just because I agreed to accompany him, it does not mean I will work for his government."

"*Our* government. Too bad they won't hear about your decision to remain independent until after you reach Washington."

"Mr. Sterling seemed confident he could change my mind." But she was certain he would not. The U.S. government had brought her only trouble. And now that she'd tasted independence, she could not give it up, no matter the cost.

"It's a long journey. He just might succeed." Jane stepped sideways, slipping on a loose board.

Sensibility grasped her elbow, steadying her friend. "He's very sure of himself."

"Anything can happen."

"So, to the States?"

Jane grasped her hand, smiling. "The States."

OTHER BOOKS BY KIRSTEN WEISS

The Metaphysical Detective
The Alchemical Detective
The Shamanic Detective
The Infernal Detective

Help an author! If you enjoyed this book (and even if you didn't!), please leave a review at Barnes & Noble or Amazon.

ABOUT THE AUTHOR

Kirsten Weiss is the author of the Riga Hayworth paranormal mystery series: The Metaphysical Detective, The Alchemical Detective, and The Shamanic Detective.

Kirsten worked overseas for nearly fourteen years, in the fringes of the former USSR and deep in the Afghan war zone. Her experiences abroad not only gave her glimpses into the darker side of human nature, but also sparked an interest in the effects of mysticism and mythology, and how both are woven into our daily lives.

Now based in San Mateo, CA, she writes paranormal mysteries, blending her experiences and imagination to create a vivid world of magic and mayhem.

Kirsten has never met a dessert she didn't like, and her guilty pleasures are watching Ghost Whisperer reruns and drinking good wine.

You can connect with Kirsten through the social media sites below, and if the mood strikes you, send her an e-mail at **kirsten_weiss2001@yahoo.com**

@RigaHayworth
Kirsten's Facebook Page
Kirsten's Google+ Page
Kirsten's Pinterest Boards
Kirsten's Website: http://kirstenweiss.com

Made in the USA
San Bernardino, CA
13 April 2015